STARG

AIR

Scott took a step and a sullen rumble echoed through the decks. He had the sudden sense of the whole ship tensing around them, like an animal coiling its muscles before pouncing; then a second tremor resonated through, and Scott felt a brief sensation of motion and velocity that faded a heartbeat later.

"What the hell was that?" said Greer.

"I don't know." Scott hesitated, then snapped out an order to the Marine. "Sergeant, get these people settled down. Start making an inventory of everything we brought through as soon as you can. Try to figure out who and what we have. No one leaves this room." He shot a look at Wallace and, as an afterthought, thrust the MagLite into his hand. "Eli! You help him!"

The guy took the flashlight and panned it around, and his face changed as he got the first good look at the place they were in. Eli's mouth dropped open.

It was then, just by chance, that Scott noticed for the first time the writing on the t-shirt Eli was wearing beneath his hoodie. It was white text on a red background, some kind of nerd joke, just three words: YOU ARE HERE.

Yeah, he thought as he walked away, *wherever the hell that is.*

SG·U
STARGATE UNIVERSE™

AIR

JAMES SWALLOW

BASED ON THE SCRIPTS BY BRAD WRIGHT AND
ROBERT C. COOPER

FANDEMONIUM BOOKS

An original publication of Fandemonium Ltd, produced under license from MGM Consumer Products.

Fandemonium Books, PO Box 795A, Surbiton, Surrey KT5 8YB, United Kingdom
Visit our website: www.stargatenovels.com

STARGATE UNIVERSE™

METRO-GOLDWYN-MAYER Presents
STARGATE UNIVERSE™
ROBERT CARLYLE   LOUIS FERREIRA   BRIAN J. SMITH   ELYSE LEVESQUE
DAVID BLUE   ALAINA HUFFMAN   JAMIL WALKER SMITH
Executive Producers BRAD WRIGHT & ROBERT C. COOPER
Created by BRAD WRIGHT & ROBERT C. COOPER

ISBN: 978-1-905586-46-2 Printed in the USA

Acknowledgements:
The author would like to thank John Scalzi, Brad
Wright, Lawren Bancroft-Wilson, Joe Mallozzi, Karol
Mora and Jon Rosenberg for their assistance in getting
some air under the wings of this adaptation.

<u>Author's Note</u>:
This novel is based on the Stargate Universe
episodes "Air, Part 1", "Air, Part 2" and "Air,
Part 3". Certain scenes and story elements have
been adapted for the purposes of novelization.

PROLOGUE

In the deeps, in the places where the light of suns burns faint and the reach of gravity fails, nothing lives.

The void is inimical to life. Out in the darkness and the unremitting, absolute cold, the sheer absence of anything but scatterings of free hydrogen, cosmic rays and stellar dust means that nothing can survive.

The frail, weak meat of organic life perishes in moments. Blood and fluids flash-boiling and freezing all at once. Organs detonating under pressure violation. Skin disintegrating, precious breaths torn away. The dark punishes anything with the temerity to invade its realm; and in the infinite emptiness of it all, those who die are lost and forgotten.

But still they come, in search of something. Knowledge and power. Purpose and redemption. Life challenges the darkness to find its destiny.

Against the reach of the endless night and the ocean of stars, the ship thundered on, its voyage unending.

It was vast, by the human scale of things. If an observer could have stood upon the dorsal hull of the vessel, they would have seen canyons of old steel and domes of azure glass, great battlements of black iron and crenellations raised high; and beyond, dwarfing all else, a steep-sided ziggurat straddling the craft's mid-line. From close in, the dimensions of the construct could only be guessed at.

If one could stand at steps removed, far enough out beyond the glowing wake of energy that sheathed the vessel in transit, then the full shape of it would be revealed. From a sword-tip bow growing out to an enormous axe-blade stern, the ship cut through the dark. It might have been a weapon, thrown far

by a defiant enemy, or a graceful carving cast adrift by arti-
sans and thinkers. It moved quicker than the pulse of starlight itself, warping the nature of space about its long, ornate
flanks. The ship's course was straight and steady, set down by
minds long dead and maintained by thinking machines that
had shepherded the vessel across countless light-years.

The kiss of the void belied the age of it. In places, the hull
metal was as shipyard-bright as it had been the day it had
been forged; but elsewhere the passage of eons was visible in
pitted, corroded towers and broken spires. And there were
other scars upon her, scars that might have been marks left
by the fury of a singularity, the blaze of a mad sun, the hammer blow of a comet. Or perhaps not; perhaps they were the
wounds of tooth and claw from enemies who had died trying to take the ship for themselves. The disfigurements of
old battles, lost to time and long forgotten.

Within, the ship was not quite silent. Through each deck,
mighty engines as large as mountains made their power
known with a steady, bass rumble that reached everywhere,
resonating up through old iron floor plates and arching walls
of dense gunmetal. The vessel had a pulse of machine-life
to it, as slow and careful systemry continued on an endless
cycle of duties, following programs that had been laid down
in an era before humans had walked upright.

But it was faint indeed. Pale traceries of oxygen ice layered the lengths of the ship's endless, frigid corridors. The
cold and dormant spaces within the hull were dark and
bleak. As it had been for so long — *Decades? Centuries?
Millennia?* — there were no footsteps, no voices, no simple
human sounds. If there were ghosts, then they did not make
themselves known.

And then, without warning, in the heart of the craft the
stillness was shattered forever.

There were many spaces inside the ship that resembled the

chamber, long halls of arching iron ribs that rose up from
a worn deck to meet a darkened, forge-built ceiling. Turns
of copper-sheathed rails guided flights of stairs up from the
lowest level to a higher ring of balconies that looked down
upon the still, cold room. Here and there, sculpted consoles
emerged from the deck plates, faces turned upward, each one
catching a glitter of faint light across glassy, inert panels.

The chamber was unremarkable but for the one thing that
set it apart, the great object that could not fail to draw all
attention. At one end of the hall, rising from a slot in the deck,
a heavy ring of metal, gray as sea-ice, dense as cast pewter,
stood sentinel. Its circumference was separated into nine sections, each bordered by a sculpted arrowhead of steel, bone
and tarnished gold; and in turn each section was divided
into four leaves of metal, each etched with a string of symbols resembling lines, circles and dots.

Reaching out across some vast and incalculable distance,
exotic energies that were the precursors of a rip in the fabric
of space-time brushed the intelligence of the device, and the
ship that surrounded it. With a groan of collapsing energies,
the tempo of the vessel's vast drives slowed, and it fell back
from the near-light speed velocities of its normal cruise to
a more sedate pace.

Steady, patient devices buried in the walls came to life
with resonant gusts of atmosphere, flooding the chamber
with breathing gasses, while concealed elements in the floors
and the walls poured new heat into the room, warring against
the void-chill soaked deep through the starship's hull. Long-
silent warning sirens came to life.

The great steel circle trembled, awakening. With a rush
of sudden motion, the entirety of the ring began to rotate
about its axis, spinning, orienting itself for the instant when
it would accept a rush of power that had come to it from far
across the cosmic void.

At once, the spin halted and every chevron about the circle flashed a brilliant, star-bright white. From the inner space of the ring, dead air was transformed into a glittering, shining wave front. It thundered outward across the chamber, punching a channel through the substance of the universe itself. The storm-roar echoed down the empty corridors of the vessel, before dying away into a ripple of light and color.

The Stargate was open; and in the next second a human being came hurtling through it, too high, too fast, too hard.

Matthew Scott wasn't exactly a stranger to pain. He'd taken enough of it in his time. Fights in bars, rough play during high school sports, and that incident during jump training... But those had just been physical impacts, just the brute force collision between meat and obstacle. This was something outside his experience.

The lieutenant had heard the theory. Once in a while, the mention slipped into the conversations of the old dogs who'd served on the early SG teams, the guys who were now instructors or base commanders. He'd heard them talk about something they called 'the Hard Gate'. It had happened a fair few times in the early days of the Stargate program, or so the stories went. Something about the way the gate on Earth wasn't initially *exactly* synched up with the gate it was dialing out to. If it was just a little out of whack, you came out the other end covered in frost. But if the mismatch was above a certain tolerance, then it off-set your kinetic energy. You took a careful, easy step through the entry gate, but when you reached the exit end of the wormhole, well, the cumulative error in synch had accelerated you up some. The bigger the distance, the worse it would be. Of course, the dialing computers were quickly upgraded to deal with this problem and the incidence of a 'Hard Gate' dropped to almost nothing, and even on those rare occasions when it did occur, it usually only affected the first guy through the puddle, as the gates quickly cross-talked and stabilized the connection. But pity that guy walking point, though.

All this flashed through Matthew Scott's mind in the half-second or so between leaving Icarus Base behind and being shredded into a discorporated matter stream, then reintegrated to find himself flying through the air like he'd been shot from a cannon. The bright light and noise of the Icarus gate room, then the rush of the wormhole, were replaced by icy blackness — and for an instant Scott was gripped by the fear that he'd emerged through a planet-orbiting space gate, like they had out in the Pegasus galaxy; but then a steel floor came up out of the gloom and slammed into him, blasting the air from his lungs in an explosive wheeze.

He rolled over on to his back, blinking away the pain. The watery shimmer of wormhole-light cast a cold, polar glow over everything, surrounding him with jumping, fluid shadows.

A woman's scream, thin and reedy, snapped him back to the moment. Scott turned, ignoring the jags of pain all down his side, and looked toward the open Stargate. People were coming through after him, boiling across the threshold in rough disorder, one after another. Another man, then a woman, both of them carrying heavy packs, both of them yelling out as they collided with the floor, crashing into each other hard enough to bruise or maybe break bone. They barely got clear before more surged through behind them, and with each new arrival the chill air filled up with cries of panic and surprise. It was like watching a flood, and in amid the mayhem, baggage and vital equipment were getting knocked around or cast away.

Scott didn't see any uniforms among them and he grimaced reflexively. *Civilians. Take them out of their comfort zone and they fall to pieces.* He turned the pain from his bruises into annoyance, and that propelled him to his feet. Someone was going to have to play traffic cop here, and he was the only person in the room with bars on his collar.

"Get outta the way!" Securing his weapon, he darted forward, waving his hands and shoving stumbling figures away from the line of exit through the Stargate. "I said get outta the way, damn it! Make a hole!"

He gave a pale-faced guy in a lab coat a forceful push and almost stumbled right into the woman standing behind him. He saw dark hair framing Asian features, and eyes that were so lost and terrified he suddenly felt bad about dismissing the fears of the civvies so quickly. He remembered her name; Camile Wray, one of the suit-and-tie brigade posted to Icarus by the International Oversight Advisory.

"Where are we?" she said, her voice high and tight with tension. "This isn't the SGC! Why didn't we come back to Earth?"

Scott wasn't about to stop and discuss the matter of their swift exit. "There was no time to explain!" he snapped, and propelled her out toward the shadowed edges of the room. "Go!"

With swift motions and barked orders, the lieutenant started to make a dent in the chaos of the evacuees, dragging dazed newcomers out of the path of those following on behind, directing them to gather up fallen packs or just move away with whatever they'd been given to haul through. It was a hysterical moving day crossed with a haunted house ride, only much less fun than it sounded.

Other people saw what he was doing and joined in. Lab coat guy came back and began to copy Scott's actions, pulling new arrivals aside, guiding them off into the dimness. It wasn't enough, though. Too many people were spilling through, and they were coming faster than the folks on this side could deal with them.

The lieutenant took a breath and keyed the handheld radio clipped to the breast of his combat vest. "This is Scott," he said, "I need you to slow down the evac! Everyone's coming in too hot, we can't handle them!" When a reply didn't come back in the next instant, he tried again, calling for his commanding officer. "Colonel, come in! Do you copy me, over?"

Still nothing. He advanced toward the gate's event horizon, threading through people picking themselves up off the deck, or bumbling around like lost children. Without thinking he reached down and helped a civilian get to his feet.

The man stood up and Scott recognized another familiar face. "Doctor Rush?"

Nicholas Rush blinked and gave him a weak nod by way of a thank you. The man had a face that hinted at a hard life, eyes that could go right through you. Scott wondered if that was for show, or if that was who Rush really was.

"Lieutenant," he said, and Scott saw right away that the man wasn't the least bit afraid. If anything, the scientist looked… *interested.* Scott moved on, leaving Rush behind. Sure, the guy was some kind of super-genius, but there was something about the man's attitude that didn't sit right with the young Air Force officer. He shook the thought away; this wasn't the time to dwell on that. He had a job to do.

Scott tried the radio again, catching sight of Curtis, one of the base's USMC contingent. The Marine had an unconscious woman cradled in his arms, and there was blood marking her face from an ugly cut over her forehead.

Curtis shouted loud to be heard over the noise. "I need a medic here!"

"Sergeant!" Scott called out to get the man's attention, and pointed away with the radio. "Get any casualties off the line. Move 'em first, patch 'em later."

The Marine scowled back at him but accepted the order with a nod and moved off.

Scott tried the radio a third time. "Icarus Base, respond!"

All that came back through the open gate were more bodies.

Eli Wallace was *most definitely* a stranger to pain. One

could even suggest that he had done his best to live a life where his exposure to any pain-causing vectors was as minimal as humanly possible. Eli considered the eating of brutally spicy food, the occasional paintball tournament and an annual game of street hockey the only places where pain was allowed into his life. He didn't view this as a failing on his part in any way; rather, Eli imagined that it made him smarter than most people, who willingly busted themselves up for what he considered to be no good reason.

So coming though the Stargate at the head of a crowd of terrified people and being slammed into a steel floor was not something he was prepared for. Eli scrambled back to his feet, fighting down the raw, animal urge to panic, and ran his hands over his chest and legs, desperately afraid that he was going to find something in the wrong place.

He'd actually been looking forward to going through the Stargate for the first time, but being forced to do it under such dangerous and near-frantic conditions had worked up a whole array of fears in his mind. He'd closed his eyes as he went through, but all he could think of was the fate of poor Jeff Goldblum in *The Fly*. Eli patted his face, and felt a rush of relief when he realized it wasn't coming off in his hands.

He barely had time to register that before a big, heavy equipment case burped through the wormhole's event horizon and whizzed past his head, narrowly missing him. The case hit the deck in front of him and cracked open along a seam, disgorging its contents in a wide fan.

Nearby, a figure in a black combat uniform was leading one of the other scientists out of harm's way. Eli saw the woman's face and his eyes flicked to her name badge — Johansen. *She was a medic, wasn't she?*

"I think my arm's broken," said the man.

"Take it easy, Volker," she told him, moving him aside so she could concentrate on people with more immediate needs.

Eli turned back to the gate in time to see the next thing

coming through; a middle-aged man, in a suit that was probably worth more than every item of clothing Eli owned put together. The first word out of the man's mouth was "Chloe?"

"Senator Armstrong?" Eli hesitated, not sure what he should do to help the politician. He glanced around. Armstrong's daughter had been in front of Eli in the scramble to go through the gate; she had to be close by.

The senator didn't seem to notice Eli and pushed past him. "Chloe? Where are you?"

"Dad!" A voice called out from across the room and both of them turned to see a young woman in what had to be the most inappropriate outfit for their present circumstances. "I'm over here!" Chloe Armstrong somehow managed to remain looking dynamite in her designer dress, even though it was peppered with rock dust.

Armstrong started forward toward his daughter, and Eli trailed after him, but Johansen blocked the politician's path. "Senator, give me a hand, please." She gestured at an injured man lying at her feet. He was one of the number crunchers from the base labs, and looking very much the worse for wear.

Armstrong was still focused on Chloe. "But my daughter is—"

"She's fine, I saw her," said the officer, her voice all hard edges and command school brusque. "But this man isn't, so give me a hand!"

Belatedly, Eli realized that he ought to be helping as well, and moved in to give some support to the pair of them. The woman gave him a nod and he placed her face. Her first name was Tamara; he'd heard some of the other Air Force guys calling her 'T.J.' She looked like the type of person who could flick from severe to smooth in a heartbeat.

"Over here," she said, and Eli and Armstrong dutifully followed her to a clear spot to put the guy down. Tamara bent

over the scientist, and so she didn't see Armstrong grimace
in pain, his face going pale. The senator's hand went to his
side, and Eli opened his mouth to speak; but the man was
already walking away, his job done.

"Are you okay?" Chloe asked, coming to her father.

"I'm fine, I'm fine," said Armstrong, covering his moment
of pain as they walked off. "Where the hell are we?"

Eli stood and watched Tamara work, suddenly at a loss for
what to do with his hands.

Nicholas Rush took the curved stairs two at a time, almost
bounding on to the upper level of the chamber — *the gate
room*, he corrected. His hands dropped to the rail around
the edge of the upper balcony and he flinched. For a second
he could have sworn he felt an electric tingle run through
him, a giddy thrill at the sheer amazement of standing here,
in this place, seeing this sight. His gaze flicked down to the
rail. The metal was old and pitted, but worn smooth from
the action of hands upon it. Rush wondered how long it had
been since a human being had stood where he stood now,
touched the metal that he was touching. *Millions of years
ago*? It was staggering to consider. The construction of the
chamber was like no Ancient technology he had seen. The
metallic structure was repeated everywhere, on the walls and
the rails. Below he'd found a console of similar design, but it
hadn't responded to any of his attempts to activate it.

He looked up and stared out across the room, across the
chaos below. Some fifty, perhaps sixty people had now arrived
through the open Stargate, disordered and afraid, some literally forming a pile of bodies and equipment in front of
the shimmering wormhole. Rush blinked and realized that
this was the first time he had looked back to actually see the
Stargate he had come through. The white glow of the active
chevrons burned hard in the dimness, illuminating a construct clearly different from the gate designs found in the

Milky Way and Pegasus galaxies.

Perhaps that's the original pattern, he wondered, *the classic model?* He filed away the thought for later consideration.

People were still trickling through, fleeing in panic from the calamity unfolding back at Icarus, all that distance away at the far end of the wormhole. Rush knew that on some level he was supposed to be afraid, but he didn't feel it. He looked down at the people, at the soldiers and civilians, his so-called colleagues and the rest of the make-weights, and he found himself looking right through them.

He took it all in, the Stargate, the walls of gray steel and the air of old and ancient days; and it was all he could do not to break into a smile. The only emotion he could bring to light was pride.

Scott had given up on the radio and gone back to doing what he could at his end — namely, motivating the Icarus refugees with sharp words and in some cases, your actual kick in the ass. By this point, a good percentage of the people coming through were airmen and jarheads, and they were trained well enough that when a motivated-looking young first lieutenant barked an order in their direction, they did what they were told, double-time.

The civilians, though… They were utterly unready for this. Icarus was supposed to be a cushy, low-traction posting where scientists did things with boxes of blinky lights and generally had nothing more to worry about than running low on pudding in the mess hall. They just weren't trained for everything to go from fine to FUBAR at the drop of a hat.

So, like they told him at OCS, *if in doubt, shout.* Scott drew in a breath and snarled at every civilian in earshot. "Clear this area! There could still be more incoming!"

Airmen and Marines would have moved. The civilians mostly just hesitated. They were still working off the shock of it all, and the gate journey was just one more thing on top of everything else that had happened.

It was Ron Greer's voice that cut through the stunned silence. "You heard him, people!" he roared, drill-sergeant loud. "Move move *move*!"

That lit a fire under them, and finally the people in front of the gate began to shift away, but not quick enough.

Greer threw him a look and Scott nodded to the stocky, dark-skinned Marine. "Where's Colonel Young?" he asked.

"He was right behind me," said Greer, nodding back toward the open wormhole.

Scott turned to the gate in time to see the last man come through; and he pitied the poor son-of-a-bitch, because the black-clad figure was buoyed on a brilliant blast of fire and smoke that crashed out of the gate behind him. The force of the discharge blew hot, charred air into the gate room, bringing with it the stink of burnt plastic, ozone and other smells that Scott didn't want to think too much about.

He barely had time to process all that when the Stargate gave a rattling hum and went dark. The wormhole vanished into quantum foam and all illumination in the chamber was extinguished. The screaming started a second or two after that.

Someone shouted "Lights!" and a bright beam stabbed out of the darkness, sweeping across the room. Scott saw smoke-dirty faces caught in the sodium glare, staring out into the dark, desperate and afraid.

More flashlights blinked on, and Scott snatched a MagLite from the grip of a nearby airman and went searching. A cold, unpleasant certainty was settling in on him, and as much as he didn't want to confirm it, he knew he had to.

His beam fell on the crumpled form of the last man through, and Scott's jaw set. "Colonel?"

Colonel Everett Young grimaced with pain and tried to lever himself off the deck without success. Scott moved closer, and tried very hard not to think about the fact that Young was the first survivor he had seen that outranked him.

The colonel blinked owlishly and focused on the other officer. Scott's CO looked ten years older than his normal hard-edged forties, the pain taking all the life out of him. "Where are we?" he coughed.

Scott bent down to support the colonel's head, holding him up so they could converse face to face. "I don't know, sir." *Kinda hoped you'd have that answer.* "Are you…?"

Young tried to move but the effort drained him. "Lieutenant," he began, and Scott knew what he would say next before the words left his lips. "You're in charge."

He was going to argue, but the colonel put an end to that by losing consciousness. Scott cursed under his breath and settled the man back on the deck; and that was when he realized his hand was wet. He shone the flashlight on his palm and it was crimson with Young's blood.

In an instant he was standing and calling out. "T.J.! Get over here!" He turned and spotted her bent over an injured scientist.

Tamara ignored the order for a moment. She took the hand of another civvie — a woman, one of the other eggheads from Icarus — and placed it carefully over a wound she'd just bandaged. "Keep pressure here until the bleeding stops." Then she was striding over to him, her expression unreadable.

Scott stood back and let her take a look at Young. "Is he okay?"

The medic bent down. "I don't know."

"We *need* him," he hissed, in a low, intense voice.

Tamara didn't look up. "Yeah. I got that. Just back off, Matt. Give me some room to work."

"Right." He did so, and found his hands tensing into fists. How all of this had landed on his shoulders was beyond him. It wasn't what he'd expected. Not at *all*.

Scott's flashlight caught a thickset figure in a hoodie at the edge of its illumination and he went after him. "Wallace!"

The genius turned to him. He looked as dazed as everyone else. "Uh…"

"What is this place?" demanded Scott. "Do you know what planet it is, or if it's a ship, or whatever?"

Eli held up a hand, apparently afraid that he was about to get blamed for something. "Look, I just did what Rush told me to—"

Scott seized on the mention of the other man's name. "Where is he?"

"I don't know, he went through the gate ahead of me."

The lieutenant nodded. "Yeah, he made it, I saw him." He moved into the middle of the chamber, calling out "Rush! Rush, where are you?"

Greer approached, jerking a thumb over his shoulder. "Went that way, I think. Up the stairs over there."

Scott accepted this with a nod. If anyone was going to have answers, it would be the Brit doctor. He took a step and a sullen rumble echoed through the decks. He had the sudden sense of the whole ship tensing around them, like an animal coiling its muscles before pouncing; then a second tremor resonated through, and Scott felt a brief sensation of motion and velocity that faded a heartbeat later.

"What the hell was that?" said Greer.

"I don't know." Scott hesitated, then snapped out an order to the Marine. "Sergeant, get these people settled down. Start making an inventory of everything we brought through as soon as you can. Try to figure out who and what we have. No one leaves this room." He shot a look at Wallace and, as an afterthought, thrust the MagLite into his hand. "Eli! You help him!"

The guy took the flashlight and panned it around, and his face changed as he got the first good look at the place they were in. Eli's mouth dropped open.

It was then, just by chance, that Scott noticed for the first time the writing on the t-shirt Eli was wearing beneath his hoodie. It was white text on a red background, some kind of nerd joke, just three words: YOU ARE HERE.

Yeah, he thought as he walked away, *wherever the hell that is.*

72 hours earlier

CHAPTER ONE

*T*he skies above the planet Omegus IV were a curtain of
   atomic flame.

   SkullCruisers from the nine fleets of the Star Mongols lay
in orbit, their neutronic blasters raining blazing particle death
down upon the last bastion world of the Phoenix Brigade.
Time ebbed away; soon the photon shell protecting the planet
would break open like a Y'kin'la egg, and the peaceful Omegusi
would perish...and all because they had been unlucky enough
to evolve on a world that had once been a home to the time-
lost Precursors.

   The warriors of Phoenix Brigade, the galaxy's most steadfast
defenders, had tracked the hyper-advanced Precursor technology from star to star, in hopes of uncovering the most powerful of the super-science relics the lost civilization had created—the device the Earthmen had nicknamed 'Prometheus';
but the Star Mongols, the pirates of a million looted planets,
were not willing to let the device fall into the hands of the law-
ful and the noble.

   If they could not have Prometheus, then they would oblit-
erate it.

   Queen Xaria of the Omegusi bent her knee before the elite
Phoenix Brigade warrior and bowed low, her golden hair cascading down over her blue-skinned shoulders and the low-cut
gown that revealed the swell of her breasts.

   "Lord Captain," she began breathlessly, indicating the stone
temple before them. "Our laws forbid us from entering the
Temple of Dakara, but it is said that the force you Earthers
call Prometheus lurks within. I grant you passage into the holy
spaces, so that you might deliver us from the space brigands who
come to pillage our world." The Queen waved her scepter and

the mystic force wall crumbled. "Enter, hero, if you dare."

The warrior began to move, but the Omegusi ruler had one more thing to say. "Warrior. If you do this, I will give you my hand in matrimony. All that I have will be yours. I ask only that you give me your true name before you embark on this final test."

The Phoenix Brigade warrior paused before answering. "Oh, yeah, right. My name is, uh, ELIsDaMan.*"*

"That is a sucky handle, though," said the tinny male voice in the headset. *"It doesn't have...whaddayacall, dignity."*

Eli paused, lifting his hands from the keyboard of his computer to reach for the open can of Mountain Dew at his side. He snorted into the microphone at his mouth. "Oh, right. And I suppose *Babes_DigMeee* is a noble and heroic name?"

"It's an accurate one," came the reply, winging its way across the continental US from Kansas, where Eli's gamer buddy Josh was busy fighting hordes of Vacuum Dragons instead of working his night shift at the local branch of Buy More.

"In your dreams."

"Yes," agreed Josh, *"Frequently, in fact."*

Eli sipped his Dew and rolled his eyes, before hunting out a slice of cooling pizza from the box at his feet. As he went for it, his gaze passed over the clock atop his bookshelf and he very carefully ignored the fact that it was past two in the morning. Instead he drummed his fingers in time to the opening riff of Van Halen's 'Atomic Punk' as it issued from a well-worn iPod.

"How can you listen to that dinosaur rock, man?"

Eli made a face. "You have no appreciation of the classics. No wonder you keep getting ganked."

He heard Josh cough out a denial. *"I'm not the one wasting my time. That puzzle, with the Queen and all? It's a fake-out."*

"Beg to differ with you." Eli squared his shoulders and leaned in, hands dancing across the keyboard. On the screen, the noble warrior *ELIsDaMan* stormed forward and vaulted into the Temple of Dakara, toward a wall covered with heavy buttons made of stone. "It's just a question of figuring out the code sequence. Get it right and you win. The core of the planet is the power source. You have to channel it into the weapon to destroy the enemy command ship."

Each of the buttons bore a set of symbols; some of them were blocky shapes that resembled letters, while others were strings of lines and circles. The latter reminded Eli of old Morse Code dot-dash notations.

"Can't be done, dude."

Eli thought otherwise. It all came down to math, and numbers spoke to Eli Wallace in a way that he couldn't really articulate, even if he tried. It was just a thing that he did. He could see the figures strung together, even when they were cloaked under funny-looking symbols like they were right now. Get them in the right order and they fitted like the parts of a well-oiled machine. It was something he'd been able to accomplish ever since he was a kid.

He tapped the keys and used the mouse to start his computer game avatar working at the stone buttons. "I'm doin' it," he reported. In moments, he'd unlock the game's big prize, blast the bad guys and get the alien space babe.

Josh's confidence in him was underwhelming, however. *"It's one'a those programmer's jokes. It can't be solved. They just put it in there to mess with your head. Nobody has ever beaten it."*

Eli felt a grin cross his lips. He saw the solution in his mind, plain as day. "Already solved it."

"You did not." Josh was adamant.

Pausing to take another sip, Eli cracked his knuckles and put his hand back on the mouse. "Shut up and watch this." He knew Josh was peeking in on his feed from the *Prometheus* game server, and that was fine. He wanted a witness to his stunning victory. Eli tapped the controls and on the screen, his avatar pressed home the final glowing symbols. "Yeah. That's it. Take that!"

What he expected next was some fully-rendered, high-spec CGI cut-scene of *ELIsDaMan* smiting the Space Mongols and winning ultimate power. Instead, the on-screen view flickered and jerked, then reset, placing his character on a mountaintop that was many, many virtual miles from the Queen and her temple.

"What the hell…?" He blinked, waiting for an error message pop-up, but nothing appeared. He'd simply been bounced right back to the start of the instance that had led him to the temple. Reset, just like that; and with it, months of careful gameplay wasted.

"*What happened?*"

"Nothing." Eli rested the urge to curse. "Nothing happened. I'm back at the beginning of the level…"

Josh made a negative noise. "*You are so full of yourself. Guess you're not so smart after all, huh?*" He broke up into sniffy giggles.

Eli ignored him, shaking his head, annoyed at the arbitrary unfairness of the game's glitch. "It worked," he insisted. "The firing code locked in."

"*Whatever. Look, I'm going to gear up with ChezeGod and the other guys for a raid on the Mecha-Centaurs, you wanna come with?*"

"No." In disgust, Eli pulled off the headset and glared at his virtual self on the screen, as if it were the fault of Elite Lord Captain *ELIsDaMan* that the game had suffered some kind of brain-fart. "That was extremely unsatisfying."

For a second, he thought about bringing up his router dashboard, maybe checking the settings to make sure there hadn't been some weird lag between his PC and the *Prometheus* game servers, but then his fatigue caught up with him and Eli realized that his eyes felt like sand and he hadn't taken a pee in over ninety minutes. All those sodas had to go somewhere.

Thoroughly irritated, Eli vowed that tomorrow morning would be spent posting a stinging rebuke on the *Prometheus* message boards about the glitchy puzzle, and he padded away to the bathroom, composing his retort in his mind, already thinking about sleep.

Because of this, he was out of the room when the lights on his wireless modem began flashing furiously, as his anti-virus and firewall programs were swiftly and effortlessly penetrated.

He awoke from dreams about cute girls with blue skin, to the sound of his name being shouted in that particular tone that only female parents are capable of making. *The Mom-Sound.*

"Eli!" The door banged open and Marion Wallace, late like she always was, waded in through the debris of her son's slacker lifestyle, fixing a 'Hi! How Can I Help?' badge to the top of the blouse they made her wear at Bobbi's Fine Dine.

Eli's awareness rose slightly from his sleep-addled state, but not enough to form a cogent reply. He lay face down amid the snarl of sheets, sprawled and unkempt.

"You didn't even set your alarm…" she continued, then raised the gain on her shout an octave higher. "*Eli!*"

That was enough to shock him fully awake, and he blinked back to something approaching alertness. "What?" he managed.

Marion was now in the process of smoothing down her outfit, simultaneously fixing her son with an acid glare. "I don't have time for this. I thought you had a job interview today?"

"They cancelled," offered Eli, his words muffled by a faceful of pillow. "I was up all night."

Neither explanation was satisfactory. Marion glared at Eli's inert computer, which occupied one corner of his room with so much hardware and strewn cables, it resembled a freeze-frame of an explosion in an electronics store. "Playing those stupid games?" She rounded on him, her disappointment bubbling over. "*They* cancelled, or *you* cancelled?"

Eli gave her a hang-dog look. "Not my skill set, Mom. Seriously."

She'd heard that before. "Nothing is." Marion glanced at her watch and hissed between her teeth. "I'm late. We'll talk about it later."

The lack of reply she got made it likely that her son had already slipped back into a doze, and she made her way to the door, pausing on the threshold to sigh. Eli was a smart kid, all the tutors had said so, but nothing could keep him focused for more than a short while. Marion despaired of the fact that Eli might never actually find the one thing that could hold his attention. Frowning, grabbing her keys, she jogged swiftly down the stairs and snatched up her coat on the way out. Marion hoped that Eli would be able to buckle down long enough to actually find whatever 'it' was, because she was damn sure opportunity wasn't going to come knocking at the door.

He folded the report closed and dropped it on the seat next to him, before pausing to flick a tiny piece of lint from the front of his uniform jacket. "You're sure this is the one, Doctor?"

The man sitting opposite him in the limo made a face. "You saw the report."

"I saw that some kid busting the high score on *Donkey Kong* is apparently a reason to get me out of bed at oh-dark-thirty hours."

"It's a little more complicated than that, General. The decode test requires a unique mindset and no little skill to complete. You read the boy's academic records. High IQ, low self-esteem, intelligent but an under-achiever. Potential without purpose. Just the kind of resource the program needs that gets lost in the cracks."

"If you say so. I just thought we had enough brains on board without have to do this whole *Sword in the Stone* thing."

"As I said," continued the doctor, his tone cooling, "it's more complicated than that."

"It so often is." The general reached for the door handle. "Wait in the car till I call you," he said.

"Uh, sir—"

He ignored the other man, picking up his service cap and setting it squarely on his head. "Don't worry, the uniform makes a strong first impression." He tapped the file. "I got a read on this kid. Believe me, I know the type pretty well."

"Geniuses?"

"Geeks." He stepped out into the overcast day, and even though he didn't need them, put on his pair of service-issue HGU-4/P sunglasses to add a final touch of Air Force cool.

The house was pretty much the same as every other one on the block: small, suburban, two-bedroom. There were signs of neglect here and there, though. A patchy lawn, peeling paint. The file filled in the gaps. Home payments in the black, but just a little too short of money for anything above the line.

He strode up to the door and gave what his dad had always called a 'soldier knock'. *Bang-bang*, hard and fast. *Open Up*, it said.

The door opened and on the threshold stood the kid, a little doughy, a little lazy-looking, wearing a t-shirt, a hoodie and baggy pajama bottoms. He blinked when he saw the dress blues and a new alertness snapped into place in his expression — it was very much an '*Oh Shit*' moment for him.

The general had seen his picture in the file, an unflattering shot scanned from a college yearbook, but he had to ask the question anyhow. "Eli Wallace?"

"What's going on?" The kid's eyes went, like most civilians did, straight to the wedge of ribbons and bars that represented the officer's numerous decorations.

He fixed Eli with a hard stare that went right through the sunglasses. "I'm General Jack O'Neill."

The next emotion on Wallace's face was barely suppressed panic. "Actually, Eli's not here right now…"

Satisfied he'd made the right first impression, O'Neill glanced over his shoulder and nodded at the limo.

Eli kept talking. "Look, whatever you think I did, I swear you've got the wrong guy."

He turned back, his gaze as steely as ever. He had to admit, he was actually enjoying making the lad squirm. "Do I look like someone who would be standing here if I didn't already know everything about you?"

Eli considered this for a moment, and saw the truth of it. "Not really," he admitted. "Who are you people?"

The doctor was coming up beside him, and O'Neill let him take the next step. "I'm Doctor Nicholas Rush. May we come in?"

Eli didn't move. "Why?"

"You've spent a great deal of time recently playing an on-line fantasy game called *Prometheus*," said Rush.

The kid's incredulity overwhelmed his terror for just a moment. "Seriously? Big Brother's got nothing better to do than to watch me grinding for cheeves?"

"I have no idea what that means," offered O'Neill.

Rush pressed on. "This morning you solved the Dakara weapon puzzle."

Now they were on the kid's territory, he got a little more confident. "Yeah, a month of my life went into that. You know what happens when you solve that thing? Nothing."

O'Neill indicated himself and Rush. "We're here. *That* happened."

The doctor smiled slightly. "To complete that particular puzzle, you had to solve a millennia-old mathematical proof written in another language. And for that, you've won…something of a prize."

"Oh yeah?" Avarice flickered in Eli's eyes. "Whatever it is, I'll take the cash equivalent."

"There isn't one," said O'Neill, as Rush produced a steel clipboard and a pen.

He offered it, but Wallace didn't bite. "It's a non-disclosure agreement," added Rush.

Eli gingerly took the document and studied it as if he thought it might be poisonous. "Non-disclosure?" he repeated. "So you guys really embedded a top secret, unsolvable problem into a videogame, hoping someone like me would crack it?"

"Yep," O'Neill deadpanned. "You'd be surprised how often that happens."

"Really?"

"No. Not really."

Eli gave them a wary look. "So if I solved it, what do you need me for now?"

Rush indicated the document. "I assure you, it will be worth your while to sign that."

The kid turned the pen over between his fingers. "And if I don't?"

O'Neill gave him a steady, intent stare. "Then we'll beam you up to our spaceship."

Eli gave a nervous chuckle, which died in moments when he saw that the general wasn't joking. He moved away a step, backing into his house. "Right. I think I want my lawyer to look at it first…"

"By *lawyer*," said O'Neill, "I assume you mean *mother*?"

The door was already closing. "Why don't we just go ahead and agree that *I* will call *you*?"

Then O'Neill and Rush were standing alone on the stoop. "I can see you've done this recruiting thing a lot, General," said the doctor, with no little sarcasm. "Good job."

"Just priming him, is all," he replied, reaching into his pocket for an encrypted cell phone. "Now we make with some *shock and awe*." He tabbed the speed-dial for a number that did not and would never exist in any kind of public record, and waited a moment.

When the line connected he spoke a terse codeword and gave his orders. "Walter? Contact Carter. Tell her she has a go."

Eli took a couple of steps into the hallway and paused, looking over the paper in his hand.

He read the words at the top of the form out loud. "Homeworld Command." That had to be a misprint, surely? Wasn't it called Home*land* Security, or something? He shook his head. And who the hell was that O'Neill guy to come to his door and play the whole *Men In Black* routine with him?

His fingers tensed around the pen. He hoped this wasn't something about all the stuff he'd downloaded off the internet. The government really frowned on that, so he'd heard.

Eli's skin began to tingle and he gasped. From out of nowhere, a brilliant white glow was forming all around him, blotting out everything. A high-pitched sound filled his ears, and he flinched and tried to scream—

—But then the white glow faded away and he was in a completely different place. A steel-walled room, like the inside of a warship or a bunker. Eli blinked, turning toward the far side of the chamber, and what he saw almost made him drop the pen and paper in surprise.

"What the...?"

One whole wall was a vast floor-to-ceiling window, and beyond it... Beyond it was the most incredible thing Eli Wallace had ever seen.

Earth. The planet lay below him, turning slowly, curtains of white cloud moving over azure seas and rich umber tracts of land. With a start, he recognized the Florida peninsula, and his eyes flicked across the sight, picking out landmarks half-remembered from geography class.

He heard the same hum, caught a glimmer of the white flash from the corner of his eye, but he could not draw his gaze away from the view out the window. Rush walked up alongside him and shared it.

"Welcome aboard the *Hammond*, Eli."

He tried to speak, but his mouth wouldn't work, so he just pointed. *Is that what I think it is?* said the gesture.

Rush gave a nod. "Yes, that is the planet Earth, and yes, you are aboard a spaceship." He said it so matter-of-factly that it shocked Eli back into speaking.

"Wh-what happened to the other guy?"

"General O'Neill had to return to Washington."

"Oh." Eli wondered how O'Neill had traveled. Did he do the *Star Trek* thing as well, or did that fancy limo they'd parked outside his house transform into a jet plane, or something? "But I didn't sign…"

"You will," said Rush. "We need your help, Eli. This is very important." He indicated the non-disclosure form, still gripped in Eli's hand. He gave a rueful smile. "To be honest, I don't really know how long it's going to take."

The reality of his situation was starting to catch up to him. "I should call my mom…" He fished in a pocket for his cell phone. "Let her know where I am."

Rush shook his head. "That won't work up here."

Eli stared lamely at his phone. "Right." *What could I say to her even if I could call? 'Hey, Mom, guess what? I've just been kidnapped by the United States Air Force!'*

"You can speak to her en route," said Rush. "There's a cover story you'll have to follow." He nodded to himself, as if remembering something. "Don't worry, these people have been doing this sort of thing for over a decade."

Eli's brain caught up with Rush's words. "Wait, I'm sorry. En route? En route to where?"

"To P4X-351. Another planet, approximately twenty-one light-years from here."

It was getting harder to handle all this at once. The size of these ideas were crowding out his brain. Eli shook his head. "I can't go. I have things to—"

Rush interrupted. "We know about your mother's condition."

"What?" The mention of Mom's illness, so sudden and so bald, immediately dragged Eli right back to the real, the everyday and earthbound actuality of his life. He felt a momentary flash of resentment. "Well, you know everything, don't you?"

"We also know you are not currently employed and that your mother's medical coverage is an ongoing issue." Eli gave a shallow nod to that, thinking of the pile of bills back on the kitchen table. The staff HMO plan at the Fine Dine wasn't exactly up to much. "We're going to see that she gets the best care available while you're gone," Rush concluded.

Eli weighed the paper in his hand. It suddenly felt like it was made of lead. "How do I know this isn't something freaky? Like, maybe you and that General guy drugged me, messed with my head?" He thought about his mother and something twisted in his chest. "Are you people for real?"

The other man nodded toward the window. "This is as real as it gets, Eli."

He held up the papers. "And if I don't sign? What? You erase my memory?"

"Something like that." Rush smiled at him, and it wasn't reassuring. "Let's just say it'd be easier if you did sign it."

Eli sighed and found the spot where his signature was supposed to go. He scrawled it in and handed the papers back to Rush, before looking down.

Abruptly, the state of his wardrobe became clear to him. He pulled at his pajama bottoms and gave Rush a sheepish glance. "Can I get some pants?"

CHAPTER TWO

Unnoticed by all but a very small percentage of the Earth's population, the starship *George S. Hammond* left orbit, passing behind the far side of the moon before charging into the other-dimensional realm of hyperspace.

Eli had insisted on being allowed to watch it happen, despite pointed suggestions from Doctor Rush that he take "the whole space thing" one step at a time. Once he'd gotten past the kidnap-abduction bit, though, Eli was starting to warm to the idea of being chosen for something this cool. And the great thing was, he hadn't had to get to it the hard way like the Air Force types he encountered around the ship, men and women who'd clearly footslogged and fought their way up to getting a posting aboard the *Hammond*, one of — so he'd been told — a handful of advanced interstellar spacecraft that were now in service protecting humanity from the dangers out there in the dark. Eli hadn't gotten around to asking exactly what those dangers might be, because he wasn't really sure he wanted to know.

He concentrated on the cool stuff. Watching the ship hit hyperdrive was incredible, as space melted away into a tunnel of blue-white energy and the speed of light shattered like glass. Somewhere, Albert Einstein was foaming at the mouth.

They didn't let him wander all over the place, though. He had a small cabin to himself, and some USAF flunky had shown the foresight to have a bag of his clothes sent up before they broke orbit. He'd asked if he could see the bridge and they'd said no. When he asked one of the crew if they had a holodeck, the guy had nodded gravely and then given Eli directions that took him to the female washroom. It had been, in retrospect, a dumb question.

But it was still very cool. It was like that movie, *The Last Starfighter*. He'd been picked for his gamer prowess to help save the world. The secret dream of every player since someone dropped the first quarter on *Space Invaders*.

At least, he hoped it was that. On some level, he was still holding away the fear that at any moment, the walls would retract and he would find himself on some hidden camera show called *How Gullible Are You?*

And just when he was wondering what he'd be doing all the way to planet whatever, Rush sat him down with what could only be described as a library of educational movies, which were not a lot different from the ones he remembered from fourth grade — only with the added complication of being Mega-Ultra Top Secret.

There was that line in *Star Wars* where Ben Kenobi tells Luke Skywalker that he's taken his "first step into a larger world". Eli understood exactly what he meant now, as the information films started to unfold, showing him stuff he'd never dreamed could be real. And it was clear that Old Obi-Wan had forgotten to mention that the first step was a real doozy.

On the screen, a bookish guy in spectacles walked through the concrete corridors of a military facility, the blunt Fifties nuclear-scare design mingled in with modern-day tech retrofitted over the top.

"*Hello,*" he began warmly, in the time-honored tradition of all educational film narrators, "*I'm Doctor Daniel Jackson...*"

"And you might remember me from such other instructional videos as '*Help! I was Abducted by the Air Force!*' and '*Outer Space is Rad!*'" Eli laughed out loud at his own joke, disappointed that there was no-one else in the room to appreciate his wit.

Jackson was now standing in front of a big metal ring with a ramp leading up to it. "*Behind me is a Stargate. Found in*

Giza, Egypt in 1928, we now know it was originally built by an alien race who we call 'the Ancients', many millennia ago. Over the next few hours we'll be touching on some of the things you need to know about this incredible technology and the universe of possibilities it has opened up for humanity."

The next few *hours?* First spaceships and now alien artifacts? Eli began to wonder what he'd agreed to when he signed that paperwork. "Probably should have actually *read* it first," he told himself.

As the narrator went on, Eli's attention became locked on the man's explanations. The more he heard, the more he was sucked in. Jackson explained the nature of the 39 symbols around the curves of the Stargate, each representing constellations as seen from Earth, and how the device used a seven symbol address to open up an interstellar wormhole across the Milky Way, capable of sending people and objects hundreds of thousands of light-years in seconds. Forget the starships and hyperdrive; this was like a subway system for the whole galaxy.

"The first six symbols lock down a point in space," continued Jackson, who never once seemed to lose enthusiasm for his subject, *"while the seventh represents the point of origin."*

On the screen the chevrons around the ring flashed orange-red and locked in place. Eli wasn't sure what he thought would happen next, but it certainly wasn't a thunderous whoosh of noise and an explosive plume of what first seemed like liquid silver. His eyes bugged. "Whoa."

"An unstable energy vortex emerges from the gate and settles into the event horizon or 'puddle' as we like to call it," noted Jackson, with a grin. *"Later, it was discovered that using an eighth symbol would actually dial another galaxy, like the addition of the prefix numeral one to a long distance phone call."*

Eli used his fingers to mime a phone at his ear. "Ring ring. Intergalactic Pizza, can I take your order, please?"

Each time he thought he'd seen all the recordings had to

offer, Doctor Daniel Jackson reappeared with something else to tell him, but after a while Eli began to feel beaten up by the sheer volume of information that was being thrown at him, without even a moment's pause to process it. He was like a boxer, slammed one too many times around the head, only here it was mind-busting ideas and the general level of sheer *you've-got-to-be-kidding-me* that was wearing him down.

If crossing the gaps between galaxies wasn't enough, Jackson was now talking about a *ninth* chevron that could take them still further, and some of the data Eli glimpsed on the screen seemed a lot like the code he'd cracked in the game. "*It is believed an unprecedented amount of power is required to reach the mysterious destination,*" said the scientist. "*Icarus Base was established on a planet discovered two years ago to have a uniquely powerful core made of a mineral called naquadria. The entire purpose of the project is to hopefully one day dial the nine chevron address found in the Ancient database.*"

Eli rocked back in his seat and buried his hands in his pockets, still trying to process it all. His fingers touched the worn plastic of his cell phone and he drew it out and looked at it. The device was totally useless to him, but he hadn't been able to leave it in his cabin, as if on some level holding on to the stupid thing was keeping him connected to Earth, and to his mother. He closed his eyes and sighed.

Marion Wallace grabbed the phone off the kitchen wall after the second ring and held her breath. "Eli?"

"*Hey, Mom. How are you?*"

"Okay. Work was busy, as usual." She stopped, catching herself before she launched into her regular daily round of bitching about her day at the Fine Dine and all the small indignities she suffered there. She missed not having Eli there to hear them out.

She thought about when she'd come home the day before,

the day he missed the interview, and found a very polite young lady from the military waiting at the front door. She'd had some things to tell her, and a check for a large sum of money.

"Where are you?" Marion asked. At first she was afraid that Eli had done something wrong, maybe got mixed up with bad people in one of those game things of his. She'd heard on the news that terrorists used those chat-rooms and on-line games to meet and talk about hurting people. The polite young lady has assured her it was nothing like that, as she gathered up a bag of Eli's stuff.

When he replied, there was a strange crackling echo around his voice, like you got when someone was making a transatlantic phone call. "*It's top secret.*"

She heard the sadness in his voice. "Eli…"

"*I'm serious, Mom. I can't tell you anything more than that. But don't worry, I'm fine.*"

Marion sat on the kitchen stool, and for a moment she felt a terrible, incredible sense of distance from the voice on the other end of the line. "I don't understand. Why couldn't you at least tell me you were leaving? You just upped and went, no explanation…."

"*That was part of the deal,*" he said, and she knew he was keeping something back from her. "*I'm sorry, but did you get the letter from—*"

"The Air Force, yes, I got it." She nodded across the empty room. The letter was there on the kitchen table where she had put it after the polite young lady had left. It talked about 'valuable contributions' and 'important work' and 'national security'. It talked about other things, too, without saying them. Paid doctor bills and cleared debts.

She sighed. Of all the options her son could have been looking at as a career, serving his country was not something Marion Wallace would ever have put on the list. She heard an odd rumble in the background. "Are you on a plane now?

You sound like you're in an airplane."

For a moment, he betrayed a little excitement in his words. "*No, no. Trust me, it's nothing like that. It's intelligence work. What you can know is in the letter, but I want you to know that they're going to look after you.*"

"You didn't have to do this. I pushed you too hard to get a job."

"*No, no, Mom... This is good. Really, it's the kind of thing I always dreamed of. I know it's going to take some getting used to, for both of us... But I just couldn't say no.*"

Marion felt a stab of sadness and pushed it away before it dared to become the start of a sob. "Okay. Okay, Eli. I know you'll do great. Just do your best."

"*I'll call you again soon,*" he said. "*Love you, Mom.*"

"*Love you too.*" His mother's voice crackled and faded, and for a moment he couldn't be sure if she had been crying. The channel cut and Eli put down the headset connected to the intercom in his cabin, and sat heavily on his bunk.

He sat there alone, watching the waves of hyperspace flash past the window in the steel wall, feeling every bit of the light-years of distance.

She rapped on the hatch with her knuckles, and from within came a distracted voice. "Come in."

Entering the cramped visiting officer's quarters, she saw Rush bent over a laptop and a scattering of papers, his attention buried deep in his work. Before she could speak, he gestured at a covered tray from the ship's kitchen on a nearby shelf. "I'm done with that," he said.

Her lips thinned. "I'll be sure to have one of my crew square that away for you, doctor."

Rush looked up in surprise. "Colonel Carter." He recovered quickly and gave her a flat smile. "I'm sorry." Immediately, he was closing the lid of the laptop. "What can I do for you?"

Carter kept a neutral expression on her face. "I didn't have the chance to speak to you before we broke orbit. I wanted to check in before we reached Icarus Base."

"I appreciate your interest, but I'm fine," he replied. Rush nodded at the computer. "I'm sure you understand I have a lot of last-minute checks to go over…"

He was trying to dismiss her on her own ship; Carter resisted the urge to sit and folded her arms instead. In truth, she wasn't really sure of her own motives in approaching Rush, but she felt like something needed to be said to the man. Carter had made no secret of her reservations about certain elements of Project Icarus from the get-go. "General O'Neill has given the *Hammond* clearance to remain in orbit for a few days after we drop you off. We'll provide additional sensor coverage of the planetary core for your tests."

"That's not necessary," Rush began.

"I disagree," said Carter. "The *Hammond* has the most advanced and up-to-date sensor package in the fleet."

Rush hesitated and then nodded. "No, you're right, Colonel. Your help will be appreciated." He smiled again. "Your input and experience is valuable." He paused. "I know there have been some…concerns among certain members of the SGC about Project Icarus. I know that both yourself and Rodney McKay put forward alternate approaches for the ninth chevron venture."

Carter's option had involved the use of a staged naquadria-fusion energy source for the Stargate, while McKay had suggested constructing an artificial black hole using Lantean technology to provide the mammoth power needs. Sam still found it hard to accept that the IOA had, in the end, gone with what she saw as a more risky venture. The highly volatile core of planet P4X-351 was the cosmic equivalent of a powder keg awaiting a lit match, but the colonel suspected that political issues rather than scientific ones had been the driving force here, as both Sam and Rodney had earned the ire of the IOA in the past.

The problem was, she couldn't shake the nagging concerns that had plagued her ever since Icarus had been given the green light. Carter had more than enough to do with the *Hammond* and the challenging missions the ship had taken on, but she found herself wondering if she was just a little envious at being the one to stand by and let someone else make this discovery, especially after so long on the cutting edge with SG-1 and then during her stewardship of Atlantis.

But it was more than just some rivalry. On some deep level, Sam wasn't sure if she entirely trusted Nicholas Rush; she couldn't read his motivations, and that bothered her. She pushed that thought away. "I'm ready to assist in any way I can, doctor," she told him.

Rush gave her a last nod and turned back to his work. "If the need arises, I'm pleased to know I can call on you," he said.

For better or worse, Carter thought to herself as she left, *I hope he knows what he's doing.*

If in doubt, take solace in a snack.

Okay, so maybe it wasn't the healthiest of philosophies, but it was one that Eli could connect with, and so he ventured down to the *Hammond*'s mess hall in the hopes that if the USAF could send a man across the stars, they could send some pizza and a few cans of soda with him as well.

He still hadn't quite got his head around the whole shipboard day-night cycle. The *Hammond* worked on something called 'Zulu Time', with the crew running in shifts similar to the way sailors did on submarines. Eli gathered a few things on a tray and wandered among the people in khaki flightsuits and nondescript work gear. Technicians and military types were not exactly the kind of people he had a lot in common with. And then he saw the girl.

She was *hot*. That was the first thing that came to mind, and, to be honest, the second and the third thing. She

reminded Eli of all the girls he'd ever thought were way out
of his league. Truth was, if they'd been back on Earth, he'd
have given her a wide berth and found a place somewhere
else, but here, out in the interstellar deeps, she was a fellow civilian aboard a boatload of airmen and scientists, and
that meant they had something in common. He glanced at
the other tables, the techs and the grunts. It wasn't really a
tough choice to make.

She looked up at him and smiled as he approached. "Hi."

He gestured with his tray at the empty seat opposite her.
"You mind?"

She gave a gracious nod. "Go ahead."

Eli sat and noticed that she'd picked a spot where the view
through the mess hall window was clearly visible. The tunnel of hyperspace effect stretched away from them, off into
infinity.

She saw him looking. "First time on a space ship, too?"

"Me?" He attempted to feign a cool, knowledgeable air. "No,
no. I've been on lots of… Various…" The attempt dried up
pretty quick, so he abandoned it. "Eli Wallace. Hello."

He got a nod in return. "I know."

The answer wrong-footed him. "You've heard of me?"

"I have."

"Wow." Eli considered this for a moment. "That almost
never happens."

"They say you're brilliant."

He was liking her more and more by the moment. Cute
and clearly an excellent judge of character. "Oh, they, *them*,
they're so…" He was in danger of trailing off again. "And
you are?"

"Chloe. I work for Alan Armstrong." She paused, and Eli
realized he was supposed to know who that was. "Senator
of California?"

He nodded sagely. "Ah, yes, yes. I've heard of California."

Chloe favored him with a brief smile. "He's also the chairman of the off-world spending committee, but you couldn't know that part. I'm his executive assistant."

"Wow," he repeated, wondering after Washington guys and their ability to attract the gorgeous. "My last job was more in the burgers and fries field. How'd you hook up something like that?"

"Well, I was a political science major at Harvard," she demurred.

Eli nodded again. "I hear that's a good school. For a while there I was at—"

"M.I.T." said Chloe. "I know."

"Really?" She knew a lot, and to be honest, Eli wasn't sure where to go with the conversation, but Chloe was pretty, and she was friendly, and he didn't know if the planet they were going to even had people on it, let alone, y'know, *girls*. He smiled winningly back at her and took a sip of his drink. "So what else did *they* tell you about me?"

The facility on P4X-351 had been up and running for a couple of years now, long enough for it to have lost that new-build smell, for the staff to have got settled in and the military contingent to learn the angles of the place. Icarus Base, as it was designated, was the only piece of civilization on the entire world — unless you wanted to count the weird little colonies of primates that existed down in the equatorial zone — an outpost of the human species far from home where people were planning on going even farther still.

Icarus was around eighty souls, all told, the split of that something like sixty-forty in favor of the eggheads. Hewn from the living rock of a mountainside, it had been picked as the location for 'the project' because it was off the beaten track and because it didn't have a Stargate. At least at first. They shipped one in from some former Goa'uld slave world, where the locals had got so sick of invaders turning up out of the blue that they just wanted to opt out of the whole gate network thing.

It wasn't hard to blame them. There was this pattern that the cultural historians at Stargate Command had noticed repeating over and over in the Milky Way and Pegasus galaxies. Civilizations that had been monkeyed with by the Goa'ulds, the Asgard, the Ancients, or any one of a number of alien races, they tended to cluster their settlements all around their gates, sometimes for commerce, but more often than not for safety in numbers. Earth had been lucky; two Stargates there, but both of them had been buried in the distant past so no damn thing could come through. Not like some worlds, planets full of people who lived in fear of the next 'kawoosh'.

It could be argued — and it often *had* — that the chain of events started when the first Earth gate was unearthed in Giza was the worst thing that ever happened to mankind. Maybe some of those threats out there would have come calling eventually, and maybe they wouldn't. All you could be sure of now is that we were all in the thick of it, players on a much bigger game board. Out of our league, some said.

But here we were at Icarus Base, about to do something else that some folks said was a bad idea. Challenging a new boundary, testing some different set of limits, because, well, that was the kind of thing that human beings did. No-one seemed to want to comment on who it was exactly that had chosen the name for the facility, though.

The irony of calling the project after a guy who had crashed and burned after pushing his own limits too far was not lost on First Lieutenant Matthew Scott. Once upon a time, he might had taken that as some kind of sign. A bad omen. But these days, Scott was more interested in the here and the now. He'd left all that other stuff behind. What Scott cared about was taking the moment, and *owning* it.

In the hot space of the compartment, there was little enough room to maneuver, but they'd gotten into the practice of it by now, so there were fewer skinned elbows and uncomfortable bruises than there had been. Scott pushed forward and buried his face in Vanessa James's chest, pressing her hard against the wall. She gasped and laughed, her arms snaking around his back, pulling him still closer. Their dogtags were caught up and bunched, digging into his clavicle. He planted a hungry kiss on her neck and she reacted.

Human contact. In the alien dark of outer space, what they were doing was practically an affirmation of the species. At least, that's what he'd say if they were caught by a superior officer. That wasn't likely to happen, though. Bases were like small towns, where everyone knew everyone else's business and kept their silence, for fear their own secrets might get out. Plus Matt and Vanessa were very careful. They made sure they knew the times when other couples were, uh, *coupling*, and kept away.

She gasped, and so did he, moving up to kiss her, and James did that thing where she looked away from him. Scott wondered about that sometimes, about what it meant. He thought he had a good handle on the dimensions of their relationship; First Lieutenant and Second Lieutenant, so they weren't fraternizing too far out of rank. No strings on either of them — and in the military where you could be transferred or, y'know, *killed*, at the drop of a hat, that was standard operating procedure. Vanessa seemed to treat sex like it was an extreme sport, and that was just fine with Matt. She'd never made it seem like there was any more to it, and he didn't need the complications of all the other stuff. The *baggage*.

Any more thoughts he might have had on the subject were abruptly cancelled by the growl from his walkie, hanging from his gear vest by the door. "*Scott, this is Colonel Young. Come in please.*"

All the passion bled out of the moment like air from a stuck balloon, and Scott cursed silently, glancing in the direction of the radio.

Young's voice continued. "*Our guests have arrived a few*

minutes early, Lieutenant. What's your position?"

James snapped out a laugh at the question, sultry and mocking in equal measure. He sighed and disengaged an arm, reaching for the walkie. She grabbed his wrist and her eyes glittered. "Not yet."

"*Lieutenant.*" Young was moving from terse enquiry to full-blown order now. "*Drop whatever you're doing and get your ass up here.*"

He let James go and she fell back with an amused yelp. "You heard him." Pulling himself together, Scott snatched up the radio and squeezed the talk button. "On my way, sir."

James was laughing behind her hand. Scott shot her a look and tossed her undershirt back to her. There was a second when their looped dog-tags caught, but then he was stepping away. "Duty calls?" she whispered.

"I, uh…"

She snorted at him and turned away. "What, you wanna cuddle? Go on, get going."

He zipped up the vest and opened the storage compartment door. Satisfied he wouldn't be seen exiting, Scott pushed out and broke into a jog, working hard to erase any lasting impression of his non-regulation activities.

The second time around Eli closed his eyes when the teleporter thing swept over him, but what struck hard was the immediate and instantaneous shift in the sensory environment around him. On the trip from Earth, he'd quickly gotten used to the temperate atmosphere of the *Hammond*, with its recycled air and quietly humming deck plates. But now he was somewhere else, under a bright, hot sun that burned yellow-orange. He felt lighter on his feet and a little bit dizzy. Eli took a couple of experimental breaths and tasted air that was hot, clean…and *alien*.

He turned slowly in place. Chloe, Rush and the senator were standing nearby, taking it all in along with him. The first thing Eli saw were concrete battlements, like some modern rendition of an ancient stronghold, with piles of sandbags and guys in desert-pattern camo looking watchful and ready for anything. He looked to see what they were facing and realized he was less than six feet away from the sheerest drop he'd ever seen. "Holy…"

The jagged stone fell away, down toward a rocky desert plateau that ranged away toward the far horizon. At the foot of the mountainside he saw the dark ribbons of runways, and parked on them were weird boomerang-shaped aircraft that looked nothing like any fighter plane he'd ever seen. In the distance, Eli could make out another range of razor-tipped peaks scraping the underside of a massive storm cell. Once again, a tremor of amazement ran through him. He'd felt it in the *Hammond*'s observation room over Earth, then in hyperspace, and now again. On some level he was glad he wasn't getting jaded about the whole thing. Grinning, he turned back as an austere-looking officer in an all-black duty uniform came walking toward the group. Eli dropped the grin and tried to look calm, resisting the urge to scream *Dude! We're on another planet!*

The officer gave a nod to Chloe's boss, who stood looking as pressed and poised as he would have stepping out of a limo at some swanky bash for D.C. politicos. "Senator, it's my honor to welcome you to Icarus Base."

"Colonel Young," replied Armstrong, shaking the man's hand and flashing a practiced smile. "Let me introduce my executive assistant, Chloe."

Chloe was just as poised, and if anything, she looked even better than she had the first time Eli had seen her. He dimly registered another arrival from inside the base — a younger male officer, flushed with the effort of running — but the majority of Eli's attention remained on the girl. He was starting to entertain the vague idea that perhaps they could have…a thing.

Chloe smiled at the colonel. "It's a pleasure to meet you, sir."

"The pleasure's mine," said Young.

"She's also my daughter," the senator added seamlessly.

Eli's hand twitched and he had to resist the almost physical need to slap himself in the forehead. *A senator's little girl? Oh right, good call, Wallace. Yeah, you were so in with a chance with her.* He ignored the sarcastic voice in the back of his head and looked away. Eli's gaze crossed that of the young officer — his nametag read 'Scott' — and they shared an instant of mutual guy telepathy. *She's real cute, but she's off-limits.*

Young stepped up to him, and Eli felt the man's eyes measure him in a single look. "You must be the—"

"Contest winner," said Eli, and for a moment he had a ridiculous vision of himself in a tiara and sash. "This place is...amazing." He glanced up again and stared at the blocky muzzle of a very large cannon. "And that is a big gun."

The young guy gave a nod. "M-995 Glaive Kinetic Impact Weapon. Rail gun, five hundred rounds per minute."

Eli thought again about the things the information films hadn't mentioned, and wondered what would need that much firepower turned against it.

Young indicated the other officer. "This is Lieutenant Scott, Mister Wallace. He's been assigned to you."

Eli blinked. "I need a bodyguard?"

Scott cocked his head. "Tour guide."

"Oh," he replied, a little crestfallen.

Rush spoke up for the first time since they'd arrived. "Shall we go inside?" He had an expression on his face that Eli has never seen him show until now — excitement.

The doctor took the lead, and he seemed to have no trouble winding his way through the corridors of the base. Eli glanced up as they passed inside, seeing a huge sigil on one wall. The symbol of the base was large, repeating the image of a single white feather over an orange sun that appeared on Young and Scott's uniforms. It sat in a blue ring with nine stars. *Nine, like the chevrons on the Stargate,* Eli thought.

Ahead, the senator kept pace with the doctor while Chloe and the colonel followed on. Armstrong frowned as he walked, adjusting the sleeves of his shirt. "I'll be interested to see where all our appropriation money is going in this place," he began. "I'm thinking you could probably shave a few dollars off the budget just by turning the heat down in here."

"Actually, cooling the place is what costs money, sir," noted Young.

Rush gave a nod. "We located the project here precisely because the core of this planet generates so much power. A lot of heat comes with that."

Eli had to admit, the temperature was a little uncomfortable. He watched the concrete walls and marble floors pass by and wondered why, with a whole empty planet of real estate out there, the Air Force had kept to the same identical style of narrow-corridored bunker they used on Earth. He glanced at Scott. "Ever get claustrophobic down here?"

"Safer in here than out on the surface," replied the lieutenant.

"Why?"

Scott didn't look at him. "Dinosaurs, man."

Eli gaped. "Really?"

"No."

Another officer passed them, a woman with the nametag 'James', and Eli could have sworn he saw a smile pass between them. He elected not to press the point about the dinosaurs for the moment.

"This way," he heard Young saying. "I'm sure Doctor Rush is eager to check the preparations." The group turned a corner, and ahead Eli glimpsed a partial view of a chamber full of light and motion.

"What's in there?" he asked.

The lieutenant gave him a crooked smile. "The star of the show."

Scott stepped into the room just a beat before Wallace did, just so he could watch the expression on the guy's face when he saw the gate room for the first time. Eli's jaw dropped open at the sight of it and Scott grinned. It got everyone like that. It didn't matter how many times you'd seen it on video or in pictures, in the flesh the Stargate was a stunning sight to see. Even now, with technicians clustered all around it and a ton of diagnostic equipment hooked up to the thing, it was still striking. Armstrong and his daughter were being led around by Rush and the colonel, and they made a good play at being guardedly impressed, but Eli wore all his reactions openly, hiding nothing.

To Scott's eyes, it was somewhere between a sculpture and piece of perfect engineering. It was a remnant of something far bigger than the human race, than Earth and everything else, and it seemed to radiate great age and huge power even when it was silent and motionless. He remembered the first time he'd plucked up the courage to go up and actually *touch* the thing. It looked like burnished steel, but it felt like no metal on Earth.

"Unbelievable," managed Eli.

"Yeah, it is." Scott nodded. "Good to remember that. It's weird how fast you can start to take something like this for granted." The Icarus gate room was a little different from the one back at Stargate Command, slightly narrower in span, and built on raised, shock-absorbing platforms to handle the backwash of power transfer.

Not watching where he was going, Eli almost tripped over a cable snaking over the floor, and he caught himself. "So... If the Stargate can instantly transport you to another planet, why did we have to fly here in a spaceship? They got one of these on Earth, right?"

"We had to take this one off the grid. Something to do with how this one is tied into the planet for power." He indicated the festoons of cables crowding the base of the gate like roots from a tree. "Apparently, it's been modified to only dial out, because incoming wormholes are too dangerous. You're the genius. You can probably tell me better."

Eli gave a rueful smile. "All I did was solve a puzzle in a videogame."

Scott felt a pang of sympathy for the guy. He was in deep here, and still scrambling to get it all straight in his head. "Hey, you figured out something that Doctor Rush has been trying to figure out for *months*. Which, by the way, a lot of people were glad to see happen."

That seemed to lift the guy's spirits a little. Scott looked away and saw Young leading the others to where the Icarus expedition team were standing at parade-ground attention. He beckoned Eli after him. "Come on. The dog-and-pony show's this way."

Rush was talking with Senator Armstrong as they came closer. "We're prepared for anything," he said.

"I'm sure you will be."

Armstrong moved down the line of the team members to the man himself, the mission commander standing tall closest to the Stargate. "And of course, you know Colonel David Telford."

The senator nodded. "Ready for this, Colonel?"

Telford gave Armstrong the same no-nonsense stare he turned on Scott and all the other junior officers. The guy had a face like tawny granite, so Vanessa had once said; he was every inch the poster boy for the Air Force's new, bold expedition into the unknown. He gave a crisp nod. "Just give the word, sir."

Armstrong spared Rush a sidelong glance. "I gave the word quite a while ago, Colonel. I'm just here to see how my one-point-six billion dollars is being spent."

Scott gave a flat smirk as a polite chuckle went down the row and stopped short of rolling his eyes. He caught Young watching him and made sure his expression was neutral again.

Rush was as animated as he got, indicating the silent Stargate with the sweep of his hands. "As you know, Senator, up until now we have been unable to channel the precise, massive amount of power into the gate necessary to unlock the Stargate's ninth and final chevron." He smiled slightly. "However, thanks to some ingenuity from young Mister Wallace, that problem has finally been solved."

Hearing his name, Eli gave a sheepish smile and a wave. "Hi."

Colonel Young didn't seem that convinced, however. He turned a dour look on the doctor. "With all due respect, we've heard that before."

"This time we're sure," insisted Rush.

"That's what I figured out?" said Eli. "A lost space-phone number?"

Rush ignored the comment. "I embedded the Ancient mathematical proof we required to solve the ninth chevron equation into the game, and then engineered Eli's solution into a practical and workable application."

Armstrong accepted this, tapping his finger on his lips. "What do you say we get on with it, then?"

The doctor nodded to one of the technicians over at the main control console. "Go ahead."

The group moved clear of the gate room's central space as power began to flow into the systems. Hunter Riley, the sergeant on the dialing computer, looked up and caught Scott's eye. A few days ago, over Icarus's floating poker game, Riley had made a bet that Rush would give the gate a run-up less than an hour after arriving. Scott checked his watch and frowned. He owed the non-com a ten-spot.

Riley started the sequence and the inner ring of the Stargate began to rumble around, chevrons clanking and illuminating as they locked into place. A trio of the civilian techs — Park, Brody and Franklin — were working in unison with him, monitoring every moment of the process.

Eli studied the gate as the chevrons began to lock, one after another. "We're dialing now?" he asked.

"A test," said Rush. "To see if we can get a connection."

Young nodded. "If we do, we'll send an automated reconnaissance drone through, see what's on the other side."

Armstrong's daughter was close by. "And then they'll go?" she asked, looking at Telford and the expedition team.

Rush shook his head. "No, we'll shut down again and assess the data we get before we send the away team."

Scott glanced at Eli. "*If* it works," he said, his voice low.

"Just as long as they don't dial up a black hole, or something," muttered the civilian.

"Don't sweat it, that won't happen again."

Eli paled. "*Again*?"

"Chevron eight encoded," announced Riley, but his words were lost as a heavy rumble reached up from the stone beneath their feet. In moments, an earthquake-tremor vibration was shaking the whole room.

"What's happening?" Eli asked.

"I don't know," Scott told him. "We've never got this far before."

The clattering gate continued its spin, and Scott knew that something was wrong. It shouldn't have taken this long to engage. Jets of steam vented from emergency heat ducts in the support frame, and random sparks of power fluttered around the heavy clamps holding the Stargate off the ground. Rush was leaning forward, his brow furrowed, almost like he was willing the alien machine to work.

"Chevron nine..." Riley read the data from his screen. "Will not lock."

The doctor's head bobbed in defeat, before he straightened. "We matched the power requirement down to the last EMU. It must work."

Over Riley's shoulder, Scott saw indicator tabs shifting higher, toward the critical end of the dial. "Power levels in the gate capacitors are going into the red," reported the technician, calm and clear despite the millions of gigawatts he was running through the system.

It was Young, as base commander, who had the authority to drop the hammer. "Shut it down."

Rush turned. "Wait…"

The tremors were getting worse every second. "We're reading fluctuations from the output in the core," said Riley. The digital gauges were all passing the red-line.

"Shut it down," repeated Young. "Now."

The sergeant didn't hesitate a moment longer, and slapped the emergency switches to bring the spinning gate back down to zero power. The rumbling died away like a passing thunderstorm, and the static in the air faded with it.

No-one spoke, leaving Rush to break the silence. "It should have worked," he insisted.

Scott saw Telford exchanging quiet words with one of his men as Young peered over Riley's console to see the data track. "But it didn't, and drawing power from the planet's core is—"

"Dangerous," Rush broke in, his tone rising. "Yes, we're all aware of—"

Young gave the scientist a hard look, but what he said next was addressed to everyone in the gate room. "Regardless of what's been spent and what is at stake, my first priority is to ensure the safety of the people on this base." In Scott's experience, the colonel wasn't much for talking when he didn't have to, but when he used *that* tone of voice, you could be sure that everyone damn well listened.

The doctor relented. "Of course." He stepped back from the control console and beckoned to Wallace as he walked away. "Eli, we'd better go over your equations again. Make sure that nothing was missed."

Eli's hand went to his chest, pointing at himself. "You're not seriously putting this on me?"

Scott looked at him and raised an eyebrow.

"Not my fault," insisted Eli, shaking his head.

CHAPTER THREE

Rush felt the problem like an ache behind his eyes.
He stood before the whiteboard and the scrawl of equation after equation, scanning the trains of numbers and mathematical symbols for what had to be the thousandth time, searching for the place where the disconnect was hiding.

How many times have I been here? The question burned in him. There had been so many close calls, so many moments when he had been absolutely certain that the key to it all was just within his grasp. Ever since the beginning, since the day he'd discovered the theorem of the ninth chevron and dared to guess at its purpose, Nicholas Rush had been consumed by the hunt for the proof that would unlock it. But it always stayed one step away. Close enough that he could sense the shape of it, lurking just outside his comprehension, but always out of reach. It drove him on like a hand at his back, pushing him and pushing him. He stared at the numbers and saw them like an enemy he could not defeat, and Rush reached up and massaged the bridge of his nose, taking a long breath.

It was galling enough that he hadn't been able to solve the proof, not after years of research, first at Area 51 and then out here at Icarus. It dented his pride to admit that he'd been forced to accept the proposal of the blind test hidden in the *Prometheus* game. He'd actually laughed when that suggestion had been made — General O'Neill had been right, with all the collected intellects working on the Stargate program, the fact that none of them could solve the formulae was, well, *embarrassing*. It was a radical way of trawling for an outsider's viewpoint, for a fresh take on the problem, but Rush had never believed that the game would net a solution, not in a million years.

But you didn't count on Eli Wallace, did you Nick? The voice in his head, warm and lightly mocking, was that of his wife. *A slacker wunderkind solves your puzzle and suddenly everything is turned upside down.*

Rush had taken back every reservation he'd ever had about the secret test when Eli's solution had been brought to him, stamping down the slight sting of resentment with the weight of elation at finding the final piece of the puzzle. After all, the majority of the work had been his, and while Wallace clearly had some level of raw, untrained insight, this was still Nicholas Rush's project. Still his destiny to fulfill.

Except it wasn't working. It all looked right, but the numbers were mocking him. After everything that had happened, the puzzle was still missing a final piece.

"There has to be an error in here." He glanced over his shoulder, and saw Eli scanning the equations, his lip curled.

"Seriously, who uses a whiteboard any more?" Eli nodded at one of the monitors nearby. "You have computers everywhere here."

"It helps me to think," Rush muttered. He tapped a subset of figures with the marker in his hand. "Power flow was within the target range. Why wouldn't the chevron lock? Why wouldn't the address connect?" Not for the first time, Rush briefly entertained the thought that the code they were dialing might be a dead end. In all the countless millennia since the Ancients had traveled the stars, there was nothing to say that the location they were trying to reach even *existed* anymore. He shook his head slightly. *No.* The feedback through the gate would have given a null reading, and they hadn't seen anything to indicate that.

"Wrong address?" offered Eli.

Rush shot him a look. "There is only one. Rodney McKay and his people found it in the Ancient database on Atlantis, out in the Pegasus galaxy."

"With no instructions."

"No." Rush had to admit, the Ancients were careless that way. They tended to leave their technology littered about the cosmos with little concern as to what might happen to those who found it; then again, when your entire species had ascended from corporeal form into something of near-god-like infinite energy, he imagined that matters of the physical suddenly became far less important. "But that's not the issue," he continued. "It has to be *your* proof."

Eli spread his hands. "My proof works," he replied. "How do I know? Because you said it did."

Rush's lips thinned, but the terse reply he was forming was lost as Colonel Young entered the room. "Gentlemen, how's it coming?"

Acting on a sudden impulse, fuelled by irritation and frustration, Rush snatched up the eraser pad and wiped out the lines of numbers.

Eli took a step forward, holding out his hand. "Whoa, what are you doing?"

"Starting from the beginning," Rush replied.

"Wait! Save save save!" Eli looked stricken as the figures were obliterated by the sweeps of the eraser.

Rush caught sight of Young evaluating the situation. The colonel did a lot of that, he'd noted. He had a dogged sense of tactics that played itself out in everything he did, from the smallest interaction to the biggest. Rush imagined that Young was the kind of man who wouldn't go anywhere or do anything without a plan.

"Mister Wallace?" said the colonel. "I'd like you to join me for dinner in the officer's mess." Which really meant: *Rush is pissed off, so give him some distance.* The scientist had to admit that the commander of Icarus Base had got just as much a read on him as he had on the colonel.

Eli seemed not to notice. "Thank you. I'm starving."

Food could wait, though. "We're very close to a breakthrough. I'd like Eli to keep working."

Young had a look that he used every time he wanted Rush to know that the scientist's 'requests' were only ever that, and he employed it now. "We've been here for six months," he said, leading Wallace to the door. "It can wait a few more hours."

Despite himself, Rush couldn't stop from shooting the colonel a glare as he exited, and with an irritated twist of his fingers, the scientist bent forward and began to quickly and carefully write out the equations from scratch.

Eli followed Young to a cafeteria-type space a short walk from the command levels, and he made a couple of attempts at conversation that netted him polite, if curt, replies.

"Why'd they call it a 'mess hall', anyhow?" Eli gave a faint grin. "You military guys don't exactly seem like sloppy eaters."

"It's from '*mes*'," said Young. "Old French word for a portion of food."

"Oh."

"They make us read books in the Air Force."

"Right," he nodded lamely. "I thought it was all just yelling and shooting and blowing stuff up."

Young shook his head as he opened the door for him. "You're thinking of the Marines," he replied, and Eli couldn't be sure if the man was making a joke or not.

He got himself a seat and an Airman served Eli what was actually a pretty passable steak dinner, which he ate with gusto. Around him, the conversation was mostly in the direction of the officers on Colonel Telford's side of the table, the jut-jawed, clear-eyed members of the expedition force who each exuded a *Right Stuff* vibe utterly at odds with anyone Eli had ever known. He saw Lieutenant Scott a few seats down, talking quietly to a female officer with a strong face and a crop of blonde hair; the name 'Johansen' was visible on her uniform jacket.

Nearby, Senator Armstrong and his daughter were intently focused on every word that Telford said. Chloe especially, Eli noted, seemed quite taken by Telford's flyboy charm.

"When you go through the Stargate, you don't really feel it." Telford used his hands to demonstrate the wingspan of an aircraft. "But I'm telling you, the moment you break through the atmosphere in an F-302 and you see the stars…" He paused, nodding to himself. "It's incredible."

"Could I go for a ride?" asked Chloe.

Telford nodded again. "Sure, I can arrange that."

Eli rolled his eyes. "So, Colonel," he broke in. "You really have no idea where this nine chevron Stargate address is going to send you?"

Telford was unfazed by the question. "No idea at all. But the Ancients built the Stargate with nine chevrons around it, and they weren't the kind of people to do stuff just for show." He took a sip of his drink. "It's got to go somewhere."

"That's a little vague, don't you think?" Eli pressed. "I mean, when NASA did the moon shots, they could see where they were supposed to be going. You're flying blind, here." The room went a little quiet, and Eli realized that perhaps this was the wrong crowd for those comments. He glanced around, looking for support, and didn't get it.

"That's true," Telford offered, "up to a point. But the fact is, Columbus had no maps when he set off. People thought that Chuck Yeager's airplane would explode if he tried to break the sound barrier. The first missions through the Stargate to Abydos, and then to Atlantis, they were all a roll of the dice. There's always a risk."

"And if we don't take risks, we don't advance," added Scott.

"Well said," nodded Armstrong.

He ran out of numbers, and Rush's hand stopped dead. Stepping back, he studied the whiteboard and his brow furrowed. Nothing had changed. The board looked almost identical to the way it had appeared before he erased it, the same lines of symbols and digits in Rush's swift, looping hand, and more importantly the same damn solutions in the same damn places.

The board loomed in front of him like a sheer wall, and that was exactly what it was. A blockade made of mathematics, stopping him from making that last step toward the solution. And as hard as he tried to force it, Rush could not find the connection that eluded him.

You need Eli, said his wife's voice. *You know it. It doesn't make you weak or wrong to admit that.*

Rush let out a sigh of exasperation, and reluctantly turned away.

It was evening on the base, and the corridors were sparsely populated; even so, he didn't register the handful of other people who passed him by, his focus buried deep in his own thoughts. Rush approached the officer's mess. Despite what Young said, this couldn't wait any longer. He was *so close*. Couldn't the man understand that? And Eli, Eli Wallace could give him the boost he needed to surmount the last obstacle.

Rush detoured through the mess hall kitchen and caught the sound of Young's voice as he came closer. "We've also known for some time that the only way to unlock the ninth chevron was to solve the power issues."

Armstrong's daughter replied immediately. "If anyone's going to solve it, I think Eli will."

He stopped. The kitchen lighting was low, so Rush doubted that anyone was aware he was outside. Through the half-open door, in the mess hall beyond he saw Eli give a smug grin, playing up to the attention of the room. "Yes, it's true. I'm Math Boy."

And all at once, the annoyance and the irritation churned up inside him, and Rush turned away on his heel, his face set in a stony grimace.

"Doctor Rush?" He turned and saw the duty cook, an air-man named Becker, offering him a food pack. He took it without comment and went back the way he had come.

The quarters the Americans had given him on Icarus Base were basic but comfortable — twice the size of those given to the junior officers or the second-string scientists, apparently — but in truth, Rush had spent hardly any time in here during his weeks at the facility, returning only to crash out on the bed when fatigue pushed him to it. There were a few books, mostly unread. A tablet computer, for those moments when he awoke in the middle of the night with some insight. But little in the way of personal effects. When he left Earth for the first time to come here, there hadn't been much he really wanted to keep. Nothing that could not be replaced, nothing of value, except...

Except the picture. He sat on the bed and his hand strayed to the bedside cabinet without conscious thought on his part, opening the drawer to pull it out. The two of them in better times, arm in arm. That smile on his face that he'd always said was amazement at how lucky he was; and her grin, her laughing eyes. They'd been in Germany when it was taken, for her star turn at a concert with the Berlin Philharmonic.

Rush ran his finger over the image and he felt his breath catch, his vision mist. The moment seemed so distant to him, but yet so close as well. How was it possible to be both things at once? The equation refused to resolve itself.

He sighed and put the picture away again.

Eli accepted his moment in the spotlight with what he considered to be good grace, and he ignored the voice inside his head reminding him that, if Rush was right, the whole reason the gate hadn't opened today was because *he'd* missed out a decimal point somewhere.

Chloe's father picked up his glass and got to his feet. "I would like to propose a toast," he began.

"I'm flattered." Eli gave a bashful smile. "But that's not really necessary."

Armstrong shot him a look. "Not to you."

The grin fell off his face. "Oh."

Armstrong went on, scanning the faces of the men and women in the room. "When the proposal for the financing of this project first crossed my desk, I was not going to approve it."

Chloe's expression became brittle, and she buried her head in her hands. "Oh my God, no…" she muttered.

"It seemed clear to me at the time," continued the senator. "There were enough terrestrial matters of importance that needed that kind of money."

Eli blinked as Chloe downed the remainder of the wine in her glass and helped herself to another. Her cheeks were taking on a blush of color, and he looked on, wondering where she was going with this sudden change in behavior.

Armstrong was into full flow by now, and didn't seem to be aware of her newfound thirst. "It was my daughter Chloe who reminded me that there is no greater endeavor than seeking an understanding of the universe in which we all exist."

Chloe glanced at Eli and spoke quietly to him. "Not in those exact words," she whispered, before going for another quick refill.

"It was also her idea to embed the Ancient mathematical proof in a medium that would give us access to brilliant young minds we would have otherwise overlooked."

Eli gaped. "You came up with the game thing?" *Chloe is responsible for me being here?* He had to admit, he hadn't seen that coming.

Armstrong's daughter was clearly unhappy in the limelight, however, and suitably fortified with a few gulps of a nice Napa Valley white, she spoke up, intent on stopping her father from talking about her any further. "And so," she piped, "to all of the brave men and women who have volunteered for—"

A sound like distant thunder cut short her words. Eli felt it through the soles of his sneakers and the back of his chair, heard it in the clink of glasses and cutlery against plates. Overhead, the lights swayed slightly.

"Okay." Chloe asked the question on everyone's mind. "What was that?"

Young was out of his seat in a flash, snatching an intercom phone from the wall and pressing it to his ear. "Ops room, this is Young—"

It happened again, and this time it was louder and closer, and it wasn't sounding like thunder any more. Eli knew the noise of an explosion when he heard it. Particles of dust shaken free from the ceiling overhead rained down, catching in the drifting, flickering light; then the sirens began to wail, and red strobes stuttered into life on the walls.

The military officers were already up, but Eli froze for a long second, watching them rise almost as one, food and drink and polite conversation immediately forgotten.

Young put down the phone and gave them a look. "The base is under attack," he said, as matter of fact as he had been about words in old French. Without pause, he snapped out orders in a tone of voice that made it clear he expected to be obeyed without question. "All non-combatant personnel report to your designated safe areas, everyone else to your battle stations. This is not a drill."

This is not a drill. Eli thought people only talked like that in the movies. But this was real, just like all the rest of it was real, and it was happening to him right now. He belatedly got to his feet, trying to remember where his designated safe area actually was, while Telford and the other officers raced away down the corridor.

Young gestured to Armstrong. "Senator, I need you and your daughter to go with Lieutenant Scott…" The colonel turned his gaze toward Eli and he saw something new in there — not fear, not concern, but *duty.* "You too, Eli," he said.

He turned and found Scott watching him with the same look in his eyes. "Follow me," he said.

In the main corridor, Young found a sergeant handing out equipment and secured himself a gear vest, a MICH helmet, a radio and a M4 carbine in short order. Boots pounding the marble floors, the colonel donned the equipment on the run, the action as easy as muscle memory from hundreds of deployments and combat operations. He checked the carbine's loads and then barked into the radio, ordering the technician in the ops room to get him hooked up with the *Hammond*, orbiting somewhere up above them.

When his first attempt to raise the starship failed, Young felt a stab of ice in his gut. There had been no alarm, no call from the *Hammond* or Icarus's suite of sensor satellites, nothing to warn them of the arrival of an intruder — and that could mean any one of a whole galaxy of problems was now at his front door, throwing down fire.

If the Hammond *is already gone...* He shook his head and pushed the thought away. There was no point in making guesses until he had the facts.

Young shouted at a pair of non-coms to make a hole, and taking two steps at a time, he vaulted up a gantry toward the battlements. He got halfway up and hesitated. If an attack was coming, he was going to need every fighting man he could muster. His *best*. Young turned and made a quick detour, grabbing some extra kit as he went.

Ronald Greer felt the next impact, and then the next, and his hands went out to walls, a sweat breaking on his forehead. Whatever the hell was going on out there, it sounded like a giant was using a sledgehammer the size of a football stadium to wale on the side of the mountain. The bombardment was rattling him around like a stone in a can, and the only thing worse than that was the annoyance he felt at being stuck in here, unable to stand a post.

Greer felt a horrible, cold chill at the idea he might die in here, locked up in a holding cell. He looked down at the bruises on his knuckles and cursed himself. It was no way for a Marine to go out, caged like an animal while the roof caved in and buried him alive.

Then keys rattled in the lock and the heavy door cranked open. Standing behind it, armed for bear, was Colonel Young. "Sergeant," he said. Over the man's shoulder he saw his fellow Marines Curtis and Spencer, and Lieutenant James gearing up for a fight.

Greer immediately shot to his feet and attention, ram-rod straight. "Sir!" he snapped, in his best Parris Island snarl.

"We're under attack," continued Young. "Don't know why. Don't know who."

Greer said nothing, remaining stock still. Young was a man of few words, and the Marine liked that about him. He was okay for Air Force. If Young had something to say, he'd get to it.

"I need every able body I can spare." The colonel had a G36 and a gear belt in his hands, and without ceremony he tossed the weapon and the kit in Greer's direction. The sergeant caught them with ease. "Consider the charges dropped. Now go take your anger out on *them*."

Greer strapped the belt about his waist and checked the assault rifle's ammunition clip. *Locked and loaded.* "Yes sir," he said, and bounded out into the corridor, without looking back.

A firestorm of energy streaked down through the darkness and slammed into the shields of the U.S.S. *Hammond*, the invisible bubble of force suddenly flashing into existence as exotic radiations collided with one another, spilling out jagged ripples of lightning.

The angular carrier ship powered into a turn, coming

about to present its stronger ventral barriers to the enemy onslaught. *Hammond*'s attackers crowded in toward it, like a trio of street thugs moving in to take down a victim. The vessels were towering brass pyramids ringed with planes of black steel; the Goa'uld who built them called them Ha'taks, and these three ships had once been warcraft in the service to a minor System Lord called Zipacna, but his sigil had been burned from their hulls a long time ago.

The bombardment was unrelenting, each shot pounding the Earth ship, harrying it wherever it turned. White streaks of missile fire lanced out, scoring retaliatory hits, and *Hammond*'s railguns spat high-velocity kinetic kill rounds into the void on flickering tails of tracer. Close by, fighters hastily scrambled from the ship's launch bay wheeled and turned as they engaged Death Glider elements launched by the Ha'taks. The battle was brutal and swift, but the balance of it was turning fast, and not in the favor of the Earth forces.

Here we are again.

The bitter thought crossed Samantha Carter's mind as she pressed herself back into her command chair, her arms flat on the panels at the side. Through the wide viewport that filled one side of the *Hammond*'s bridge, she could see nothing but the hot orange flares of energy transfer as the Ha'taks swept around for another fusillade of beam fire. Circuit-breakers sparked and flashed and jumping-jack shorts lanced through the support systems. She took a breath and coughed, her throat seared by the acrid stink of burnt plastic.

"Missile status," she snapped.

"Reloading…" reported Major Marks, her second-in-command. "And ready. Green lights from all gun decks, ma'am." Marks had recently transferred over to Carter's ship from the U.S.S. *Daedalus*, and like his new commander, he was no stranger to the brutal dance of space combat.

"Return fire. Hit them hard."

"Firing!" Marks stabbed a control and Carter felt the *Hammond* shiver as the ship released another wave of nuclear-tipped fury at her enemies.

"Colonel! I have Icarus Base on the comm!" called a voice from over her shoulder.

Carter nodded. "On speakers." She heard the crackle over the bridge intercom as the channel connected and spoke again. "Icarus, this is the *Hammond*. What's your status, over?"

"*About to ask you the same thing,*" came the reply. Carter didn't know Everett Young all that well, but she was familiar with the man's reputation as a careful, calm operator. Young didn't say anything to belie that now, but Carter could still sense the tension brimming in his voice. "*Who crashed our party?*"

"Three Goa'uld motherships. They started shooting the second they came out of hyperspace. Dropped out almost on top of the planet. We had no warning."

"*Lucian Alliance?*" said Young.

Carter nodded as her ship rocked again under another barrage. "That's my guess." Her lip curled. "They haven't introduced themselves and they don't respond to any hails." She didn't add the question that was burning at the back of her mind: *exactly how did a bunch of space-going drug runners find out about this base?*

As Greer and the others raced to their combat positions, Young strode forward over the blocky concrete battlements of the base, sweeping the night sky with a pair of high-powered binoculars, pressing his radio to his ear. "*Our shields are holding...for now,*" Carter was saying, "*But we're not the target. They're just making sure we keep busy.*"

Young caught sight of something high up: flashes of faint light, like distant fireworks. He let the binoculars fall on their straps and scrutinized the men and women all around him, crews on the emplaced railguns, missile quads and conventional thirty-mil cannons. They were all cranking their weapons upward, hunting for the enemy. "What's coming our way?" he asked, for a second hearing nothing but the wind through the mountain peaks.

"*It's not good.*" Static laced Carter's reply. "*We read a full squadron of gliders and a heavy troop transport. Our CAP of 302's cut them down some, but the others blew past and went straight for the surface. The rest of them will be on your doorstep in about three minutes.*"

Young considered that for a moment. A troop transport. That meant a ground attack in force. He had no illusions; this battle would be hard-fought. He sniffed the air and smelled ozone, doubtless wafting in from the places where stray shots from the Ha'taks had come slamming down into the planet's surface. Young keyed the walkie again, talking into the general guard channel. "Received and understood, *Hammond*. We'll take it from here. Colonel Telford, did you copy all that?"

"*Roger that,*" said Telford crisply.

Young moved to the very edge of the fortification and glanced down to the foot of the mountain, where stark sodium-white light was spilling across the runway apron from the mouth of an open hangar. Blade-winged shadows were moving down there, angling out to face the sky.

"*If we can get to the transport before they land their troops, we stand a chance of making them think twice.*" Telford's voice was muffled by the closeness of an oxygen mask.

"I concur," said Young. He could see the twinkling lights in the sky now without the binoculars, and they were closing fast. "Good hunting, sir."

"*And to you, sir.*" Telford's voice cut out and the next sound Young heard was the roar of turbojets as a flight of F-302 interceptors swept away down the runway. He watched them angle up into the night, raptors on the wind in search of prey.

"Keep moving!" Scott shouted the command and gestured with his free hand, the other staying close to the G36 assault rifle that he'd snagged on the way to the safe zone. He shot a glance over his shoulder at the disordered snake of people moving down the corridor, civilians and non-essential personnel who, according to the regs, were instantly deemed liabilities the moment the base attack alarm began to sound.

Part of him desperately wanted to be up there on the battlements behind a big thirty mike, ready to give a bloody nose to whomever it was that was knocking at their door; but Matthew Scott had his orders, and he had his duty — which was to get these people out of harm's way.

New impacts slammed into the rock somewhere far above them, and the whole of Icarus Base resonated with the force of the blast.

At his side, Eli Wallace choked out a gasp as a lengthy crack passed down the length of the wall. "Oh crap."

"Keep it together, Eli," Scott told him. "It's just a little further."

"Shouldn't we be, y'know, heading *out* of here, instead of deeper in?"

"Remember that 'instant transport to another planet' thing?"

"We're gonna gate out of here?"

Scott nodded. "That's the idea. We hook back up to the network, dial you out, and—"

"Kawoosh," said Eli, with a weak grin. "And then what, you and Young and the others, you're gonna follow us?"

Scott's lips thinned. "If we have to."

"But—"

Whatever Eli had to say was snatched away by another impact that hit so hard, Scott felt it in the bones of his skull. The vibration actually bounced him off his feet and he stumbled as rock and concrete gave way overhead. A rain of heavy, choking soil washed over him and he heard shouting and screaming.

Shaking himself, Scott turned to see the corridor behind

him blocked by a wall of fallen rubble. Dazed by the collapse, people were milling around in the settling dust.

The lieutenant found Eli as the young man climbed back to his feet. "What was that?"

Scott ignored the question and pointed past him in the direction they'd been heading. "You know what 'double-time' means?"

"That's like, military-speak for 'run real fast', right?"

He nodded. "So do it, Eli. Get to the gate room, and don't wait for me." He slapped him on the back. "Go now!"

Wallace and a few of the others disappeared off down the corridor, but enough of the civvies were still in shock. "Let's go, people!" he called. "You need to move to the gate room!"

Scott waded through them, pushing them in the right direction. A face rose out of the dust before him and he saw the cute girl, the senator's daughter. Her pretty face was twisted in an expression of absolute fear, tears streaking her cheeks. "It just collapsed…." she was saying, "My father… And there could still be people trapped on the other side!"

He glanced around. Senator Armstrong and a few of the other scientists were nowhere to be seen. His hand was on Chloe's wrist, and for a long second he thought about taking her to the gate, by force if need be, but he couldn't summon the sheer coldness to do it. "The rest of you, keep going!" he snapped. "Don't stop until you reach the gate room."

"I'm not going!" Chloe insisted. She went to the rock pile and pulled at the stones, dragging them away, tearing the skin on her fingers.

"Me neither," he told her, and then spoke into his radio. "Ops, this is Lieutenant Scott, I've got a dozen or so people cut off from the gate room down here, corridor six-alpha."

"*Copy that,*" said a harried voice. "*No assist available at this time, Lieutenant.*"

Chloe shot him a panicked look. "Wh-what does that mean?"

He paused for a moment. "It means we have to do this on our own."

With the base's meager flight of interceptors out gunning for the troop transporter, there was no air cover to stop the enemy's aerial strike element from screaming down on Icarus Base, bringing fire along with them.

A wave of sleek-winged Death Gliders howled over the tops of the fortifications, pulse-bolts shrieking from their heavy cannons. Rocky outcrops clipped by the blasts blew apart into scattershot fragments, taking down men like shrapnel from a fragmentation bomb. Other hits seemed to simply erase whole sections of the battlements, defenders and guns turned to smoke in a heartbeat.

Young stabbed a finger into the air, yelling out his orders over the general channel. "Concentrate your fire on the gliders! Pour it on!"

Ropes of tracer snaked across the sky and clipped the wings of one of the Goa'uld fighters, ripping divots from the scarab-shaped body in chugs of thick black smoke. The craft stalled and fell away, vanishing below the line of the fortification to explode against the mountainside. The big railguns were slow to traverse and track, but when they found their mark the electromagnetically-accelerated tungsten quarrels they fired bored right though the hull metal of the Death Gliders and out the other side. Young saw one ship take a hit through the cockpit and tumble out of control, veering into the path of its wingman, destroying both craft in a ball of flame.

But there were too many of them, and as the hot stench of cordite and laser-burned air stung his nostrils, Colonel Young saw the specter of defeat closing like an oncoming storm front.

Angry at the thought, he raised his carbine and tore off rounds into the belly of a glider as it roared over his head.

Eli pushed his way through the building knot of people crowding the entrance to the gate room and glanced around.

The sounds of hit after hit were almost a steady rhythm now, and each new impact brought another rain of dust down from the ceiling. He flinched as a long, low groan sounded through the metal decking surrounding the Stargate. He'd expected the thing to be open already, and people moving through like a crocodile of school kids on a field trip; instead it was silent and inert.

Eli caught sight of Rush over at one of the consoles. The Air Force tech, Riley, was craning over his panel. "Doctor, I'm reading a dangerous energy spike in the core." The digital gauges were flicking up toward the redline, and Eli remembered the last time that had happened. *Not good.*

"It's the bombardment," Rush snapped, shooting an angry look upwards, as if he could beam his irritation through the rock at the invaders. "Whomever is attacking us doesn't understand the instability of this planet's geological structure…"

That caught Eli's attention immediately. *Instability?* Was this planet some giant earthquake waiting to happen? He wondered again about what he hadn't been told about this project.

Rush looked up, saw him, and sprang at him, grabbing his arm. "Good, you're safe. Help me with this, Eli." He propelled him over to the dialing computer, a tower of electronics wired into the crystalline guts of an incongruous mushroom-shaped device. On the podium's surface was a red hemisphere surrounded by rings of keys, each sporting one of the gate's star-sign symbols.

"With what?" he managed.

Rush tapped the console. "The ninth chevron."

Eli jerked with surprise. "What?" Icarus Base was being taken apart, stone by stone, apparently by one of those *let's-not-tell-Eli-about-it* alien threats, but Rush was still fixated on his project. "Listen, forget that, we all need to get the hell out of here!"

And to underline his point for him, at that moment another bone-shaking blast rocked the base. Rush met him with a steady eye. "If that bombardment continues, the stability of this planet will fail. The radioactive core of P4X-351 will go critical."

Eli felt the blood drain from his face as the full import of Rush's statement registered with him. "You mean explode? The whole planet?"

The doctor nodded. "It took us two years of deep space surveys to find this site. The properties of this world are unique." A strange intensity glittered in Rush's eyes. "This may be our last chance."

"If my math works…" began Eli, thinking it through.

Rush spoke over him. "We can't assume that—"

"I said *if*," he insisted. "If I'm right, then it's not a power issue, it's the gate address."

Rush was shaking his head, turning away. "We've known the first eight symbols of the sequence for years." He tapped the dialing panel. "The ninth symbol has to be the point of origin. That's how the Stargate works, that's how it's always worked."

Despite the desperate circumstances, despite the looming threat of death — or maybe because of them — Eli felt a sudden surge of excitement. This was the game puzzle all over again, a problem he knew he could solve, if he could just come at it from the right angle. "So, what…. What if this *isn't* the planet you're supposed to dial from?"

Rush snorted and gestured at the walls. "This is where we *are*."

"Yeah, I get that." Eli nodded back at him. "But I'm just saying, what if we're not supposed to be *here*? What if we, you and Icarus and all of this stuff is supposed to be somewhere else?"

The scientist became silent. And over their heads, rock ground on rock as fire fell from the heavens.

CHAPTER FOUR

Telford pressed the F-302's throttle up to zone five full military power, and flicked the switches to bring the AIM-120 missiles beneath its wings from 'safe' to 'armed' status. "Red flight, our target of import is the heavy troop transport," he began, speaking into his mask mike. "Valens, DeSalvo, Kanin, you three give their fighter cover something to think about. Chavez, you're with me."

The colonel got a chorus of acknowledgments and he nodded to himself as the shapes of the enemy landing force became clear on his engagement-range radar. "Here we go, gentlemen. Break and attack."

Red Flight Two, Three and Five flicked into high-g turns and roared away from the v-formation, and from the corner of his eye Telford saw Captain Chavez's Red Four move up to a strike posture.

Then the screen of eight Death Gliders was on them and the night sky became a storm of orange fire. Telford slammed the 302's joystick over hard, and the interceptor responded instantly, standing up on one wing to vector right past the diving shape of an enemy fighter. They were so close, the colonel's jet wash buffeted the ship, but he had no time to spend worrying about it. Telford was relying on the rest of the pilots to keep the gliders off Chavez and him long enough to put a dent in the plans of the invaders.

"Tally," called Chavez, spotting their target. "Eleven high, angels fifteen and descending fast."

"Roger that," said Telford. "Designate target."

"Copy. Red Four has the lead."

The two interceptors split and angled up toward the bulky shield-shaped starship. So intel said, each one was capable of holding hundreds and hundreds of men, and if they were bringing down mobile ring transporters into the bargain, then they'd have a line back to the big motherships in orbit and enough reserves of troops to occupy a small country. Telford's scanners pinged a warning tone. "They see us." He knew that on the ventral hull of the transport, heavy-wattage energy cannons had to already be tracking them.

Out of nowhere, a flash of brilliant white appeared off in the distance and Telford heard a blare of static over his helmet speakers. "This is DeSalvo," called a voice over the general channel. "Red Two is down, I repeat, Major Valens is down."

"No chute, no chute visible..." Kanin was gruff. "He's gone."

Telford cursed. The numbers were against them, and every second the enemy was allowed to push closer to Icarus was a second closer to the end of them all. "Just keep the bandits off us," he replied.

Beam fire streaked down past his cockpit and Telford heard Chavez give an annoyed grunt. "Incoming."

Telford's air-to-air missiles signaled a lock on the transport ship and his finger hovered over the firing stud. "Red Four, I got your wing."

"Copy," said Chavez. "Fox Three!" The captain snapped out the firing call and Telford saw an AIM-120 leap off the rack and blaze away on a spear of white fire.

"Fox Three," he repeated, and released his own warshot, tracking in on the same target. The heavy transport veered away, turret cannons turning as it did, still spraying fire across the path of the F-302s.

Chavez's missile ran straight into a fan of energy bolts streaming from the enemy ship, but Telford's shot spiraled pass the ball of smoke and fire and managed a glancing impact on the port aft quarter. The transport lost a chunk of hull metal and flames spat from the wound in the metal — but it was still airborne, still on target.

"Hell no—" Chavez began, turning to follow the target as it dropped past their ascent. He didn't see what the colonel saw, the winged shape trailing behind the transport, hidden in its thrust wake.

Telford called out to the other pilot, but it was too late. The Death Glider pacing the troop carrier caught Red Four as it turned and unleashed a barrage of murderous pulse-fire into the F-302. The aerospace fighter came apart in a storm of metal; there was no explosion, only a whirlwind of steel and plastic.

"You son of a bitch!" Telford's reaction was immediate and furious. The Death Glider spun away from its kill and the colonel bore down on it, the death of his wingman blinding the other pilot to his presence long enough for Telford to put his guns on the enemy. In a jousting pass, Telford raked the target with the railgun cannons in his 302's nose and ripped Chavez's killer open. The Death Glider exploded and he rode out the shockwave, coming hard about.

"Red Four lost," he said into the radio. "Red Flight, report."

"Red Five. I'm hit but I can handle it," Kanin replied.

"Red Three," grated DeSalvo, voice tight with effort. "In a turning fight. Damn, these creeps are serious."

"On my way," Kanin reported.

Telford throttled up, diving after the transport, but even as he aimed and fired his next missile salvos, he knew it wouldn't be enough. The injured ship was already bellying down toward the desert and its turret gunners were quick, throwing up sheets of fire to knock down the AIM-120s before they could strike home.

He broke off and went down on the deck, swooping low over the grounded, smoldering vessel. He grimaced as he saw a horde of troops boiling out of the craft, and strafed them with the railguns, but the damage was already done. The enemy was advancing on Icarus Base. Small arms fire licked at his wings as Telford pulled up and turned for another pass.

The colonel toggled the ground communications channel. "Icarus Base, do you read? This is Telford."

"*We read*," said a voice. It was Colonel Young, and in those two words he made it clear he knew this wasn't going to be good news.

"We didn't get to the transport before they offloaded..." Telford turned a practiced eye over the lines of enemy soldiers. "You've got at least a thousand ground assault troops coming your way. I repeat, estimate battalion strength enemy foot mobiles inbound to your perimeter."

"Understood," said Young, the numbers registering in the cold, unforgiving tactical calculations of his thoughts. A glider howled overhead, low enough that he could have thrown a stone and struck the belly of it, and off to the colonel's right a Marine with a M249 SAW machine gun tracked the craft, pouring fire into it as it went, a fountain of expended brass shells arcing over his shoulder. In the next second, Young heard the snarling whoop of a Goa'uld energy weapon and a bolt of fire struck the Marine dead where he stood.

"*We can slow them down, but there's not a chance in hell we're gonna be able to stop them...*" Telford's voice was tense with exertion. "*Lock the doors, and we'll meet up back at the SGC!*"

Young let off a burst of fire from his M4 in the direction the hit had come from and ducked back into cover behind a wall of sandbags. "Do what you can, Colonel. Icarus out."

He took a breath and switched to the base alert frequency. The order he was going to give was the one that no field commander ever wanted to voice, but the choice had been taken from him the moment this planet had been targeted for conquest. His eyes flicked to the dead Marine, lying beside his still-smoking gun. *We can't win this.*

Close by, a non-com behind one of the railguns put his shoulder into the weapon and hauled it around, coming to bear on another Death Glider as it wailed through the air.

"This is Colonel Young," he said. "All non-essential personnel muster to the gate room for immediate evac. All combat personnel, fall back to standby positions and prepare to disengage." He changed channels again. "Sergeant Riley, do you copy?"

There was a momentary pause before the gate technician came on the line. "*Sir, yes sir.*"

"Override the lockout protocol and dial the Stargate to Earth."

Fire erupted from the railgun as the glider powered in toward the battlements on an attack run. Riley's reply was lost in the heavy snarl of the cannon as the kinetic kill rounds shredded the fighter's cockpit and sent it into a corkscrew spin directly toward the gun emplacement.

Moving without thinking, Young vaulted up and grabbed the gunner by the scruff of his armor vest and dragged him off the mount. The two of them spun away into safety just as the glider slammed into the railgun and detonated.

The back blast threw the pair of them, commander and enlisted man, into a head-over-heels tumble down the access gantry and back into the base.

Rush looked up irritably as a scattering of pebble-sized stones rattled off the elevated walkway leading up to the Stargate. Up above the hanging, swaying lighting rigs, the dark streaks of rents in the concrete ceiling were visible in the shadows. He frowned and absently brushed a layer of rock dust from his shoulder. The lights gave an ominous flicker as the distant report of gunfire and explosions went on and on.

Lines of people were huddled in the access wells below the walkway, fear ready and strong on the faces of every one of them.

For a moment, Rush studied them, wondering what each of them were thinking. He saw faces he knew — Park and Franklin, Brody and Volker, Boone and Palmer and all the others.

They want to go home, he thought. He couldn't blame them, but at the same time he couldn't empathize with them. They all had something to go home to, after all, but what did he have? What was there back on Earth for Nicholas Rush except another failure? The last time he had been back, to pick up Wallace and go through yet another round of meetings with the IOA, they had demanded answers from him that he couldn't give. He recalled looking into the eyes of Carl Strom, the current head of the oversight committee, and knowing that the man thought Project Icarus was a hiding to nothing. A fool's errand.

The pattern was repeating itself over and over: each time Rush would get close to the answer, but each time fate would reach in and snatch it away from him. But not this time. *Not this time, not if Eli is really on to something.*

If the power *wasn't* the problem…if it *was* the dialing sequence…

Eli was waving his hand over the keys of the Dial-Home Device podium. "The symbols on the Stargate are constellations as seen from Earth, that's what you said."

"Yes," Rush nodded impatiently, wondering where Wallace was going with his train of thought. He glanced away, to where the technician was programming in the standard seven chevron coding that would open a wormhole back to Cheyenne Mountain and Stargate Command.

Eli pointed at a specific symbol on the DHD; it was one that everyone involved in any aspect of the Stargate program remembered, the symbol that had enabled Daniel Jackson to open the gate, the symbol that every SG team wore on their shoulder patches. An inverted 'V' with a tiny circle above it. "So what if *Earth* is supposed to be the point of origin?"

Rush frowned. "We couldn't do this from Earth," he

insisted, "even if we had a hundred Lantean zero point modules. The only viable power source we could find is *here*." He indicated the floor. "Light-years away from the Sol system."

Eli shook his head, his eyes wide. "But maybe that doesn't matter. Maybe it's the only combination that will work. Like a code."

The truth of the moment locked into place inside Rush's thoughts. It was simple, but it made perfect sense. And how like the Ancients to make the final part of their greatest leap across the infinite void contingent on the world that had been so pivotal in their history. He felt almost giddy with the sense of it. *Yes. He's right.*

Rush turned to Riley. "Stop the dialing sequence."

The sergeant gave him a look and shook his head. "I have my orders, Doctor."

Rush dashed across the gantry to Riley's console, his mind racing. If they returned to Earth now, then this planet and the Icarus Base facility would be lost to the invaders, at best; or torn apart by tectonic instability at worst. Without the core's monumental power, it wouldn't matter if Eli Wallace was correct about the origin symbol. No other known energy source existed that could pass the threshold for dialing the eighth chevron to reach the ninth. Everything Nicholas Rush had worked for, all these months and years of sacrificing himself, the destiny he knew was his…all of it would be lost, and this time there would be no more chances. He felt a tremor in his hands at the thought of that. It would destroy him.

Rush glanced at the power flow gauges and a thought formed in his mind. This was his last chance. He had to take *control*.

"We… We can't risk dialing Earth," he snapped, shoving Riley aside. "Get out of my way!"

Greer moved as quickly as he could with the dead weight of a bloody, unconscious man over his shoulder. His G36 rifle bounced off his thigh from its strap, and the Marine's hand never strayed too far from it each time he turned a corner or passed a shadowed hallway.

So far, he hadn't encountered any enemy contact this deep into Icarus, but he knew the enemy already had their men inside the perimeter. He'd seen the tail end of the firefight in the hangar bay, as waves of troops had flooded in through blast holes in the doors.

All things being equal, the Marine Corps and Air Force contingent at Icarus should have been more than a match for them, but whoever was pulling the strings of this operation knew that, and had made up for it with the sheer weight of numbers. Greer grimaced. Maybe the 300 Spartans had worse odds, but that was about it. Like it or not, Icarus Base was going to fall, and soon.

He rounded a corner into the main corridor and found what he was looking for. "Medic!" he called.

Lieutenant Johansen came to the sergeant's side as he carefully lay his burden down on the floor. The injured man was barely breathing, and his face was a mess of blood.

From her shocked reaction, Johansen clearly knew the guy. "Oh my god… Doctor Simms."

Greer blinked and looked again at the man he'd rescued. He hadn't even recognized the base's chief medical officer, the officer's face so messed up it looked like he'd been attacked by a razor-wielding psycho.

"What happened?" said the lieutenant, as she started to work on Simms, tearing bandages from her medical pack.

"He caught shrapnel from an explosion," Greer explained. "He was helping pull the wounded back from the surface." The sergeant saw Johansen busy herself with a nasty injury at the doctor's neck. Blood was seeping from it, matting his collar to his skin.

Greer stepped back to let the lieutenant do her job. He'd seen wounds like that before, and he had his doubts that Simms would survive it. Without another word, he paused to check his G36 once again and made to head back the way he came.

Strong fingers gripped his arm. "Greer!" He turned to find Colonel Young standing beside him. His commanding officer was smoke-dirty and he smelled like spent cordite. "We're pulling back."

Greer jerked a thumb at the corridor. "There are still people out there, sir!"

Young shook his head. "The *Hammond* has already started beaming up anyone pinned down on the surface—"

The sergeant's mouth twisted. When the hammer came down, he wasn't the kind to rely on any of that *Buck Rogers* sci-fi crap the flyboys liked so much. "Someone's got to make sure," he retorted.

"Sergeant!" Young snapped, with enough force that Greer's ingrained Corps training stopped him dead. "I've got people cut off from the gate room, trapped by a rock fall. The base is shielded, which means the *Hammond* can't get a lock on them to beam them out. So I need you here, to help them."

Greer relented. An order was an order. "Sir, yes sir. Where are they?"

"Corridor six-alpha—" Young halted as the medic gave a shallow, choked sob. Both men looked as Johansen's desperate attempts at resuscitation proved fruitless. Tears streaked the lieutenant's face, making tracks down her dust-smeared cheeks.

"T.J.," said Young, touching her shoulder. "Tamara, stop…"

Johansen drew back her hands and gave a shuddering sigh. "I was just talking with him a couple of hours ago."

"You can't help him any more," the colonel said. "We've gotta save who we can."

Hunter Riley watched the Scottish scientist as he worked the console, erasing the Earth gate address and beginning the initialization sequence over again. He hesitated, unsure how to proceed. The man had practically tipped him out of his chair, and now he was in the process of countermanding the orders of Riley's superior officer. The sergeant wasn't exactly sure how chain of command was supposed to work with civilians like Doctor Rush. He was the lead scientist here, but this was still a military base. Rush was here on a mandate from the SGC and the IOA, though, and Riley was pretty damned sure that all those three-letter acronyms overshadowed his stripes. What the question boiled down to was, *Will I end up in the stockade if I lay a hand on this guy?* He thought about what had happened to Greer and hesitated.

Like a lot of his family, Riley was career Air Force, and the Stargate program had already claimed one of his relatives, a cousin of his who'd been lost on the Atlantis expedition. He didn't want to be the next one who had a flag sent to his parents in lieu of a coffin.

"Doctor Rush," he began, "I'm going to have to ask you to step away from the console."

The scientist ignored him and entered the final symbol of the gate address, this time substituting the local glyph for the Earth symbol. Rush stared up at the spinning, rumbling gate with hope in his eyes. It was like he didn't even see the rest of the people in the room.

Riley glanced at the console. He didn't think for a second this was actually going to work.

But then the gate vibrated with a tremor of immense power and the event horizon erupted into the air, cascading across the length of the chamber with such force that everyone flinched and instinctively hugged the ground.

The noise of the vortex's formation was louder and more intense than any active gate Riley had witnessed, invisible waves of cold and static radiating out across the room, making the hairs on his arms stand up. As the event horizon collapsed back into the metallic ring, a familiar rippling light danced over the walls and through the dust-filled air, the echo of the opening roar dying away.

"That is impressive," managed Eli, amazement and shock writ large across his expression.

And it *was* impressive. The sergeant moved to one of the other consoles, checking the telemetry from the Stargate. His eyes narrowed. The wormhole was stable and showing the same kinds of readings he would have expected from a standard seven chevron link, but at the same time there was whole different layer of data streaming in that was totally new to him. Riley glanced at the energy transfer gauges and what he saw there gave him pause. Red tell-tales were blinking furiously, consumption and distribution graphs peaking well beyond the safe zone. "Power is fluctuating at critical levels." He swallowed hard. "Doctor, we need to disengage."

Rush didn't look at him; he was staring at the shimmering silver pool of the gateway, and by the expression on his face, you might have thought the man was looking into heaven itself. "I've done it," he whispered.

The *Hammond* rocked like a boat in a storm as another one-two punch landed on her forward shields, the energy-shock from the hits radiating back to the vessel itself. Colonel Carter hung on to her command chair and rode it out, unwilling to let herself be tipped out on the deck of her own bridge. It was all well and good that the ship had Asgard-designed gravity compensators on board, she reflected, but maybe a seatbelt wouldn't go amiss either.

"Marks, report," she demanded.

The major frowned at his readouts. "Shields are holding for now, but we're not going to be able to take much more of this pounding, ma'am. Forward missile bays are off line, and we've got atmospheric venting on three decks. Damage control teams are en route."

"What about the evacuation?"

Marks nodded. "The last of the wounded are coming on

board now. Anyone else is inside the base itself and we can't reach them."

"They'll have to fend for themselves…" Carter muttered, frowning.

An alert tone sounded on the major's screen and he stabbed at a button. "The aft sensor pallet… I'm detecting a massive build-up of energy from the planet. It's almost off the scale…"

The colonel saw the spike on the sensor return. The SGC had pretty big scales, considering the amount of high-power stuff they encountered on a regular basis, so anything that buried the needle was going to be, to put it mildly, a problem.

She studied the radiation waveform on the screen and her blood ran cold. What she was seeing was an energetic resonance build-up taking place deep inside the core of P4X-351. The natural deposits of naquadria were conducting and reflecting energy back upon themselves, shaping a quantum-level effect that would grow and grow until it reached criticality. When that happened…the release of radiation from the exotic matter would be huge and devastating.

Carter called out to the navigation officer at the chart console. "Get me a course to the nearest allied world with a gate, right now." She looked back at Marks. "Recall our fighters. Radio Colonel Telford and tell him he's got two minutes to get his people aboard before we go to hyperspace."

"Ma'am, what about the others inside Icarus Base?"

Carter looked away, feeling hollow inside. "They're on their own."

Young knew something was wrong the moment he reached the corridor leading to the gate room and saw the throng of people there, people who, instead of moving in a steady and orderly manner through the gate back to Earth, were standing around looking panicky and afraid. The tremors beneath his feet were a constant, unsteady pulse now, and he wondered how much longer the walls could still stand. He charged into the gate room and saw the open gate and more people who also weren't moving through it.

Rush looked over at him from the DHD, but Young glared past at Sergeant Riley. "What are you waiting for?" he demanded. "I ordered an evacuation!"

Eli held up a hand. "He didn't dial Earth," he explained, and nodded toward the Stargate. "It's the nine chevron address."

"What?!" It took a lot for Young to break his cool, but it happened now. He was incredulous that Rush could do something so reckless, at exactly the moment the lives of every man and woman on the base were in dire jeopardy. He glared at the gate and saw glowing light in each illuminated chevron, then turned his gaze on Rush.

"The attack has started a chain reaction in the planet's core," said the scientist, his words coming out in haste, "and there's no stopping it." He pointed at the open Stargate. "The effect will be catastrophic! The blast will easily translate through an open wormhole. It was too dangerous to dial Earth!"

Young advanced to him, his anger building. "You could have dialed somewhere else. The Alpha Site, or Chulak, or Abydos. *Anywhere* else." He was face to face with the other man.

"This was our last chance," insisted the scientist.

"Shut it down!" he snarled.

"We can't," said Rush. "It's too late."

Riley nodded grimly from a nearby console. "The system's not responding."

Young glared at the other man. "We need to get these people out of here."

"We have a way out," said Rush.

"We don't know what's on the other side!" he snapped back. "We can't even get a MALP remote up here to go take a look!"

Eli spoke up from behind him. "Can't be worse than here, can it?"

For a long second, Young wavered on the edge of knocking Rush on his ass, but this wasn't the time or the place for that. The man's arrogance was unbelievable, but it was too late to cry over it now, the damage was done. The colonel knew that severing the wormhole and trying to dial out again could be a death sentence for them all. It would take too long to cycle the whole process from the start, and Everett Young was not about to leave people behind.

He turned to Riley. "Get these people prepped to go through."

The sergeant saluted. "Yes sir."

Young favored Rush with a hard, unflinching glare for a long moment, then turned and stalked away to where Greer was waiting by the doorway.

The Marine held up a gear bag. "Colonel, I got the C-4 you wanted from the armory."

Young nodded. "Follow me."

It couldn't have been more than a few minutes, but it felt like they had been digging for hours. The front of Scott's uniform was gray with concrete dust and his hands were caked with grime. At his side, Chloe Armstrong was doing her best to help him, steadily and silently crying as she pulled at broken rocks. Her soft, well-manicured hands were now as filthy as his, and blood lined her fingers where her nails were shattered and bleeding.

"Dad?" she cried out, and coughed from the haze in the corridor. "Can you hear me?"

Scott paused, holding his breath and straining to listen for a reply. He thought he could hear a faint noise from the other side of the collapsed wall, but there was so much ambient sound, with the quake-rumbles and the distant hammer of gunfire, he couldn't be sure. He started to wonder how long they could go before he had to call it quits and drag the girl out of there, kicking and screaming.

"Chloe," he began, trying to frame the words.

"Stand clear," called a voice, and he turned to see two figures emerging through the dust: Colonel Young and Sergeant Greer.

"Heard you needed an assist, Lieutenant," said Young.

"Roger that," nodded Scott. He gave Greer a look. "When did you get out?"

Greer nodded at the colonel. "Early parole, sir." He stepped in and Scott's eyes widened as the Marine began to place a series of small explosive charges on the rubble.

"That could bring the rest of the roof down," said the lieutenant.

"We don't have the time to argue." Young fixed Scott with an intense look. "I need you to lead the evacuees through the gate." The colonel included Chloe. "Miss Armstrong, you need to go with him, too."

The girl shook her head. "I'm staying here until I know my father is okay."

Young didn't press the point and turned back to the lieutenant. "Make sure that everyone carries as much of the expedition supplies as they can."

Scott gave him a questioning look. "Why?"

"You're not going to Earth. Rush dialed the ninth chevron."

The lieutenant couldn't believe what he had just heard, but the grave cast of his commander's face told him that this was the situation, and this was his part in it.

"Go," ordered Young, and Scott broke into a run.

He made it to the gate room like the devil himself was chasing him, and perhaps that wasn't too far from the reality of it. Scott found Riley loading up a train of civilians with practically everything that wasn't nailed down, dividing up

the gear from the storage spaces adjacent to this one, packs
and hard-cases for every person.

The lieutenant paused to scoop up a backpack for himself
and dragged it on over his shoulders.

"Hey," said Eli, coming closer. "We're really doing this,
then?"

"Guess so," he replied, checking his assault rifle.

Eli nodded at the gun. "You...think you're gonna need
that?"

"Better to have it and not need it," Scott said, punctuating
his words with a snap of the weapon's slide, "than to need it
and not have it."

A large piece of rock detached itself from the ceiling
and plummeted to the ground, smashing a light fixture as
it fell. The sound and the flash set a ripple of fear fanning
out through the assembled people — *refugees now*, Scott
told himself — and he moved quickly to stamp on any fresh
waves of panic. "Okay, I need everyone to listen to me." He
walked toward the Stargate. "Once I'm through, give it a
count of three and then follow, one at a time." He looked
toward Riley. "Clear?" The sergeant nodded, and started
marshalling the group behind him.

Scott turned away and approached the event horizon.
This wasn't the first time he'd been through a Stargate. Okay,
so he had never been part of an SG team, but he knew the
feel of what was going to happen next. The cold kiss of the
strange non-matter as you passed through the vertical pool.
The peculiar, vertiginous head-rush as your body seemed
to fade away for a brief moment, and then the rollercoaster
ride boost out through space, off to some distant world.

But what the hell am I walking into this time? he wondered. On the other side of that shimmering puddle of light
was the unknown, something beyond human experience,
uncharted and alien. Matthew Scott wasn't the right man
for this moment, this whole *one small step*. Telford and

his team, they had been trained for this, they knew all the
Ancient stuff, they were the first contact specialists and
spec force operators.

Only they weren't here, and Scott was. He resisted the
urge to throw a glance over his shoulder and set his jaw.
Suddenly a memory bubbled up in his thoughts, something
the old man had told him when he was still a boy, back before
things had changed for the worse.

*You play the hand you're dealt, Scott. That's all anyone
ever can.*

He took a breath and stepped through.

Greer fixed the connector to the wired remote and then
unspooled the cable, paying it out, back along the length
of the corridor, around a corner. Chloe followed him, her
expression leaden.

Young watched them go. The Armstrong girl showed a lot
of heart for someone he'd originally pegged as a society girl
riding her father's coattails, but then adversity did things
like that to people. It either broke them apart or it broke
them open, and let the strength they had inside come out.
He just hoped that what she was wishing for was still there
on the other side of the rocks. The colonel took a breath of
the thick air and shouted into the rubble. "If you can hear
me, stand back! We're going to blow the obstruction!"

The warning delivered, he jogged back around the corner to where Greer and Chloe were crouching behind some
cover. The sergeant handed him the live trigger, and Young
called out the instant before he flipped the firing switch.
"Fire in the hole!"

A split-second later the C-4 blew, sending a rolling tor-
rent of fresh dust and powdered concrete churning away
over their heads. Young held his breath, afraid that the
next sound he would hear would be the rumble of the ceiling collapsing, but Greer had proven his worth once more,

planting the charges in just the right places.

He followed the Marine back to where the rubble had stood. A hole big enough to crawl through had appeared, and Greer was already pushing loose stone out of the way as the first person pushed through. Chloe stepped up to help him, offering her hands to a dust-covered woman in a lab coat, who stumbled past Young, clutching a pair of spectacles with shattered lenses.

"Move it!" Greer was calling out. "Come on, let's go!"

Young pointed down the corridor. "You heard him, that way. Get to the gate."

As the woman ran on, the base took another hit that lingered for long seconds, shaking the walls and threatening to undo the work of the breaching charges. Young looked up at the ceiling; the noise sounded like the peak was being torn from the top of the mountain, and for all he knew, it could have been just that. If Rush was right, the attack and maybe Icarus's tap into the core, to boot, had pushed this fragile world past the point of no return.

The people coming through the hole slowed to nothing, and Greer gave his commander a look. Young reached out for Chloe's shoulder, but the girl's attention was elsewhere. "Dad?"

One more figure pushed through, a man in a suit that had once been quite fine but now looked like it had been dragged through a quarry with him still in it. "I'm all right," said Armstrong, his face splitting in a grin at seeing his daughter again. "I was the last. There's no one else."

Chloe took the senator's weight and helped him away. Greer followed, and paused as he realized that the colonel wasn't with him.

"I'm right behind you," Young called after him. "Keep going."

He reached for his radio, and for the last time he toggled the channel to the general guard frequency. "*Hammond*, this is Young!" His answer was nothing but static. "*Hammond,* come in!"

No response. He hoped that meant Colonel Carter had lit the fires and taken the ship out of orbit, and not the more troubling option. At least he could hope that some of his people would make it back home. He wondered if Telford was among them; *Boy, is he gonna be pissed that I got to make this trip instead of him.*

Tamara Johansen glanced around and felt the panic rising from the people around her, the fear in them rolling forward like a tidal swell. The thunderous quakes went on and on, ceaseless now, the terrible sound of them blurring together into one unending chorus. She saw Rush move forward and pass through the event horizon of the Stargate, but no sooner was he through than a fresh crashing salvo of explosions blew the self-control of the evacuees and they all pressed at once.

"Don't push!" she shouted. "Stay calm!"

No-one listened, and her every attempt at holding on to some kind of order crumbled. The crowed surged, funneling toward the open gate.

She heard a voice over her radio, distorted and laced with strange interference. "*This is Scott, I need you to slow down the evac! Everyone's coming in too hot, we can't handle them!*"

Tamara tried to reach her walkie to respond, but it was too late. She was already being swamped by the crush of people, and fighting the motion of them would only get her trampled. She felt herself dragged toward the Stargate, and the last sight she had of Icarus Base was of Colonel Young racing into the gate room.

Young saw the chaos at the mouth of the gate and shouted at the top of his lungs, snarling at the evacuees to get through as quickly as they could. The gate room — and Icarus itself — was coming apart as chunks of concrete and rebar fell from the ceiling, smashing through gantries where they landed. Control panels sparked and dimmed as power began to die off through the base's crippled systems, and the colonel knew that the death knell was only seconds away.

Greer was almost at the event horizon, supporting an injured civilian with his free hand. He caught sight of his commander and called out. "Sir!"

Young stabbed a finger toward the Stargate. "Go!" he shouted, and reluctantly the Marine obeyed.

Dozens of supply cases and backpacks were scattered across the floor, left behind by the fleeing evacuees, some too heavy to carry, others broken open with their contents scattered. He looked up to see the last few people passing through the gate, and Young halted, instead turning to the crates and starting a frantic search.

Another shuddering explosion brought gusts of burning hot air with it, and he tasted the sulphurous stink of searing chemical fumes. The vibrations were so strong now he could barely stay on his feet, and the lights overhead began to blow out one by one. The Stargate itself rattled in its restraints and threw great lightning-streaks of energy out across the walls.

One more container. He tore open the lid and his eyes immediately found what he had been searching for: a slim, nondescript silver case. A coded locking mechanism secured its single latch. With his rifle still in his other hand, Young threw himself up on to the gate gantry and ran full tilt toward the event horizon. It loomed ahead of him, wreathed in energetic discharges, shaking so hard it seemed to be trying to break free and escape.

Young was less than an arm's length from it when a burning wall of flame and smoke slammed into him from behind, ripping him off his feet and spinning him through the air. The fireball ripped the breath from his lungs and pitched him over into the disc of silver, the surface of it tinted crimson with the reflections of a planet wide inferno.

On the parched, rocky surface of P4X-351, a massive bloom of thermal energy erupted like a towering volcano as the churning mass of volatile naquadria went supercritical. The first shockwave event blasted up through the channels cut into the fissures of the planetary crust, seeking the path of least resistance. Icarus Base, like its namesake, was touched by fire and destroyed. In seconds, magma flows under intense pressure tore through the sublevels of the facility, melting rock, turning steel and glass instantly to gas. The eruption discharged into the sky, ripping open the mountain that had housed the base, sending a fountain of smoke and fire miles into the air. The enemy ground troops died instantly, killed by the sheer overpressure of the mountain's destruction.

And still the fireball grew, as the planet's core went mad, turning itself inside out, energy flashing over as it shattered the cowl of rock and air surrounding it. The shockwave crossed the landscape, searing everything it touched, blazing everything into ashes and fragments in its inferno. The blast fractured the atmosphere, tearing it away, the pillar of fire growing into orbital space.

The trio of Ha'tak motherships had drawn close to the planet, preparing to lock on to the portable ring transporter terminals the transport crew had set up. They were too near to escape, even as their helmsmen tried to make for open space. The blast wave reached up and swatted them from the sky, smashing the pyramid ships into pieces that collided and crackled with spilled energy.

The death-throes of P4X-351 turned the planet into a brief, glittering sun as it ate out its own heart, before crumbling into a storm of radioactive dust.

CHAPTER FIVE

It was the silences that were the worst. They were what hit him hardest, just the simple absence of speaking, and she knew that. She knew how much it bothered him. He never really talked that much, not anywhere near as much as Emily did, and that was how Everett liked it. He loved to hear the sound of her voice, not his own, always had. He could listen to her reading out the phone book and it would make him relax, make him smile; so when she went silent, it was like a light going out of the world.

She collected the dishes from the dinner table and carried them into the kitchen. Emily couldn't manage them all in one trip, though, so he picked up the rest, the glasses and all, and brought those to her while she started sorting them.

She didn't speak. Her mouth was in a thin, flat line, eyes not meeting his. She might have even cried if he hadn't been in the room with her. And finally, when he couldn't stand the silence any more, he spoke again, repeating himself.

"It's just one more year."

"It's *always* just one more year," she said, old reproach strong in her words.

"Well, this time it is." It sounded weak coming from him.

"There's always important work that needs to be done," she went on. "By you."

He sighed. "It's a command. A good posting."

"Where?" Emily loaded the dishwasher and closed it with an air of finality.

"It's classified." She started to sigh, and he pressed on. "It's a lot safer than other places I've been assigned to—"

She looked up at him. "That's not the point. You've put in your time, Everett."

He nodded. His throat felt dry, and it suddenly seemed hot in the kitchen, hot and dust-dry. "And when this tour is over, I promise you—"

Emily didn't let him finish. "You know what? Never mind. Don't bother promising anything. You always end up choosing to be somewhere other than here."

He reached for his collar, pulling at it. He could feel an odd, distant heat on his back. He had the sudden sense of fire and dizziness at the edge of his thoughts and he pushed it away. "I am not choosing my job over you!" he insisted, feeling light-headed. "I... I don't know how you can even say that."

His wife looked away. "I love you. I do. But I can't wait anymore."

"Emily—" He took a step toward her and his legs turned to water. He stumbled, the strength ebbing from him. He reached out, bracing himself on the counter. Sweat blossomed on his forehead, streaming into his eyes. The heat was at his back, all over him, engulfing him.

"Everett, are you okay?" Her voice, her beautiful voice, began to echo and distort. Her face became a blur, the kitchen with it. "Everett?"

And then there was pain, pain and silver fire and darkness and cold. Then another voice, a woman but not Emily. Not his wife.

"Colonel?"

Tamara bent down over Young, trying to pick out any signs of awareness from him, but his eyes were rolled back into his head and he started to twitch and jerk. His legs kicked against nothing, scraping across the dark floor of the alien gate room.

The medic gritted her teeth and glanced around. She found the girl from the dinner in the officer's mess, the senator's daughter. *What was her name? Zoë? Chloe?*

"Hey, you," she called. "Help me."

The girl came over, her face pale with worry and border-line shock "Is he—?"

Tamara grabbed an unused injector pen from her medical kit and opened the colonel's mouth, wedging it in between his teeth. "Hold him down," she told her.

The girl — *Chloe, yeah, that was her* — looked at her with fear as Young convulsed. "Can't you do something for him?"

She shook her head. "He's having a seizure. I'm trying to prevent him from causing further injury to himself." Tamara swallowed, dry-throated. "There's nothing else I can do."

Gently but tightly, the lieutenant held her commanding officer's head and let the spasms run their course. Chloe looked on, her expression one of shock and alarm.

Scott walked slowly down the corridor, stepping evenly, panning the muzzle of the G36 left and right in steady arcs. The assault rifle had a flashlight slung under the barrel on a rail, and he used it to throw a disc of illumination out in front of him.

Everywhere the light fell, he saw walls of dark metal, pipe work, conduits. Everything had a heavily-engineered, boiler-plate feel to it, as if whoever had built this place had decided that endurance was more important than elegance. It reminded the lieutenant of an old steam locomotive he'd seen as a kid; he actually saw gauges, the real dial-and-needle kind, bolted on to mechanical hubs in the walls. Thinking about it, there was a sort of logic to that — electronics and digital hardware were never as resilient as old-fashioned analog tech.

He reached out a hand and laid his palm on the wall. At first he'd thought the gate had spat them out into some kind of underground bunker, perhaps the Ancient equivalent of Cheyenne Mountain or Icarus Base; but there was a subtle vibration in the floor and the walls that felt like the running of distant engines, and then there'd been that weird moment of motion-sense after the gate had cut out. The metal was chilly and a little damp, and there was the faint smell of ozone and rust in the air, like a junkyard after a thunderstorm.

He moved on. Still no sign of Rush yet. The man wasn't anywhere in sight. Scott had left the gate room behind and started moving down the first corridor he came across, figuring that maybe the scientist's curiosity had got the better of him. He was just hoping now that if there were any locals hereabouts, they hadn't already killed and eaten the man; or perhaps there were lethal deathtraps scattered all over the place, and Rush had fallen foul of one and been, what, vaporized?

Ahead of him the corridor presented a broad circular hatch that was larger than any of the others he'd passed so far. He advanced on it.

Scott's boot touched a plate of decking and it gave a creak, giving slightly under his weight. He froze, and in that moment sensed something moving behind him. He spun in place, bringing up the rifle, the safety catch snapping off.

"Whoa!" The glow from the flashlight caught Eli Wallace's face and the terror in his eyes. He had his hands up like a robbery victim. "It's me!"

Scott scowled and lowered the gun, glancing at the creaky floor plate. That was all it was, not a trap, just old and a bit rusted. "What are you doing here? I told you to help Greer."

"I did, uh, for a little bit," Eli replied. "But I figured I could maybe, y'know, help you better."

"And how are you gonna do that, exactly?"

Eli didn't answer, instead halting in front of the large hatch, his eyes narrowing.

"What?" said Scott.

He pointed at lines of symbols across the midline of the hatch; dots and circles and wavy lines. "I've seen this writing before."

"In the game?" Scott recalled what he'd heard about the secret test Wallace had been a part of.

Eli nodded. "Yeah." He ran his fingers over the surface of the metal door. "Roll d-twenty, check for traps," he muttered to himself, and then touched a disc in the center of the hatch. It opened immediately and Scott brought up the rifle, pushing Eli aside.

Beyond was a wide open room populated with a few narrow support stanchions and a couple of low couches. Light fell across the chamber in waves, cast from one entire wall where the steel and iron ended and thick, age-worn windows ranged from floor to ceiling. Beyond the portal, far below a dark, metallic cityscape stretched away; but it was the remainder of the view that captivated them.

Stars, drawn by impossible speed into swirling streaks of phase-shifted light, raced past at unknowable velocity. Scott felt a momentary head-swim and shook it off; it was like standing on the prow of a sailing vessel racing into the night.

"We're on a ship?" said Eli.

Scott found himself nodding. That explained the engine sounds. He saw a figure standing at the window, his hands on the glass. Rush; the man was lit by the light of alien suns, and he seemed utterly lost in it.

"The design is clearly Ancient…" said the scientist, his voice distant. "In the truest sense of the word. Launched hundreds of thousands of years ago… Perhaps more."

Scott blinked and pushed the majesty of the sight to the back of his thoughts. The view from this observation room was breathtaking, but they were not here to sightsee. "Doctor Rush," he began.

The other man didn't acknowledge him. "We seem to be moving faster than light speed, yet not through hyperspace…"

"What are you doing?"

"How far has it traveled in all that time?" Rush asked the

question, still enrapt in the starlight.

"Doctor Rush!" Scott stepped to him, raising his voice, finally breaking the man's reverie. The scientist glanced at the lieutenant as if he hadn't even known he was there. "We've got a lot of wounded. We need to get home." When Rush didn't answer him straight away, Scott put all the force he could into the next word. "Sir?"

Eli gave him a look; wherever Rush's head was at, it wasn't here.

Young's seizure finally, mercifully subsided and Tamara settled him down on the deck, using a folded gear vest as a support for the colonel's head. His breathing was steady but shallow and sweat filmed his pale skin. She sighed and glanced at Chloe. "Thanks for the help."

"Will he be okay?"

I have no idea. The words almost tripped out of her mouth, but she forced them down and gave a curt nod. "We'll have to see." She stood up and ran her hands over the thighs of her uniform trousers, leaving trails of blood and dirt on the dark material.

Tamara glanced around. There were just so many of them, people huddled in groups or clustered around the inert Stargate, cold and afraid and hurt, and all of them were looking to her for help. *But I'm not a doctor,* she screamed inside, *I'm just a field medic. Sew you up, send you back to base where the real physicians are, that's what I was trained to do. Not this.*

A man's shout reached her and Tamara saw one of the scientists, Franklin, stumbling away from a wall, tugging at his jacket. She ran to him and caught a whiff of a pungent, acidic stink.

"Ow! Damn it!" Franklin had his jacket off now, and threw it to the deck. He was pulling at the shirt underneath, craning to look at his shoulder.

"What is it?" said Tamara.

"I don't know…" She couldn't recall ever having seen the guy this animated before. What Tamara remembered of Jeremy Franklin from the times she'd seen him on Icarus was a circumspect middle-aged man with a perpetually hang-dog expression. His shirt was slightly discolored where something had soaked into it. Tamara peeled it back and saw a patch of inflamed skin.

"It burned me," offered Franklin.

She bent and prodded the man's jacket. There on the shoulder was a blob of black ooze, gritty, with the consistency of thick oatmeal. The chemical smell was coming from it in tiny wisps of white vapor.

"Is that acid?" said the man. "Where did it come from?"

Tamara glanced around. Franklin had been sitting on a gear case, half-asleep with his back to the wall. She looked up and saw a grate a little way up, air grumbling through it from some concealed atmosphere processor. Stepping closer, she saw more of the thick goop trickling slowly from the mouth of the vent, dropping in fat gobs to the deck; Franklin had been right under it.

And then, with a rattling clatter, the fan behind the vent stuttered to a halt and the air flow ceased.

"Oh, that's not good," she said to herself. Tamara snatched up her radio and spoke into it. "Lieutenant Scott, come in. We've got a problem in the gate room."

"This is Scott," said the officer, turning away from Rush and shooting Eli an expression that said *What now?* "Go ahead, T.J."

"One of the air vents just shut down in here. It's coughing up some kind of acidic slurry."

Eli took a deep breath and frowned. "The air's getting pretty thin in here, too." He hadn't noticed it at first, thinking that perhaps he was just giddy with awe at the sight outside the window, but his chest was starting to ache. He looked for and found air vents in the walls of the observation room and waved his hand in front of them; nothing was coming through.

"What does that mean?" Scott was saying.

Rush turned away from the window. "It means that the life support systems are not working properly." Suddenly, the distant, dreamy look on the scientist's face was gone and he was back to his more typical acerbic, narrow-eyed focus. "We should probably do something about that."

Eli nodded and pointed. "What he said."

Scott raced back to the gate room as quickly as he could, and he found himself panting hard, the thinning air beginning to make itself apparent. He tried to run some quick and dirty calculations in his head, but he gave up when he realized he didn't have all the data. He didn't know for sure how many people had made it through the gate, or how many rooms and corridors on this ship had air in them, or how long those vents had been working. Trying to put a number on it was a waste of time. He wondered about what the airflow thing meant. The ship was obviously old, so was it just a matter of decrepit systems that had fallen apart when the Stargate's activation had triggered them? Or perhaps it was something else — Scott had glimpsed the size of the ship they were on. A lot of room out there. Maybe it wasn't so derelict as he thought, maybe there was a crew somewhere who didn't like the idea of gatecrashers. "We come in peace," he said aloud. The silent walls didn't answer him.

Rush had said something about finding a 'control nexus' a way down the corridor past the observation room, so Scott had sent him and Eli off to take a look at it in hopes of stemming this newest problem. *Maybe we'll catch a break*, he thought, *we're due it*. Bombed by raiders, thrown who-knows-where through the Stargate, lost and alone and now facing the threat of suffocation; this wasn't exactly how Scott had expected his first field command to go.

He halted before reaching the gate room and took a second to compose himself; his instructors at officer candidate school taught him that a commander had to look capable and sound confident in order to engender conviction from his men, even if he didn't feel it. Like it or not, these people were relying on him now — at least until Colonel Young woke up.

If he wakes up. Scott frowned at that thought and dismissed it. *One damn problem at a time.*

He came back into the room to find a knot of people clustering around Johansen, bombarding her with questions that she couldn't answer. Most vocal of them was the senator. Alan Armstrong; Scott had seen the guy on the news one time, arguing over some point of military spending. He was using the same tone of voice on Tamara as he had back then.

"You need to start giving us some answers," he demanded.

Scott slung his rifle and called out. "Can I have everybody's attention? Please, be quiet!" When that didn't work, he snapped out a shout. "*Hey*! Listen up!"

That got him about a second of actual calm before Armstrong felt the need to fill the silence. "What is going on?" The man's words were a little gaspy; he was practically hyperventilating.

Scott figured he wouldn't sugar-coat it. "We're on an Ancient spaceship. That's all I've got." A murmur went through the crowd as they processed this new piece of information. "What that means is—"

Armstrong butted in. "It means that we need to use the Stargate to get us all home!"

Scott raised his hand. "That is definitely on the list of things to do, sir, but—"

The senator wasn't listening. "You can consider that an order, Lieutenant!"

He could feel the mood of the evacuees turning angry and fearful behind Armstrong's lead. "Colonel Young put me in charge—"

"Then do your job and get these people back to Stargate Command right now!" snapped the senator.

"We're working on it." Scott's cool fractured. "But do you see a DHD anywhere?" He gestured around angrily.

"A what?" snapped Armstrong.

"Dial Home Device," offered Tamara. "Runs the Stargates." There were a couple of copper-colored consoles lurking at the back of the room, but nothing that resembled the usual dialing podium.

Armstrong changed tack. "I want to speak to whomever is responsible for this. Where is Doctor Rush?" The politician's face was coloring, his voice rising. "He sent us here! This is his fault!"

Scott's patience was about done. "Just shut up for a second, will you?"

Armstrong's nostrils flared with anger. "Don't you dare talk to me like that—" He choked off the end of the sentence and coughed hard, one hand reaching up to clutch at his chest. He dove into a pocket and came back with a pill bottle, tapping a red and white capsule into a shaky hand.

Scott's annoyance subsided and he pulled his canteen from his belt, offering it to the other man. Armstrong waved it away and took the pill dry, swallowing it with effort.

His daughter came to him, taking his arm. "Dad, please…" she began, leading away to a place where he could sit down.

The lieutenant took a breath. "Look, I'm sorry," he began again. "I'm trying to explain the situation. We are on a ship but we have no idea where we are in relation to Earth." *Or anywhere else, for that matter.* He fixed Armstrong with a firm look. "With all due respect, sir, the reason you may be having a hard time breathing right now is because the ship's life support system is not functioning properly."

That piece of information finally got Scott the quiet he'd been wanting all along. He nodded in the direction of the corridor. "Doctor Rush is working on that problem right now, but I need everyone with any knowledge of Ancient systems. We need all the help we can muster." He scanned the faces in front of him. "Adam Brody and Lisa Park, are you here?"

Two people gingerly raised their arms. One was a guy in his forties, the other a woman with shoulder-length hair. Both had the look of career academics about them, and both were clearly way out of their depth in the current situation.

"Okay, you two come with me."

Brody hesitated, indicating one of the nearby panels. "These consoles just came on, shouldn't we—"

Scott shook his head. "Nobody touch anything yet. Right now, Rush needs your help." He saw Sergeant Greer standing nearby and gave him a look. Greer didn't need to be told and just nodded, gathering up his weapon. "Everybody else, just stay calm, and stay put. Please."

Tamara spoke close to his ear. "I'll try to make sure no one else wanders off, but I'm swamped down here."

"I know." Scott saw Young where he lay on the floor. "What about—?"

She answered his question before he could finish it. "The colonel's still out."

"Keep me posted," he told her, and stepped away, with the Marine and the two scientists following on behind.

Greer insisted on taking point even though the lieutenant explained he'd already checked out the corridors. It never hurt to have a set of Marine Corp eyes look over things, just to be sure. Park and Brody talked amongst themselves, half excited by what the saw all around them, and half terrified.

Scott pointed. "It's just up this way." Greer threw the officer a look and Scott's brow furrowed. "What? You got something on your mind, sergeant?"

He shrugged. "I was thinking. You just told a United States senator to quit his bitching back there. I guess you're not in a hurry to get those captain's bars."

Scott made a face. "Ah, who cares if he puts me on report," he said, after a moment. "Joke's on him. We're probably all gonna die out here anyhow."

Greer gave a gallows-humor smirk. "And here was me thinking you were a ray of sunshine, sir."

Scott had a retort, but he forgot it as the sound of raised voices filtered down the corridor toward them.

"That's Doctor Rush," said Park.

Then Greer very clearly heard the Wallace kid say "Stop! You're going to kill us all!"

"Ah hell," said Scott, "what now?"

They broke into a run and raced down the length of the corridor, turning into a hexagonal-shaped room with a complex thicket of cables, tubes and conduits snaking up from the center, rising from floor to ceiling like a ragged pillar. Angled consoles like those in the gate room were arranged around it, and Rush stood behind one of them, his face back-lit by the glow of an active screen.

"What's going on?" Greer demanded. He saw lines of blocky lettering — Ancient text, it looked like — streaming across the display. Rush was working a circular interface pad, like a scaled-up version of the one on the front of an mp3 player.

"The life support system is on," said Rush, "but for some reason it's not working properly. The atmosphere is too thin, we can all feel it." Greer couldn't argue with that. He had a headache that just wouldn't quit. "I'm attempting to reset the system."

Which all sounded reasonable enough. But Wallace wasn't buying any of it, shaking his head, pointing at Rush. "He has no idea what he's doing."

Greer did not like Rush, not even a little. The man was unfriendly, arrogant and clearly convinced of his own superiority. The Marine had heard all about him from the other jarheads on duty in Icarus, as well as seeing the man's behavior for himself once or twice. And like Armstrong had said, none of them would have been in this mess if Rush had just let Riley dial Earth. By now they could have been in Colorado, with a cup of coffee and a debrief instead of waiting to choke to death.

He raised his G36. "Step away from that thing," he said.

Rush paid no attention to the Marine and ran his hands over the control pad, locking in commands one after another. He reached for the interface disc.

"That screen says what you're doing is going to overload it!" Eli snapped.

Rush gave the kid a pitying look. "Eli, please. Don't interfere with what you don't understand."

"Is that what it says or not?" insisted Wallace.

The scientist glanced up as Park and Brody appeared at the doorway, and looked at them as if expecting support. When he didn't get it, Rush's manner turned stormy. "Eli, you only *think* you know what this screen says because we embedded a rudimentary version of the Ancient language into that game you played." He tapped the console angrily. "*This* is not a game! This is life and death!"

"Don't touch it, Rush," said Scott. From the corner of his eye, Greer could see the lieutenant also had his hand on his weapon. Greer started thinking about where he could put a round into Rush that would knock him down but not kill him.

"Oh, for the…" Rush's hands tightened in annoyance. "Listen to me. When oxygen levels aboard this ship fall below a critical level, it will become increasingly hard to concentrate! We have to do this now!"

"What you're doing could blow the whole ship," insisted Eli.

"Are you sure of that?" said Scott.

"No!" snapped Eli. "But I don't think he is either!"

Greer saw a flicker of doubt in Rush's eyes and he knew immediately that the kid was right. The scientist was taking a big risk with all their lives. He gestured with the barrel of the rifle. "Back off now, or I will shoot!"

"No," said Rush.

He felt a hand on his shoulder. "Lower your weapon, sergeant," said Scott.

Greer's hand stiffened around the grip of the G36. "He's already screwed us once. I'm not going to let him do it again."

Scott hesitated, his gaze shifting from Rush to Eli and then back again.

Rush was stock still now, his hand hovering over the console's interface wheel. "I am going to press this button," he said, calmly and firmly, taking on a lecturing tone. "It is going to fix life support and then we'll all be able to breathe much better and think more clearly. You can shoot me for it if you want, but if, however, there *are* any negative consequences to resetting the system, I suggest you might still need me to help resolve them."

Eli threw up his hands, and Scott knew this was on him now. He spoke directly to Greer. "I know we're in a tough situation, Sergeant, but I am giving you an order." He took a breath. "Hold your fire."

There was a moment when he thought that Greer might just go ahead and put a bullet in Rush anyway, but then the Marine relaxed and let the G36's muzzle drop, his thumb flicking the safety catch.

Rush didn't want for him to change his mind, and stabbed the control key. The room went silent, and Scott found himself holding his breath. After a couple of long seconds, he glanced up at one of the air vents in the ceiling. There was no sound of fans turning, no rattle of the grilles. "So?"

The scientist's shoulders sagged and he glared at the read-outs on the console. "I suppose that would have been too easy," he muttered to himself. "At least I didn't get shot for it."

Eli looked up. "Apparently, that did nothing."

Scott turned and beckoned Brody and Park into the room. "Okay, show's over. Get in here and make yourselves useful."

"I don't need any help—" began Rush, as the other two scientists moved to study the consoles before them.

Scott indicated the silent air vents. "Clearly, Doctor, you do. Just get it done." The tension in the moment and the lack of oxygen was getting to him. He rubbed his eyes and stepped away into the corridor. Out here, the air tasted worse, all tinny and metallic. He spoke into his radio. "Gate room? Scott here."

Tamara held her walkie to her ear. "Go ahead." The lack of airflow already made it clear that whatever was supposed to be working, wasn't, but she tried to keep the weariness from her voice.

"*This may take a little more time, T.J.,*" he told her. "*Just hang in there.*"

She wanted to ask him exactly how the hell she was supposed to do that, but instead she just nodded to herself and said "Copy that."

Tamara clipped the radio back on her gear vest and gave a shallow sigh. All around her, the Icarus evacuees were sitting down on the deck, not moving or talking, trying to conserve what oxygen they still had. She felt the energy draining from her, moment by moment, and silently cursed whatever fate it was that had dragged her into this situation. *Tamara Johansen had plans*, she told herself, *and who was it that got to say she couldn't fulfill them?* A flare of resentment flickered inside her, but it had nowhere to go, and it guttered out just as quickly.

She looked to where Young was lying. He was probably

going to sleep through it all, she reflected, never once wake to know what outcome would befall them. From the corner of her eye she saw another face she knew, all distressed dark hair and anxious eyes. Camile Wray, the IOA's human resources liaison at Icarus. *Former liaison*, she corrected.

The last time she'd seen the woman was in her office. Tamara remembered it clearly, standing in front of her desk, the letter of resignation and all the attendant paperwork in a neat pile under Camile's elegantly manicured fingers.

Wray hadn't even bothered to read the letter, instead asking "Does Colonel Young know about this?"

"He knows." Tamara didn't waste time with specifics. She thought that would be it. Forms signed, paperwork done. A rubber stamp in the right place and it would all be over.

But Wray wouldn't drop it. "Are you sure I can't change your mind?"

"No," she'd insisted. "This is something I've wanted to do for a long time." It almost sounded like she meant it.

"Two weeks ago you told me you would be re-enlisting," Wray went on. "You said this was the best experience of your life." The woman had leaned forward and given her a hard look. "Something has to have happened."

Tamara had replied with the answer she rehearsed. "The scholarship came through. I guess I've just been too afraid to admit what I really want. Afraid I'd fail if I tried." Wray didn't call her a liar, but her expression had said it plainly. "Come on, Camile," she said. "I know better than to try and hide anything from you."

Wray gave a small smile at that. "You didn't even tell me you had applied."

Tamara Johansen had plans, said the voice in her head. "There's nothing else going on. You know I'd tell you."

"Unless you were protecting someone."

"I'm not," she'd insisted. "Like I said, I guess I hadn't made up my mind."

And that was where she'd ended it, walking out of the office, the choice written there on the papers, in black and white.

But all that happened before some force bigger than her had snatched the wheel of her life from Tamara's hands and wrenched it hard over, off the road she chose and on to this path.

She blinked away the moment of reverie, and snapped back to the present. Tamara watched the colonel there on the floor, his chest rising and falling, rising and falling.

Eli snuck a look across the room at Rush, past the tower of control interface systems, but the scientist didn't seem to notice. He felt pretty guilty, actually, considering what he had thought to be a difference of opinion had turned into a situation where his big mouth would have resulted in Rush catching a bullet.

He winced at the thought of that and wondered if he should apologize. Eli shook his head slightly and tried to focus. The lack of oxygen was making his mind wander. He'd already caught himself thinking about how he could apply lessons learned from watching episodes of *Lost in Space* to their current situation, and wondering if one of the compartments along the corridor was actually the home of a cute-but-sassy robot.

That's the hypoxia talking, Eli, he told himself, *get a grip.* He had full-blown nausea, coma and blue skin to look forward to unless they could fix the air.

He moved past Brody and Park, both of them engrossed in their own explorations of the Ancient consoles, seeing Scott and his Marine buddy by the doorway. The military guys looked bored; without anything to shoot at, they probably both felt a little surplus to requirements.

Eli took a breath of stale air and moved closer to Rush, glancing over his shoulder. The scientist was using the rotary interface to spin through panels of text, jumping from one menu panel to another. As the strings of lettering whirled past, Eli suddenly spotted something that seemed out of place. "What's that?" He was asking the question before he was even aware of thinking it.

"I don't know," admitted Rush. "Another subsystem?"

"Doesn't look like life support," he added.

"I know." He completely missed the irritation in the other man's tone.

Eli extended an arm and pointed at the screen, invading Rush's personal space. "Why don't you try this—"

The scientist glared at him. "Do you mind?"

Eli tried to look around the other man. "I can't see otherwise."

Rush let out a sigh. "Fine." He spooled back to the data-panel Eli had been talking about and flipped through a layer of menus before pressing the screen.

Immediately, a glimmer of light flickered along the far wall of the room, drawing everyone's attention. Projected from some hidden source, a large window of holographic light phased into being, and it filled with thousands of dots of light. Park and Brody left their consoles behind and came closer, eyes wide.

"What are we looking at?" asked Scott.

The display was moving, drawing back, zooming out from the initial starting point. The dots of light merged, forming a banner of glowing color. Eli gasped as he recognized the shape of a galactic spiral arm.

"It's a star map," breathed Rush. "A navigational chart, perhaps."

The hologram continued to pull back, the spiral arm becoming more defined. "That's the Milky Way," said Park. "That's *our* home galaxy."

Rush nodded. "I believe what we're seeing here is a visual log of this ship's route."

Eli saw a faint blue dot that stood out among the white and yellow of the stars, and pointed at it. "So this is where we are right now?"

"No," said Rush, flicking a glance down at his console. "That is where the ship originally embarked from."

"Earth," said Brody.

Eli felt a curious smile on his lips, and suddenly the ship didn't seem quite as alien as it had a moment ago. They were all from the same place, more or less.

Rush turned back to the console and began manipulating the keypad. In response, a glowing line marking the ship's course drew out across the star map like a lengthening thread, and the image continued to change, the barred spiral of the Milky Way shrinking as the line moved into the void of inter-galactic space.

Park spoke again, awed. "It's leaving the galaxy."

"It did," Rush corrected. "Long ago."

The line went on, passing by another pool of shimmering stars. "That was Pegasus," said Brody.

The galaxy-shapes grew even smaller, contracting into dots as more and more points of light crowded in from the sides of the screen.

"So, those points are more stars?" asked Scott.

"No." Eli shook his head, and the words came from his mouth, but he could hardly hold the magnitude of them in his thoughts. "They're *galaxies*." Eli felt giddy and put out a hand to steady himself on the console. This time, he knew it wasn't the bad air. He couldn't look away from the screen. The distance was incredible, unthinkable. It was literally *astronomical*.

"This ship has traveled a very, very long way," Rush said quietly.

"How far?" Scott insisted, the scale of the image clearly lost on him. "Rush, where the hell are we?"

Eli watched the line moving on and on, further and further.

"Several billion light-years from home," said Rush.

CHAPTER SIX

The evening rain drummed hard on the roof of the staff car as it turned on to Jefferson Davis Highway, heading south past the Arlington National Cemetery toward the imposing edifice of the Pentagon. Jack O'Neill blinked away a twinge of fatigue and glanced down at the file on his lap, before frowning and putting it to one side. He tried to remember that last time he'd been in a car where he *hadn't* had a landslide of paperwork with him. It had gotten so that he was still in the office even when he wasn't in the office, even the brief moments of respite he liked to take during the drive into DC snatched away by a mountain of reports and requests...

Not for the first time, O'Neill wondered how his former CO General Hammond had managed to handle all this stuff and make it seem so effortless.

The car took the Pentagon exit and made its way through a series of priority checkpoints before pulling to a halt outside a nondescript side entrance along the flank of the massive building, far from the public eye. Inside, along with all the myriad other components of America's military machine, was a department whose nature and purpose was unique among them all.

Homeworld Command was a global joint-ops division, something that had evolved out of the USAF's Stargate Command and the sister organizations in the nations that were part of the International Oversight Advisory. Gone were the old days, back when it was just the Air Force poking around in outer space. Jack recalled a time when there were only a handful of SG teams on sorties through the Stargate, when the whole program was viewed as some massive boondoggle that would likely blow up in their faces. Now the

Stargate was a major factor in the military structure of not only the United States of America, but of the planet Earth. It still amazed him that the existence of the gate remained a secret to the world at large; but then that dumb *Wormhole X-Treme!* TV show had helped a lot, ruining the credibility of anyone who came sniffing around. It was O'Neill's understanding that the Air Force had borrowed the idea from the FBI, who had set up a similar disinformation strategy back in the early nineties to draw attention away from one of their secret departments.

A woman in a captain's uniform came down the steps with an umbrella in her hand and opened the car door. O'Neill walked back with her toward the building. "Captain Sharpe."

"General." Helen Sharpe was a recent addition to O'Neill's staff and she had a manner that was brisk and direct. A former officer aboard one of the SGC's starships, she'd returned to Earth and turned her fiercely competent skills to Homeworld Command's advantage. "I'm sorry we had to recall you from the senator's dinner party, but this couldn't wait."

"Yes, I'm quite disappointed," O'Neill replied, pokerfaced. "Because you know how much I love being in a room full of politicians, with nothing to eat but those little sticks with cheese and pineapple on them."

They entered the Pentagon and moved swiftly toward an elevator, which dropped sharply into the sublevels below the street. "I took the liberty of having an airman get you a club sandwich, sir."

Damn, she's efficient. "So, on a scale of one to ten, how big a deal is this gonna be?"

They arrived at the next security checkpoint. "With respect, sir, I can't discuss that with you until you've been cleared." She gestured at a tall scanner archway that was of noticeably off-world origin.

O'Neill saw two Marines in full body armor, one with a

loaded and ready P90, the other with an active zat'ni'katel energy pistol, guarding the door. He knew that two more would be on the other side, and another squad of five were in a room just down the hall in case the panic button was pushed.

Someone had turned the security dial way up, and he frowned. "Is this really necessary?" he asked. "I was here about three hours ago. We talked about how much I was looking forward to the party, remember?"

"General, you're the one who has faced off against invisible monsters, parasitic aliens and shape-changing killers. You know that there's security, and then there's *security*." Sharpe took O'Neill's identity pass and swept it through a reader.

"Identify for voice print check," said a soft, synthetic voice.

"Oh, for cryin' out loud—" began the general.

"Voice print check approved," replied the computer. "Proceed to imaging scanner."

"Fine." O'Neill stepped through the arch and no alarms sounded. "Am I still a person?"

Sharpe nodded and the two Marines went from combat stances to attention. "Welcome back, sir."

The main nexus of Homeworld Command was a tactical information center linked to a network of similar facilities scattered around the world, in IOA-member nations; China, Russia, Europe and the UK, all of them had their own equivalents of this room, all of them working in real-time on the one thing that every nation could agree about — keeping the planet safe.

Digital charts of the world, near-Earth space and the solar system adorned the walls, and in the middle of the room there were ranks of desks with operations staff parsing a constant stream of data from ground based sensors, orbital satellites, as well as feeds from the new lunar base facility and even hidden scanner arrays aboard the International Space Station. Other members of O'Neill's staff monitored information from much further afield, sifting intel from starships like the *Apollo* and the *Odyssey*, or from allied extraterrestrial groups like the Free Jaffa and the Tok'ra.

Sharpe left O'Neill to address a question from a junior officer as the general crossed to his office. A familiar face intercepted him; Master Sergeant Walter Harriman had been a vital part of the Stargate program from the very start, and O'Neill had made damn sure the man came with him when he relocated to Washington. Harriman's expression was much the same as Sharpe's; something serious had happened.

"Sergeant?"

"A six, sir," said Harriman, anticipating the question he'd already put to the captain. "Maybe even a seven."

O'Neill followed him to one of the wall screens. "Let me guess. Icarus?"

Harriman nodded. "We received a garbled subspace signal that cut out before we could make sense of it. All the evidence points to heavy localized jamming. All communications in that area have been completely cut off. The SGC can't reach them either, but we managed to get in contact with the *Hammond*." He tapped a few controls on a keypad and the screen switched to a standby mode. "I have Colonel Carter for you, sir."

The general turned to the display as Samantha Carter's face appeared on it. Behind her, O'Neill could see a slice of the *Hammond*'s bridge, and what appeared to be members of a damage control party working at blown-out consoles. *What the hell happened out there?* he wondered.

Carter looked grim, and she wasted no time with preamble and got straight to the point. "*General, we barely got away,*" she said. "*The enemy came out of nowhere with an invasion force, hit us before we could react.*"

"Who did this?" he demanded.

She frowned. "*We think it was the Lucian Alliance.*"

"What about Icarus Base?" He was dreading the answer.

The colonel's lips thinned. "*We now have visual confirmation. The planet was destroyed. Vaporized.*"

"Good grief," whispered Sharpe, from behind him.

"That explains why we haven't been able to dial in." O'Neill's mind was already racing, thinking quickly on every possible outcome, every ripple that could spread out from the center of this terrible incident.

Carter went on. "*We managed to beam aboard most of our people from the surface before jumping to hyperspace. We believe that the enemy forces were also destroyed in the planetary collapse.*"

That meant no prisoners, and no prisoners meant nobody to interrogate as to the reasons why the Lucian Alliance — if they were to blame — had come to Icarus with malicious intent.

"*Any word on how they may have gained intel on our base?*" Carter was thinking the same thing.

O'Neill glanced at Harriman, and the sergeant shook his head. "No. We don't even know why the attack was launched." The general's frown deepened; the last they had heard of the Alliance, that loose gathering of interstellar criminal factions were in the midst of an internal struggle, fighting one another to fill a power vacuum largely created by the actions of SG-1. *Maybe they solved their differences and turned on us instead,* he thought grimly. He looked up at the screen. "Casualties on our side?"

"*Twelve,*" said Carter. "*Eighty plus MIA. Icarus's bunker shielding technology prevented us from beaming out anyone inside. How many got through the gate to Earth?*"

Harriman shook his head again.

"None." And there it was; eighty people's lives, cut down to one word.

The signal from the *Hammond* flickered, brief cosmic static washing across the image. "*None?*" repeated Carter, her brow creasing in confusion. "*Our sensors indicated that their Stargate was active for a full six minutes before the planetary core went critical.*"

"Well, they didn't show up here." O'Neill saw Harriman turn away and ask urgent questions of one of the desk operators.

"*Then where did they go?*"

"Good question," said the general. "I'll let you know when I have an answer." He paused and offered his old friend a rueful smile. "Glad you're okay, Colonel."

Carter nodded. "*Thank you, sir.*"

"Safe trip home," he told her, and she cut the connection. O'Neill turned and Harriman was already there, holding a tablet screen and talking with Captain Sharpe.

"No," Sharpe was saying, "if they'd gated to one of the other SGC sites, we'd have heard about it straight away."

"It's possible they could have opened a wormhole to an allied planet," offered the sergeant. "A Free Jaffa world, maybe."

O'Neill shook his head. "Even if they dialed a random gate address, something from the SGC general database — and there's no reason I can think of why they would — there's nothing to have stopped them just re-dialing Earth once they were through." He paused, considering. "All right. Send flash traffic messages to all our ships, bases and off-world teams, apprise them of the situation with Icarus and warn them about a possible new threat from the Lucian Alliance. Then get me everything we have on those scumbags, 'cos the joint chiefs are gonna want a briefing." He paused. "And I still want my club sandwich."

Another non-com approached with a print-out and offered it to the captain. Sharpe scanned the paper. "Casualty report from *Hammond*, they sent it on a side channel. Looks like Colonel Telford made it out alive…"

"Let me see that." O'Neill took the list and studied it, his eyes dropping to the names beneath the header reading *Missing In Action*. "Where did you all go?" he asked quietly.

Across a billion light-years of distance, huddled inside an iron dart racing through the dark, the survivors of the destruction of Icarus Base waited in the shadow of the Stargate.

Matthew Scott walked around the edge of the group, looking for Lieutenant Johansen, and saw her still attending the injured Colonel Young. As he approached, he caught a snatch of conversation between Armstrong and a woman.

"Senator," she said, introducing herself, "I'm Camile Wray. I believe, as the highest ranking member of the International Oversight Advisory here—"

Armstrong grunted and spoke over her. "Wray... You're in Human Resources, right?"

"With the IOA, yes," she insisted.

"Don't worry," the senator said, dismissing her, "I'm going to get things organized."

Scott's lip curled and he moved away before either of them noticed him. He didn't want to get into another fight over who was in charge, not right now. Tamara looked up and saw him as he approached.

"His vital signs seem to be stable," she said, nodding to Young. "He's strong."

Scott nodded. That was about all any of them could be right now, *strong*. He turned, looking for Greer and found Armstrong instead.

Despite a tone of gray across his face, the senator was clear-eyed and not about to be avoided. "Do we have any idea how long the air will last if we don't get the life support fixed?"

There was no point in lying to the man. "No, sir. Doctor Rush and the other scientists are working on that right now."

Armstrong made a face. "That's not good enough,

Lieutenant. We need answers."

"I agree," said Scott. He glanced around and saw people turning to look at him, drawn by the sound of their conversation. Armstrong was right, they wanted answers, they *needed* them; otherwise they were just sitting around, waiting to die. And inaction could be more toxic to a group's morale than any amount of bad news.

Now he had their attention, he decided he was going to use it. "Okay, listen up. Everyone who is able, we're going to search this ship from top to bottom…" He trailed off, thinking of the acres of vessel he'd seen from the observation room window. "Or as much as we can, at least. Get yourselves into teams of three." He glanced at Greer. "Sergeant, how are we set for weapons?" he said quietly.

"Twenty-three firearms," said the Marine, "including handguns."

Scott nodded back to him. "One per group, get them distributed." The lieutenant returned his attention to the crowd. "Use flashlights and radios only when necessary. Once those batteries are dead, they are *dead*. I want regular check-ins with Doctor Rush in the control room from all teams every ten minutes." He got a series of nods in return and saw men and women getting to their feet, a new sense of purpose in their eyes. "Keep in mind," he continued, "as far as we know, this bucket is really freakin' old, and there may be areas of damage where life support is unstable." Scott turned to go, then hesitated, another thought occurring to him. "Look, just be smart, okay? Don't touch anything that might be dangerous."

An airman at the back of the room raised his hand. "How are we supposed to know what's dangerous and what isn't?"

Scott had to think for a moment to place the man. "Becker, right?"

"Yes sir," said the airman. "I work in the mess. I mean, I did."

The lieutenant considered it; Becker had a good point. "Don't touch. Just…look. That's all." He stepped away, finding Greer. "Sergeant, you take Corporal Gorman and one of the eggheads with you."

"Got it," said the Marine.

Scott beckoned to two other figures standing in the shadows; one of them was Riley, the gate technician, and he fought down a jolt of surprise to see that the other was Vanessa James. It seemed like a lifetime ago since they had seen each other. He was pleased she was alive, but suddenly guilty as well. Their previous associations — if you could call them that — were not something he could let cloud the concerns of the moment. "You're Lieutenant James, right?" he asked, the question as casual as he could make it.

"Yes, sir," she replied, with a pointed look.

"You two are with me," he added.

Greer smirked and walked away. "Subtle, man, subtle…" he muttered, just loud enough that Scott could hear him.

Armstrong was still standing nearby, and the lieutenant looked back at him. The senator was watching everything he said and did, judging his command ability. "If it's okay with you, sir," Scott said to him, "it might be best, given your obvious skills, if you could hang back here and keep the rest of these people calm."

The other man's gaze never wavered for a moment. "Don't patronize me, son."

"No, sir," Scott replied. "Wouldn't dream of it, sir." He gathered up his rifle and moved out, following Greer's team back into the corridors.

Eli had been so engrossed in the depths of the alien computer system that he hadn't even noticed that Rush has slipped out; but he saw him now as he came back into the control room, nexus chamber, whatever you wanted to call it. He had a case in his hand, one of those slim-line impact resistant types made out of stainless steel, the sort that bad guys in action movies used to transport wads of cash or top secret bio-weapons. "Did you go back to the gate room?" Eli asked. "What's that?"

"Nothing you need to be concerned about," Rush replied, glancing at the consoles. "Any progress?"

Park and Brody were clustered around one of the panels, and both of them looked up. Having something to keep their minds off the thinning air was certainly helping. "Well, fortunately for us," said Park, "the life support system activated automatically when we dialed the ship, probably emergency reserves, but only in these sections." She gestured at the walls. "And now the reserve is gone."

Brody was nodding along with the woman's explanation. "Life support has been breaking down section by section ever since then. Resetting it doesn't help."

Rush's expression turned cold. "I asked if there was any progress. Can you tell me something I don't already know?"

Park frowned at his tone. "Unless something changes, based on my readings, we only have about six to eight hours of breathable air left."

Eli swallowed hard. To hear it put into numbers made it all seem horribly, inescapably real.

"Anyone got any good news?" Rush's gaze found him. "Eli?"

He indicated the console in front of him. "I've got some sort of a main menu over here, I think."

"Try to find an internal schematic or a map of the decks."

Eli rolled his eyes. "Yeah, I'll just go ahead and look up *Google Space Ship*." He blew out a breath, feeling a tightness in his stomach. It seemed like a long while since he'd had that steak. "Hey, I don't suppose there's any food in that case? I'm starving."

Rush's grip on the case's handle tightened reflexively. "No," he said, heading back to the doorway. "Keep working."

"Where are you going?" Eli demanded.

Rush threw a comment over his shoulder as he left. "To see if I can find a bathroom."

Eli considered the scientist's comment for a moment. "Yeah," he agreed, "that'd be good too."

What Nicholas Rush actually wanted was privacy, but there was no telling how long he might have it for. Back in the gate room, he'd heard Scott rallying the escapees with his make-work jobs for them all, and taken the opportunity to pick up the case while people's attention was elsewhere. Rush had seen the case soon after they arrived on the ship, close to where Young had fallen coming through the gate, but there had been too many people around, too many people to ask questions and get in the way. His heart had leapt when he saw the silver container; he knew that it had been a part of Telford's expedition inventory, but there was no guarantee it had come through from Icarus, and Rush had been unable to locate it before he had left the base.

Young had done the job for him; and like the colonel, Rush knew the value of the artifacts inside. All of which made it imperative that *he* utilize them as soon as possible, before Young woke up.

Off one of the side corridors, there were a series of small rooms that had clearly been designed as quarters for a human-oid crew. Rush chose one at random and entered, closing the door behind him. Inside, illuminated by sparse subsistence lighting, there was a pallet, a low couch, a table and an alcove leading to another sub-chamber. He sat and placed the case on the table, thumbing the latch codes and flipping open the locks. Inside, recessed on a bed of protective foam, there was a small device resembling a flat glassy plate, and three identical stones no bigger than the palm of his hand. Each of the stones was a smooth-edged, almost oblate shape, and their obsidian surfaces were whorled with intricate carvings of layered detail.

Selecting one of the stones, Rush activated the plate-device and laid the stone on it.

The objects were alien technology, relics crafted by the same minds that had built the ship around him. Fashioned by the Ancients, the so-called 'communication stones' were actually one single component of a much larger system. Like the Stargates, they had a reach that was unbound by conventional physics; so theory went, they operated using some form of quantum entanglement, whereby the physical distance between the stones and their base unit was immaterial, even if it was a matter of cosmic scale. The stones had been known to operate over intergalactic distances in the past; Rush hoped that they would do so again.

The plate chimed and Rush reached for the stone. *Moment of truth,* he told himself.

William Lee sipped his coffee and walked quickly down the corridor, shifting the bundle of paperwork under his arm to a more comfortable position. He'd been busy with a different project when the word came down from the tactical room about the attack on the Icarus, and immediately shelved what he was doing to assist in the follow-up. He hadn't had much involvement in Project Icarus, aside from being in the loop at the high-level proposal end of things, and while he'd seen the merit in the science of it, he had to admit that he'd been soured by the attitude of the man they'd brought on to lead the program. Nicholas Rush, the one time Lee had met him, had been brusque and dismissive of his work, even refusing to take a look at the lengthy document on the minutiae of chevron programming Lee had put together in his own time as a pet project.

But he put all that aside now. Elsewhere in the halls of Homeworld Command, General O'Neill and his staff were working hard to figure out exactly what was going on with the Icarus Base attack, and that meant that every extra helping hand was, well, *helpful*.

And anyhow, it wasn't as if Bill Lee had anything to rush home for. He blinked as he considered that. He'd been down here in the sublevels for quite a while, eating in the commissary, catching some sack-time on a cot in his office... Just when had he seen the sun last?

He sniffed and waved the question away, wandering into the communications lab. He threw a jaunty nod to the two Marines guarding the door and as always, they didn't respond. Across the room, where he could be seen by both the guards, a man in the same cut of lab coat as Lee was sitting at a desk, reading *The Washington Post*. A video camera and a slew of sensor gear was aimed at him, showing normal readouts on a panel of screens.

"How are you doing, Frank?" said Lee, putting down his burdens.

"Hey Bill," said the other man, "just fine." On the table in front of Frank was a flat metallic plate; the man was idly turning an etched stone in his fingers.

"Anything?"

Frank shook his head and put down the stone. "Nah." He stood up, rolling his newspaper, and the two men signed their names on a time-in/time-out board.

"See you tomorrow, then," said Lee, sipping his drink and glancing at the camera. He put the stone back on the plate and activated it. "Initializing communication stone..." he announced for the camera, and touched the whorled artifact. "Stand by for... Nothing to happen."

Lee made a sour face and sat down, resigning himself to another shift of sitting in this uncomfortable chair, watching the clock, and being watched by two armed men who would probably have shot him if he made any sudden moves.

"So," he offered, smiling weakly. "Either of you guys see the Redskins game this—"

His voice cut out in the middle of the sentence and Bill

Lee's entire manner changed; his expression, posture, all of it shifted.

One of the Marines reached for the intercom phone, while the other reached for his gun.

He had expected it to be something like the Stargate; the same sort of giddying effect of moving across the event horizon from one location to another, but what Rush experienced was something much more subtle. It was almost like the fade between scenes in a film, or the slow blink of an eye. One moment he was there in the dimly-lit cabin of an Ancient starship, the next he was in a bright room staring at the faces of two armed men.

He felt peculiar, strangely out of proportion to his body's image of itself. He looked down at his hands and saw a black communications stone gripped in one of them. *It worked.*

Using means that human scientists had only begun to guess at, the communications stones were capable, by the simple interface of dermal induction, to open up a two-way quantum conduit between the beings holding a pair of stones linked to a single base unit. But rather than transmitting voice or a visual component, the stones enabled the transmission of a consciousness.

He turned his head and saw a face looking back at him from the monitor near the video camera, bespectacled and slightly unkempt. *Lee,* he thought. *Couldn't I have connected with someone more…important?*

It wasn't as if Rush's actual brain was now inside the body of William Lee, however, or vice-versa. What made him who he was, was still inside his skull, in his body back on the ship—but the stones allowed him to move and speak through Lee's body, controlling it like an operator working a telepresence robot. Rush frowned for a moment, hoping that his erstwhile partner in this message wouldn't damage *his* body or walk it into some as-yet unseen danger aboard the Ancient ship; but that was a chance he was going to have to take.

He looked back at the Marines, and when he spoke it sounded odd and distorted. "My name is Doctor Nicholas Rush," he said. "I want to talk to your commanding officer."

"Are we sure it's him?" said O'Neill, following Harriman toward the comms lab. "We have a procedure for this kinda thing, right? Like, code words or something?"

"It's Doctor Rush, sir," said the sergeant. "I'm sure."

O'Neill entered the lab and saw Bill Lee sitting on the edge of the table and looking at his fingernails. When the man glanced up at him, the general felt an odd twinge of recognition. Even though it wasn't Rush, *yeah*, it was Rush all right. Something in the turn of the lip and the look in the eyes were just like those of the man he'd accompanied to Eli Wallace's home a few days ago. It was like Lee's flesh was just a coat that Rush had slipped into for the interim.

"General, I am reporting from on board an Ancient space ship, which seems to be well beyond our known universe." It was strange to hear a Scottish accent coming from Lee's mouth, but if O'Neill had any lingering doubts about who was talking to him, the tonality of the voice swept them away.

He held up a hand. "Wait, back up. You're on a ship, not a planet. Who's with you?"

Rush shrugged Lee's shoulders. "I don't have an exact count. Several dozen. Someone else was working on that." A smile crossed his face. "The point is, I did it. I successfully made a connection to the nine chevron address."

O'Neill folded his arms. "What you were supposed to be doing was evacuating non-combat personnel." He pointed at the floor. "To *Earth*."

The other man nodded. "Colonel Young gave that order, yes," he admitted. "I overrode that decision."

O'Neill's first impulse was to demand to know exactly *why* Rush had thought it was okay to ignore a ranking officer's command in favor of a science experiment, but he held back on that for a moment. "Where's Young now?" he demanded.

"At the moment, he's unconscious. I'm sorry to say he's not doing well, actually. He was injured during the attack."

"And what about Senator Armstrong?"

"He's fine…" Rush/Lee took a step closer. "But if you'll let me explain… Dialing Earth was not an option. The core of P4X-351 had become unstable as a result of the attack and—"

O'Neill spoke over him. "The planet's been vaporized."

Rush nodded Lee's head. "And if the resulting blast had come back through the wormhole to Earth, it would have been catastrophic!"

He was right, of course, but the man's explanation was still pretty damn thin. "So, instead of dialing any number of other planets in our galaxy, you took a bunch of unqualified people halfway across the universe? How was that a better idea, Doctor?"

"I took what I thought was our last chance to try and dial the ninth chevron," he insisted. "We were successful. At that point, we couldn't shut the gate down again." He spread Lee's hands. "I saved these people's lives."

A nerve twitched in O'Neill's jaw. "Not yet you haven't. Get them home."

"General," he pleaded, "this may be the greatest opportunity for exploration mankind has ever known…"

"Rush…" He couldn't believe the man's arrogance. Here he was, one second taking credit for a rescue, the next talking about lofty ideals without any concern for the people on that ship.

He kept talking. "We are determining the possibility of dialing Earth. I will do everything in my power to keep these people alive and safe."

"Doctor," began O'Neill, raising his hand; but then he halted as the expression on Bill Lee's face shifted and returned to its more usual aspect. Rush had hung up on him.

"Doctor Lee?" said Harriman.

Lee nodded and reached into a pocket for handkerchief to mop his brow. "Oh, wow," he began. "You're never gonna believe where I've just been."

"You alright?" said Scott, as they walked.

"Solid, sir," James replied, without looking his way. "I'm trained for this."

He lowered his voice. "I didn't mean…" Scott noticed that Riley was listening to their exchange and fell silent.

Over the sergeant's radio, the interchange between Greer and his team was also audible. "*How exactly do we know this ship is unoccupied?*" Franklin was asking.

"*Rush said the air came on just before we got here,*" Greer told him.

"*What about aliens that don't breathe air?*" insisted the scientist.

Scott scowled and toggled his walkie. "Keep the chatter off the comms, people."

"Franklin's got a point," said Riley, panning the MagLite in his hand slowly over the walls of the corridor. "I mean, if it's this big, seems like an awful lot of ship for no-one to be on it."

James shot him a wry look. "Atlantis was empty when they found that. The Ancients are all dead, Sergeant. Didn't you read the special memo?"

"No ma'am, lieutenant," he replied. "Those are only for officers, and I work for a living."

"Maybe there *were* crew, one time," James said, her tone turning sinister. "Maybe they got eaten by something. Or infected with some space virus." She gave Scott a sideways look. "Maybe they died off and became extinct when there weren't enough of them left to breed."

"This isn't the school yard, boys and girls," said Scott,

without looking back at them. "Talk less. You're burning up our oh-two."

Up ahead, the trio had to halt where the corridor came to an abrupt end in front of a large, heavy-gauge door. The lieutenant ran a hand over the surface of it, searching for a locking control he didn't find.

"Can you open it?" said Riley.

Scott shook his head and reached for his radio. "Rush, this is Scott, come in."

Eli heard the lieutenant's tinny voice and found the source; a walkie-talkie sitting on top of the console Rush had been using. He stepped away from his own panel; as he'd been told to, Eli had dutifully pored over the multiple panels of the menu screens and found what seemed to be a map of the ship, although so far he'd had no success isolating exactly which sets of lines and chambers were those nearest to the evacuees.

Leaving Park and Brody to continue their work, he picked up the radio and spoke into it. "Hello? This is Eli. Uh, over."

"*Where's Rush?*"

"The bathroom, I think. If he found it." *And didn't flush himself*, he almost added.

He heard the irritation in Scott's voice. "*I'm at what looks like some kind of bulkhead door. I was hoping that Rush could tell me how to open it.*"

Eli felt a little thrown. "Oh. Should I go look for him?"

"*No,*" came the terse reply. "*We'll do it ourselves.*"

Scott clipped his radio back on his vest and shouldered his rifle, examining the surface of the bulkhead for possible handholds. "You two, give me a hand with this."

Riley was hesitant. "What happened to being smart, sir?"

"Don't touch, just look," James reminded him.

"I changed my mind." The lieutenant shot them a glance.

"This could be the engine room for all we know. We gotta at least open a few doors."

"Do we?" said the sergeant. "Do we really?"

"Space virus," muttered the other officer darkly.

Scott ignored the comments and put his shoulder to the door, trying to force it. The metal creaked under his weight, and reluctantly Riley and James stepped in to assist him. With all three of them working it, the door gave a groan and shifted slightly.

A strident tone issued out from the console where Eli had drawn up the map, getting the attention of everyone in the control room. He dashed over in time to see the map moving and re-orienting itself. Text he couldn't decipher moved across the upper corner of the screen in a slow train. "Hang on!" he said into the radio mike. "Whatever you did, stop it."

The tone ceased immediately, and Eli took control of the panel, navigating around the map of the vessel.

"Is there a problem?"

"No." Eli hesitated. "I think. I don't know. Just keep doing what you were doing."

"All right…"

The tone sounded again, and this time Eli managed to realign the map to show what seemed to be a length of corridor. Blocking it was a thick line that was highlighted in stark crimson.

"I think I found where you are," Eli told them. "The door is flashing red."

"Can you open it from there?" said Scott.

Eli hesitated. "Red is usually bad, isn't it?"

"We don't really know if the Ancients actually saw color the same way we do," offered Park, "or even if they had the same cultural cues, so red might not—"

Eli waved her into silence as Scott spoke again. *"Maybe it means the door is stuck. Just try."*

His finger hovered over the touch screen; suddenly Eli was glad he was in here instead of out there with them. "Okay… You should probably step back."

He leaned in and swiped his fingertip across the door symbol.

Scott and the others moved away a few paces and waited. For a long second, nothing happened; then it happened all at once.

There was a loud, crashing grind of eons-old gears, and with slow, stately progress, the bulkhead door began to slide open, a thin patina of old rust flaking off it. The moment the lip of the door cleared the frame, a rattling rush of air whipped around the opening.

"*Whoa!*" called Eli "*Not good! I see more red! That whole section is flashing now!*"

Scott was transfixed for an instant, seeing past the opening doorway and into the compartment beyond. A corridor the mirror of the one they stood in stretched away, but only a few meters distant it became a torn, jagged mess of shattered metals and broken panels. Long sections of the walls and the ceiling had been ripped away, leaving great gouges like the claw-marks of some massive beast. A sparkling sheet of energy was visible through the holes, and beyond it the void of space.

"We're venting atmosphere!" shouted Riley.

"Close it!" Scott bellowed into the walkie, feeling the pull of chill vacuum dragging the breath from his lungs. "Now!"

"*Eli!*"

He heard Scott shouting his name and he almost panicked, his hands trembling over the panel as death and darkness came thundering into the ship through a door that he had opened. He swiped the icon again, and nothing changed. Fear was rising like a tide through him, and Eli felt himself sweating as the massive hatch continued its slow, inexorable motion toward the open position.

Maybe it had to open all the way before it closed again? Maybe the door won't close without some code key or something? The thoughts tumbled around in his mind. *Maybe I've just killed three people and am about to flush out all the air for the rest of us?*

"I'm trying!" he snapped, working the screen, flipping back through the interface panes, stabbing at anything that looked like it might be the right symbol.

Then in the next second the shrill alarm fell silent and the screen blinked back to the state it had been in before anything had happened.

Eli gingerly reached for the radio and keyed the mike. "Hello? Did...that work?"

He heard Scott panting. "*We're all right. The door shut. You did great.*"

He sagged against the console, relief washing over him. "Let's not do that again."

"*Yeah,*" agreed the lieutenant, with feeling. "*Okay, we've established why that hatch was closed.*"

Now he knew what he was looking for, Eli swept around the local area on the map-screen, finding more doors with the same flashing red halo. "It looks like a lot of others are closed for the same reason. We're only occupying a fraction of the ship right now, but it goes on forever..." He halted, as a sudden and unpleasant thought occurred to him. "But if there are damaged areas of the ship that aren't sealed off, that could be our problem. We could be bleeding air every second..."

Eli looked up as Rush entered the room, still holding the case, with an expression of self-assurance on his face.

"Good timing," began Eli. "We just figured out that—"

Rush stepped forward and snatched the radio from Eli's hand without even the slightest glimmer of interest in what he was saying. He toggled the radio to the general channel and spoke into it. "This is Doctor Rush. All of you, stop what you're doing and meet me in the gate room immediately." Then he bothered to give Eli a look. "That means you too."

The scientist walked back out of the control room as briskly as he had entered, leaving Eli, Brody and Park watching him go, nonplussed.

"So," ventured Brody, "did he find a bathroom, or what?"

CHAPTER SEVEN

The course of action was clear to him; someone had to take authority over the situation, and do it now. There was no sense in waiting for one of the military to step in — they were just soldiers, out of their depth in this place and for all their weapons and bravado, unprepared for the kinds of challenges they were all going to face.

What was needed was a calm, rational mind. Someone of intelligence and foresight. Someone like *him*.

Rush glanced around at the assembled crowd in the gate room, the groups who had split off to wander aimlessly around the decks of the ship trickling back after his summons. He saw Eli watching him with confusion; the young man was bright, there was no denying that, but he lacked focus. Rush could give that to him, use his skills and those of people like Brody, Park and the others to make this mission work. Rush caught sight of Armstrong and saw the pale, sweaty cast to his face; the senator might be a problem, though. He was used to being obeyed, and he'd already challenged Scott. The man clearly thought that he was the person who should be calling the shots here...but they were a long way from the Senate floor, and surviving in an environment like this was doubtless well outside the politician's experience. Nearby, the medic Johansen was checking Young's pulse, and by the look on her face it was long odds that the colonel would pull through. All the more reason to have a strong leadership in place as soon as possible.

Rush nodded to himself. He was doing the right thing. The others would see that and follow along.

Lieutenant Scott and his group were the last to return to the gate room, and Rush noted they all seemed fatigued and twitchy. A loaded look passed between Scott and Eli, something Rush couldn't read.

"What's going on?" said the lieutenant.

Rush climbed up a few steps toward the balcony so he was above the heads of everyone else, looking down on all of them. He held up the silver case so everyone in the room could see it. "In this box are three Ancient communications stones," he began. "They connect to another person who is also holding a preprogrammed stone across vast distances, in real-time—"

Armstrong got it immediately. "We can talk to people on Earth. Why are you only just telling us this now?"

He ignored the question. "Except, unlike conventional communication technologies, the stones allow you to actually take control of the body of the individual on the other end." That earned him some incredulous looks from everyone who had a low security clearance. "I brought these with us in the event that we ended up somewhere out of range of normal communications."

The senator held out his hand. "So let's use them," he insisted.

"I already have," Rush replied. Murmurs washed out over the crowd.

Brody spoke up, voicing the question they all wanted an answer to. "Are they sending help?"

"No." Rush shook his head gravely. *First the bad news. Make them afraid.* "The only means of dialing this gate from our galaxy was destroyed in the attack. We're cut off."

"The whole planet?" he heard one of the airmen say. "Gone?"

Armstrong pointed at the case, drawing himself up. "I want to use one of those things, now."

"I have spoken with General O'Neill—"

The politician didn't let up. "I am a United States senator—"

Rush spoke over him. "And I have explained our situation clearly," he went on. *Now give them hope.* "In light of my knowledge and experience, General O'Neill has placed me in charge—"

Armstrong couldn't let that pass. "He did?" Disbelief dripped from the words.

"It was the original mission of this expedition to explore the universe," Rush went on. "I believe we can still do that."

Eli gave Scott a brief, pointed look. "We only have a few hours of air left...maybe not even that much. How much of the universe are we gonna be able to cover?"

The muttering in the group took on a fearful edge at the young man's announcement, and Rush frowned. "I have faith in our ability to work together and to repair this ship," he insisted. "But if we're going to survive this, we need leadership and a clear chain of command—"

Once again, Armstrong interrupted, his condescension evident. "Get off it, Doctor! I want to talk to the general myself!"

Rush fixed him with a hard look. The last thing anyone needed was this pompous fool interfering. For a moment, he considered a lie; he could tell the man the stones were programmed for certain individuals, and Armstrong wouldn't know it wasn't the truth.

Scott stepped between them. "Give it to him, Doctor." There was an implied threat in there somewhere, and Rush hesitated. He didn't want to make an enemy of the young officer, not while he needed him to strengthen his authority.

With a sigh, Rush held opened the case and showed the contents to Armstrong, who seemed on the verge of snatching it from him. For a moment the senator studied the contents, his face an angry red. It mattered little; Rush doubted that the man even had the first clue of how to use the artifacts.

"Dad..." Armstrong's daughter was close by him. Surely she could see he was being unreasonable?

The politician reached forward, intending to pick up a stone; what followed Rush hadn't expected at all. Armstrong tensed and froze in place. Then in the next second, he gasped in pain and dropped to the metal deck. His daughter called out in alarm and went to him, eyes wide with fear.

Rush quickly closed the case and put it aside.

Scott was glaring his way. "What did you do to him?"

"Nothing," Rush said in all honesty, securing the case. "He didn't even touch the stone…"

Johansen parted the group around Armstrong and knelt by his side. "He's conscious, still breathing."

"I…I think he might have hurt his side…" offered Eli. "After we came through the gate, he looked like he was in pain…"

"He was caught in a rock fall," added Scott.

The medic nodded and pulled up the man's shirt. Rush winced at the sight of a string of heavy purple-black bruises down the length of Armstrong's torso.

Chloe's hand flew to her mouth. "Oh my God."

"I saw him taking pills," said Johansen. "What were they?"

"Warfarin, for his heart," Chloe replied, her voice catching.

Johansen frowned. "Blood thinners are the last thing he needs if he's bleeding internally."

"Please do something!" Chloe begged.

The other woman's firm expression suddenly crumbled. "I told you, I'm just a medic! I mean, I have morphine but I don't…" She trailed off.

Rush could feel the situation slipping and he took a breath, speaking loudly so his voice would carry. "People, listen!" he demanded. He could hear them becoming more agitated by the moment; if he didn't take control now, then he never would. "There is no need for us all to congregate in one place!" He looked down at the medic. "Lieutenant Johansen, please locate reasonable accommodation for the injured. As for the rest of you—"

Before he could finish, another challenger stepped up; Wray, a woman he barely remembered from one of his first meetings on Icarus Base. "I don't recognize your authority, Doctor Rush! As the IOA representative here, I—"

His opinion of the IOA was somewhere below that of politicians and imbeciles, and Rush ignored every word she said, growing more frustrated by the moment. "We've found quarters nearby, more comfortable than this," he said. "Go there and stay there until you are asked to do something useful."

Andrea Palmer, one of the geology team, shot him an affronted glare. "Something *useful*?" she echoed. Palmer's annoyance rippled out into the crowd. Rush was suddenly aware that he had lost them, and sensed their mood veering toward an angry pack mentality.

"We don't want to settle in!" snapped Wray. "We want to get out of here!"

"She's right," Volker added. " We should all be working on getting home."

Rush hesitated; *all right*, he thought, *if all else fails, tell them the hard truth*. "I don't even know if that's possible."

The words had barely left his lips when the group exploded in uproar. Wray stabbed finger toward the silent Stargate. "What? You haven't even tried!"

Spencer was nodding along with her. "Maybe you should do something instead of standing around talking about being in charge."

From the side of the group, a hatchet-faced Marine eyed him coldly. "If that's even true." The man stood up and took a menacing step.

People were pushing forward now, all talking at once, crowding toward the staircase where Rush was standing. He resisted the urge to draw back and put some distance between himself and them. It was all falling apart! Didn't they understand? Didn't they realize he was doing this for the good of the mission, for the good of all of them?

Scott stepped up, making his rifle evident on its sling, and a couple more of the Air Force officers backed him up. "Curtis," said the lieutenant, addressing the Marine, "back off!" Curtis hesitated, and Scott used the moment to raise his own voice. "Everyone calm down! The fact is, Colonel Young put *me* in charge, and I expect all SG personnel to follow my orders." As that sunk in, he scanned the faces of the civilians. "As for the rest of you, if you get out of line we will lock you down." He threw Rush a quick look over his shoulder. "Now. Doctor Rush is right about a couple of things. One: we have to work together and Two: we don't all have to stay here. So let's move out."

And just like that, the simmering resentment was damped down, the potential riot forestalled. As the crowd broke up into smaller groups, Rush let out a weary breath, unable to grasp how the situation could have spiraled out of his control so fast.

He found Scott looking at him. "I think we need you, so I've got your back for now," said the lieutenant, his voice low. "But if I were you, I'd start figuring out how to dial that gate back to Earth."

The lieutenant walked away before he could frame a reply.

Once the civilians had got themselves into the quarters, Greer gathered a handful of people, and got them to work moving the cases and backpacks that were scattered all over the gate room into an empty chamber that he'd arbitrarily decided was a storage compartment. The gate tech, Riley, had offered to keep inventory of what they had, but without something to write it all down on, he wondered how the man was going to manage it. Along with Spencer, two of the science types — Palmer and a guy called Volker — were lending a hand. But much to the sergeant's irritation, that snooty witch

Wray from the IOA was also there; although she seemed to be spending more time eyeballing Greer than actually helping out.

Riley was bent over an open airdrop case. "I've got some sort of testing equipment here…" He gave the device a rattling shake. "Looks broken."

Greer nodded. "We'll come back to that."

"Did no-one think to label anything?" Volker grumbled.

"There's a bar code on every case," noted Riley.

"Anybody find the bar code *reader*?" Volker replied.

Greer shook his head, joining the chorus of 'No's. He unzipped a bag and found what appeared to be a collapsible tent and some desert-pattern camouflage gear. He showed it to Riley, who nodded.

"I guess the reader got left behind along with the food and the water," said Spencer.

"We got food," Greer looked up again and caught Wray watching him. She quickly turned away.

"Oh, yeah, power bars," replied Palmer, "and that powdered stuff. *Yum*."

Greer noticed Spencer pocket a handful of the ration bars from the open case as Palmer looked away. He didn't say anything about it for the moment, but made a mental note to give the guy a firm one-on-one talk.

Volker held up some silver packets, all of them carefully color-coded and compartmentalized. "Hey everybody, look," he said sarcastically. "We're saved!"

"Seeds?" Riley squinted at the packages. "You've got to be kidding."

As Volker tossed the packets aside, Palmer went to the next box and opened it to reveal a set of blocky packages. "This is like a very depressing Christmas morning," she said.

"What's that?" said Riley.

"I've got a case of blank paper," came the reply.

"Maybe we should start a suggestion box," offered Volker.

From the corner of his eye, Greer saw Wray giving him the look again and his composure snapped. He turned on her. "What are you staring at?" he snarled.

Wray held her ground. "You were in detention, back on Icarus."

"Yeah, that's right," he replied, challenging her.

"For good reason," Wray went on. The room became quiet.

"What did you want him to do?" Greer snapped. "Leave me there?"

"Of course not," she said, looking him up and down. "I was just wondering what to do about it now."

Who the hell did she think she was? "It's not up to you."

"We'll see," replied Wray.

Greer's lip twisted in annoyance and he took a step toward her. Wray hadn't expected that, and she showed a flash of fear, backing away.

Riley stepped into his path. "Don't, man."

Greer turned his glare on the Air Force sergeant, who had placed a hand on the Marine's chest. Greer looked down at it, and Riley pulled it away.

Then he heard Lieutenant Scott calling his name over the radio. "*Greer, do you read? I need you to help check for any open bulkhead doors that lead to damaged parts of the ship. Rush will direct you from the control room.*"

He picked up the radio, giving Wray a last, iron-hard glare, and replied. "Copy that. On my way."

A few corridors away across the span of the ship, Scott moved down the middle of a long passageway, his eyes flicking to every shadowed corner, his rifle slung across his chest. So far, they hadn't encountered anything that could be classed as a threat aboard the vast Ancient derelict — *not unless I want to count my own damn stupidity*, he chided himself — but Scott wasn't about to slack off on his vigilance. Now, as the falling oxygen levels would start to take their toll on people's alertness, it was more important than ever to be careful. He'd already screwed up once by opening that hatchway; he wasn't going to make that kind of mistake a second time.

"*Go past the next junction.*" Rush's voice crackled over the open radio link. Scott kept walking, glancing up at the low iron ceiling, wondering if the scientist was even looking at the same piece of corridor that he was in. So much of the interior of the ship had a similar, modular look to it, like a lot of Ancient construction. He could imagine the walls and the floors being stamped out of moulds or cut from massive plates of red-hot steel, welded together like warships in old newsreels of dockside shipyards.

"*There should be an elevator at the end of the hall.*" Rush's voice snapped him back. Scott blinked. His mind was starting to wander.

"Copy that," he replied. "I see it." Scott found an open hatchway and a conventional-looking elevator car behind it. Stepping carefully inside, he looked for and found a small control panel.

"*We've got what looks like another compromised area one level down,*" continued Rush. He sounded a lot more in control now he was back in his comfort zone, Scott reflected.

"Okay," he said. "I'm on my way." The lieutenant reached out to press one of the keys on the control pad and saw movement out in the corridor, back the way he had come. He stopped dead, snapping his G36 to the ready.

He wasn't alone. From around the corner of the curving corridor came a spherical object, not much bigger than a softball, floating at chest height with no apparent means of support. It had a silvery, metallic tone to it, similar to the careworn steel walls all around him. Gently, it drifted past, and on one side of its surface he saw something that might have been the impassive mono-optic gaze of a lens. It kept moving, and Scott pulled his rifle up, taking aim as it drifted on. He blinked. *What the hell was that?*

"Are you there yet?" Rush's voice was so sudden and so loud over the open channel that it made him twitch in surprise.

The lieutenant toggled the radio and hissed into it. "Radio silence, please. Scott out." Leading with the rifle, he left the elevator and went after the floating sphere, his finger resting on the trigger-guard.

Pain rushed in from every corner of him, and he gasped as his eyes opened. He tried to focus, but all that he could feel was a pounding series of dull impacts coming from the inside of his skull.

Young turned and realized he was lying on some kind of bed, in a room where the lights were soft. He felt groggy and it was a struggle to focus.

"Easy, Colonel. It's okay." He knew that voice. *Tamara.* For a second, he thought he had been talking to Emily... But then memory caught up with him and he remembered where he was.

"What's going on?" he managed. His tongue felt thick, his mouth bone-dry.

"We almost lost you, sir," she said. "You were thrown clear across the room." Young tried to sit up, but his pain had other ideas. Tamara put a gentle hand on his chest. She shook her head. "I need you to stay still."

He relented, and for the moment, eased back down. He blinked at the walls around him. The place looked familiar and alien all at once. "Where are we?"

She checked his eyes with a pen-light. "Aboard a ship. It's Ancient. Rush says its thousands of years old, and we're probably on the far side of the universe." Tamara paused. "I say that out loud and it still doesn't seem like it's real."

Young tried to process all that, and a question immediately rose to the top of his thoughts. "What's he doing to get us home?"

"He says he's working on it, but right now we have bigger problems. The life support system isn't working properly. We may not have much time left if it can't be fixed."

The colonel nodded. He'd already noticed the air seemed thin in here.

Tamara went on. "You should also know he used the communication stones to contact Earth. He says General O'Neill put him in charge."

Young's jaw stiffened, and he felt a surge of anger. Typical of the man to take advantage of any situation. "Oh, I don't think so," he began, and tried to rise again.

"Sir…"

He got only a little way before his body betrayed him and the pain forced Young to give up the attempt.

"You shouldn't be trying to move yet," insisted the lieutenant.

"I don't have a choice." He bit out the words and took a shaky breath. "I can't… Feel my legs."

Tamara rested a hand on his arm. "Neurapraxia is a temporary paralysis that can follow a concussive injury," she told him, with book-rote diction.

"But you don't know if it's that."

Her hesitation answered the question before she did. "You'd need an MRI scan and a qualified doctor to read it to know for sure if there's any spinal damage." Tamara's face fell. "We don't have either. Hopefully, it's just the nerves in shock. Best I can do is insist you remain still."

He studied her; right now, she should have been the one giving him the support, but Young sensed rightly that Tamara needed it more than he did. "Your tour of duty was over two weeks ago. You should be in some classroom in San Diego."

"I was going to go back on the *Hammond*," she admitted. "And it's Seattle, sir. That's where I got my scholarship."

He nodded. "I'm sorry."

She looked away. "That part is not your fault."

He was silent for a moment before he spoke again. "Tell Rush I want to see him."

"Yes, sir." Tamara got up and left him there.

In the dimness, Young tried to move his leg, just a little. Tried, and failed.

Scott paced the sphere-thing down the halls of the ship, watching it bob gently like a feather caught in an updraft. He wasn't sure, but he thought he could detect the faintest humming sound coming from it, perhaps the noise from some kind of propulsion system. Then he checked himself; he was automatically assuming the thing was a device, a mechanical construct, maybe a robot — but there was nothing to say it wasn't an organic, living being instead, albeit of a kind he couldn't fathom. He thought back to when he'd been in the corridor before, that whole *Star Trek* moment he'd had — was this the ship's way of answering him back?

Still, he had no idea if the sphere was harmless or of hostile intent, so he was erring on the latter. For all he could know, the object might be like the lure on an angler fish, encouraging him to follow it so he would walk himself straight into a trap.

Out of nowhere, a side door along the corridor opened and Eli Wallace stepped out in front of the lieutenant. He balked at the sight of the assault rifle being aimed in his direction. "*Whoa*!" he shouted. "Not again!" Eli stepped carefully out of the firing line.

Wallace seemed unconcerned by the presence of the sphere, which continued on its way down the corridor. "What is that thing?" said Scott.

Eli's face split in a grin. "Oh, it's cool. Come here, I'll show you."

He ducked back into the room he'd just left and Scott warily followed him. The chamber was laid out in a similar fashion to the control room they'd found elsewhere, with the same kind of consoles; but the large mechanism on one wall was a new feature.

"Check this out," said Eli, indicating a screen on one of the consoles.

Scott peered at it and saw a bobbing first-person view of a corridor; the image had to be coming from the lens he'd seen on the front of the sphere. "It's a camera."

"*Flying* camera," Eli corrected. "I was gonna call it a *Kino*, you know, after the Russian word for—"

Scott made a winding up motion with his free hand. "Moving on…"

He shrugged. "I figure maybe we can use it to check out damaged areas of the ship."

"That's good," admitted Scott. They could operate the thing like an unmanned aerial vehicle, as a drone scout. "Where is it going now?"

Eli shrugged again. "I don't know, doin' its thing. I haven't figured out all the controls yet, but there's lots more of 'em." He moved to the mechanism on the wall and reached into it. Eli's hand returned with another of the spheres and Scott understood that the machine had to be a dispenser unit, of sorts.

Eli tossed the sphere at Scott and the lieutenant went to grab it; but instead the device just floated in mid-air. Eli gave it a gentle tap and it drifted across the room, orienting itself to aim a lens at him. "See?" said Eli, pointing at the console.

Scott looked and saw the sphere's-eye view of him. He looked tired and not really in the mood for games.

Eli went back to the dispenser again. "Here, you want one too?"

"It's not a gumball machine," snapped Scott, frowning.

Eli drew his hand back like he was a kid caught reaching into the cookie jar. "Okay, okay," he said.

Scott paused and slung his rifle, which Eli liked a lot better than having it waved in his face. After all, as far as he knew, he only had the one pair of underwear with him. "Sorry," said the lieutenant. "Guess we're all feeling a little…"

"Crabby?" offered Eli helpfully.

The other man gave him a nod. "Something like that." He took a breath. "So, you found where they keep the, uh, kinos. What else have you figured out?" Scott beckoned him out into the corridor and Eli followed him.

"What, that's not enough?"

"It's a start," said Scott, "but remember the air thing? Tick-tock."

His shoulders sagged. "Ah, come on, give me a break. This is only my second spaceship, man. And the first was like, yesterday."

Scott eyed him, and Eli suddenly felt bad about griping. The lieutenant had to be feeling the pressure a heck of a lot more than he was. "Icarus Base was my first SGC assignment after training," he admitted. "I haven't been at this much longer than you."

Eli considered that. "Did they beam you out of your house?"

Scott showed a brief grin. "No, you got me there."

They walked in silence for a moment. "You, uh, got any food on you?" said Eli.

Scott shook his head. "No."

"Tylenol?"

"Headache?"

Eli rubbed his face. "Yeah."

Scott nodded, and Eli knew that the other man was feeling the same tight pressure behind the eyes, the same bone-deep throbbing in his skull. "Me too."

They headed back to the control room and found Rush at work on the main console, scrutinizing the schematics of the ship Eli had discovered earlier. The scientist was using the interface wheel to move back and forth across the deck plans of the vessel. Scott immediately noticed a series of red indicator glyphs blinking steadily on the plan view.

Rush looked up as they entered and his eyes widened as one of the drone spheres followed them in, drifting behind Eli like an obedient dog at heel. Scott hadn't even noticed it moving with them.

"What is that?" said the scientist.

"Flying camera ball," Eli announced, with a flourish. "I'm calling it a Kino."

"Don't ask," Scott added.

Rush's expression turned to one of charmed amazement and he came over to take a closer look, smiling widely. "Wonderful…"

Eli pulled a hand-held device from his back pocket and showed it off. "Comes with a remote," he said. "I thought we could use it to look around."

Scott interrupted the two of them before the conversation went off track. "What do you have, Doctor?"

Rush snapped back to his usual default glower. "Unfortunately, more bad news." He wandered to the screen. "These processing nodes are scrubbers responsible for cleaning carbon dioxide from the air." Rush pointed out the red symbols. "Here, here and here. This is indicating malfunction, and more are failing."

"What kind of malfunction?" Scott was thinking about the metallic ooze that Tamara had told him about.

"I'm not sure," admitted Rush. "Someone needs to take a closer look." He zoomed in on an area of the map. "This one is closest, in the gate room."

Scott sighed. Right now all he wanted was a moment to sit a spell and take a breather, but he knew that if he stopped moving his fatigue was going to knock him down. He nodded. "Okay, I'll check it out." He toggled his radio. "Greer? I'm heading to the gate room. Meet me there."

Chloe took a little of the water and bunched up her handkerchief, then wet it and dabbed her father's clammy forehead. There wasn't a lot in the canteen, but Lieutenant Scott had just handed it over to her without question, without her even needing to ask for it. She wondered if that was all the water he had; how much did any of them have? So far, from what she could understand, none of the people who had gone out exploring had found anything that looked like a supply of drinking water.She sighed. All this thinking about it made her thirsty, but there were more important things to worry about.

"Pat?" said a quiet, tired voice. "That you?"

"No, Dad, it's me, Chloe."

Her father's eyes flickered open and he focused on her. "Oh, hey, princess." He was drawn and haggard. "Where are we?"

"One of the rooms, the quarters I mean," she explained. "It's not the Four Seasons, or anything..."

"Better than the floor," he managed. "What happened? There was Rush, and that stone..."

"You collapsed," she told him, holding back the fear from her voice. "We brought you here."

"How long was I out? What's going on?"

"I'm not sure. I've been here with you."

He shifted on the couch, flinching with pain. "You need to know what's happening, Chloe. This is important."

She felt the tears welling up inside her. "But I was so worried about you... And I'm so scared." Chloe barely got the words out before she broke into a sob.

Her father reached out and took her into an embrace. "One step at a time, honey," he soothed. "One step at a time. You've always had an angel looking over your shoulder. It's going to be okay, I promise."

She let him go and wiped her eyes. Chloe saw him grimace as he moved, pain lancing across his chest.

"My pills..."

Chloe shook her head. Lieutenant Johansen had been clear

about the tablets. "You can't take any more of those. Your ribs are very badly bruised. You'll bleed internally." She handed him Scott's canteen and he took a shallow drink.

He fought down the ache. "If I don't take those pills, a bruise is going to be the least of my problems."

She felt a terrible weight pressing down on her. "I know." More than anything, Chloe wanted to wish this all away, to open her eyes and wake from a terrible dream, to be back home on Earth. To have all this strange, alien gloom dispelled from her life, like storm clouds fading before sunshine. Her father met her gaze and he hid his pain well, trying hard not to let it show, trying to be strong for her. Chloe loved that about him, the selfless nature that he hadn't let time or the compromises of political life strip away. It was a face he rarely showed the rest of the world.

"Don't worry about me," he said gently, "I'll be okay. Go. Find out what's going on out there."

"I want to be here with you." When she said it, all she could hear in herself was the scared little nine-year-old girl whose daddy had chased the monsters from her bedroom closet.

He heard it too. "And I want you here. But right now, I want to know what's going on just a little bit more."

She smiled slightly at that. Alan Armstrong was still as much a senator as he was her father, and always had been.

"I'll be here when you get back," he assured her.

After a moment, Chloe nodded, got to her feet and left him there.

Her father kept a tight smile on his face until she was gone; and then he released a shuddering, pained sigh and pulled himself, inch by aching inch, into a sitting position.

Scott and Greer exited the corridor and entered the gate room. The sergeant was wound tight with annoyance, and it was something the lieutenant had seen before, more times than was healthy. Ron Greer was a good Marine, one of the best, but he had real difficulty with his impulse control, and right now Scott didn't want to add that to the laundry list of other problems that were stacking up.

"I'm just sayin'," Greer went on, "she better stay out of my face."

Scott nodded. Camile Wray had no business interfering with a matter of military justice, and if Colonel Young had judged it field-expedient to drop all charges against Greer for his previous transgressions, then it was so ordered. "I'll explain your personal space issues to her the next chance I get."

They walked into the room and looked around. Scott could see several of the air vent grilles in the walls and he cast around looking for the right one. "Rush," he said into his radio, "we're here. Where's the node?"

"*Back of the room,*" came the reply. "*Near the staircases.*"

Greer nodded and pointed. "Oh, yeah. I see it."

Rush had his hands on either side of the control panel, leaning into it like a preacher over a pulpit lectern. "Have you located it?" he asked, glancing at the schematic on the screen.

"*Wait one,*" Scott's voice came over the walkie on the console.

"What do you think they're gonna find in there?" said Eli, his face pinched in worry. "The vent could be blocked, maybe. Rusted shut."

"Unlikely," Rush snapped back, dismissing the young man's concerns. "There wasn't even any moisture in the air until we came through the Stargate a few hours ago." He drummed his fingers on the panel impatiently.

"A few hours," Eli repeated, glancing at his wristwatch. "Wow, you're right. It just seems like we've been at this for, I don't know, days on end."

"Well, time is relative," Rush said airily,

"Yeah," Eli went on, "But—"

Rush gave him an exaggerated look. "Unless you actually have anything productive to add, please stop talking to me. You're using up both the oxygen and my patience."

"Oh," said Eli, deflated. "Okay."

As he went back to the control panel, one of the Air Force officers entered the room, the medic Johansen. "Doctor Rush? Colonel Young is awake and he wants to see you. Right now."

He held up a hand in a terse gesture. Couldn't she see he was occupied? And as for Young, he wasn't in any hurry to visit him. Rush knew full well what the dimensions of that conversation would be.

Instead, he spoke into the radio. "There should be something of a grate over the processor node. You'll feel air coming through it."

"*That's a negative,*" said Scott. "*There's no airflow at all.*"

He frowned. "Can you remove it?"

"*I think so.*"

"Give me a hand with this." Scott drew his combat knife and used it to lever open the lip around the outside of the grille across the air vent. Greer leaned in and did the same. With both of them working it, the metal frame creaked and shifted.

Scott got his fingers around the edges and pulled hard; the grille came off in one motion with a squeal of metal. An acrid smell assaulted his nostrils and his face wrinkled. "Gah."

"What is that stink?" muttered Greer.

Scott trained his flashlight into the compartment in time to see a smooth-sided canister slide out of the wall on an automatic mechanism, probably triggered by the grille release. As he watched, the top of the canister rose up, and from within a thick black chemical slurry bubbled up, dripping down the sides in resinous strings. The flashlight's glow revealed more detail behind the main part of the node; a nest of pipes and conduits. All of them were caked in gelatinous layers of the ooze.

"That can't be good," said the Marine.

"*What do you see in there?*" Rush was asking.

Fat plugs of the viscous matter were dripping out of the open vent now, and pooling on the floor. "A problem," said Scott grimly. "We see a very big problem."

CHAPTER EIGHT

Greer left Scott to deal with Rush's problem and headed back out into the ship. Right now, aside from brute force or shooting something, there was nothing he could add to the situation, so he moved on. Standing around watching the science types debating made him itchy with the inaction of it, and he was wound tight. He hated the idea that he couldn't do a damn thing to get out of this situation, and that manifested itself in annoyance; the nagging headache gathering at the base of his skull didn't help any, either.

Ron Greer did not deal very well with being helpless. It was one of the main reasons he'd joined the Corps in the first place, back when he was searching for someplace to aim his life. He didn't want to go back to that feeling, not now, not *ever*.

Ahead down the corridor, he saw Franklin and Lieutenant James at one of the doors. Franklin was working the control panel, sealing the hatch shut.

James looked up as he approached. "What's going on?"

He shrugged. "I don't know, man. The air filter's full of crap."

Greer's matter-of-fact pronouncement seemed to rattle Franklin. "That doesn't sound good," he ventured.

"No," the Marine agreed. He gestured ahead, up along the corridor. "Come on, they want us to keep looking around."

Franklin nodded. "I think there might be a larger compartment through here. That's if the design follows the pattern of the other levels."

"Show us," said James.

The scientist moved forward, peering at the walls, pausing every few steps. After a moment, he came to another hatchway. "Here." He pressed the door control and it grumbled open, letting a wisp of dust out into the passageway.

Greer immediately stepped past the man and moved around the width of the door before entering, scanning the room beyond. It was a basic tactic for room clearance called 'slicing the pie', used by SWAT teams and soldiers in urban warfare, minimizing exposure while maximizing target awareness. So far, no one had encountered anything resembling other life aboard the derelict, but Greer knew that was no reason to get sloppy.

Content that the room was as empty as all the others, Greer stepped in, with James and Franklin close by. It was an open space, dominated by four large tables and angular chairs arranged in a cross formation. Along the walls there were alcoves and storage lockers of some kind.

"Looks like a mess," said James.

"Seems pretty tidy to me," said Franklin.

"Mess *hall*," James added, with a roll of her eyes.

"Oh. Right."

Greer moved to one of the lockers and opened it. Inside there were odd-shaped plates and cups, along with empty containers.

"Lots of stuff to put food on," noted Franklin.

"But no food," sighed the lieutenant.

Franklin sniffed the musty air. "I suspect it would be a bit stale."

Greer went to one of the alcoves; it seemed to be a service station of some kind, with a draining sink and what had to be a faucet. He licked his lips, suddenly feeling thirsty. The Marine reached for the tap and halted, throwing Franklin a questioning look. The civilian gave him a none-too-helpful shrug.

He frowned and turned the tap; the Ancients had been like human beings, so it wasn't as if they drank acid or anything. It took a little effort to move it, and Greer was rewarded with a single, solitary drop of rusty-colored water.

James gave a snort of cold amusement. "Bar's closed," she said.

Tamara watched Brody as he carefully twirled a test tube full of oily liquid, dipping a testing strip into the mixture. Scattered around him was the contents of a chemical analysis kit and the metallic canister Scott had recovered from the inside of the air unit. Scott and Eli looked over Rush's shoulder as the scientist probed at the mass of dark slurry with a pencil, while Volker and a few of the other civilians hovered nearby. Everyone had heard about the mess inside the pipes by now, and everyone wanted to see just what it was that was strangling the air from them. Tamara saw Chloe enter the gate room and approach. The girl looked like she had been crying.

"Are you okay?" she offered.

Chloe gave her a shaky smile, but said nothing.

"It's highly caustic, alkaline..." Brody was saying, peering at his results.

Volker nodded. "Which is why it burned Franklin."

"Everyone's respiration rate is elevated," Tamara added. "People are reporting headaches, so it has to be—"

"What?" demanded Scott, more interested in effects and not facts.

Brody showed him the test tube. "This is the used-up residue of whatever magic compound the Ancients used to scrub carbon dioxide from the air."

"So now we have two big problems relating to the life support." Scott shot a look at Rush.

The scientist didn't look at him. "Our first priority is to seal off any of the leaks." He prodded the oily goop, and it smoked slightly, thin wisps of acrid vapor twirling upward. "If we can do that, I believe we can buy ourselves another day or so before the build-up of carbon dioxide kills us." Tamara blanched at the man's cold evaluation of their survival possibilities.

Scott was frowning. "As it stands right now, how much time do we have?"

"I don't know," Rush admitted.

Brody gave a bleak sigh. "A couple of hours at the most."

"Awesome," managed Eli.

Rush got to his feet. "Mister Brody, there was medical grade soda lime in the supply manifest for the expedition—"

The geologist, Palmer, spoke up from the edge of the group. "It never made it."

"Unfortunate," said Rush. He was quiet for a moment. "Well, a ship this old... There are bound to be systems that are far past their designed life span."

Tamara's hands bunched. She couldn't believe how blandly Rush was taking the whole thing.

"Okay, let's say we fix the leaks," said Scott. "Can you fix this?" He pointed at the black mass of residue.

Rush considered the question. "I doubt this could be cooked off. We can't reuse what is here. Perhaps, if there are stores of this substance in a clean form, or something else capable of carbon dioxide sequestration..."

"What does that mean?" said Chloe quietly, her voice trembling.

"Stale air passes through the scrubber, the chemical compound," Tamara explained. "It filters the CO_2 out of the atmosphere. Without it, carbon dioxide builds up in the bloodstream, causes something called hypercapnia...which will kill you just as easily as suffocation."

Rush looked to Brody and the others. "If I had some calcium carbonate or lithium hydroxide... Then, yes, I could fix it."

Tamara could tell from the expression on the faces of Palmer, Volker and the others, that what Rush needed they didn't have; and Chloe sensed it too, taking a shuddering breath that was on the verge of tears.

Scott saw the girl's reaction and spoke up before the fear could spread anew. "Okay, well, that's not going to matter, because you're going to get that gate dialed back to Earth before it becomes an issue." The lieutenant gave Rush a hard look. "Right?"

Rush's reply carried the smallest hint of condescension. "Lieutenant… You're taught to say that sort of thing in officer training for the benefit of those who don't know any better. But we do."

Before Tamara could react, Scott stepped up to the scientist and she was afraid he was about to lose his temper and lash out; but in the next second the look of fury on his face softened and became earnest. "Please," he said quietly, almost as if he were begging a favor.

"What makes you think I won't try?" said Rush. That, it seemed, was the closest the man would come to a 'yes'.

Eli tried to keep his focus off the ticking death clock in his head and on the job at hand. Returning to the control room, he turned the kino drone loose on the ship and used it to search parts of the decks where human teams hadn't yet ventured. In short order, he was able to direct groups to places where open doors were bleeding precious atmosphere out into unsealed sectors, and with every success they pushed back the moment when the air would grow so thin that nobody would be able to move anymore. Some of the less robust members of the evacuee group were already starting to succumb, and Eli found himself sweating as he wondered when the first of them was going to die. The thought crawled down his spine like ice; how long would *he* last, he wondered? Would he survive long enough to see the others perish before he did?

Eli pushed the grisly notion aside and peered at the console in front of him. The kino's-eye-view passed through another of the heavy bulkhead doors that lay half-open, and then into a smaller space that had an internal design different from the other corridors he'd seen so far. The kino floated through the dim chamber, turning, and its field of vision fell across a heavy chair that immediately reminded him of a jet fighter's ejector seat, but more curved and over-engineered. The kino kept turning, revealing more consoles, until it settled upon a viewport that looked out into space. In front of it, Eli saw what had to be a dashboard of flight controls. "I think... I think I've got something interesting here."

Rush looked up from his console across the room as Eli grabbed a radio and spoke quickly into it. "Greer? Listen, I found what looks like a cockpit. Maybe a shuttle, or something. It's close to where you are, past the next junction."

"*Copy that,*" said the Marine. "*We'll go take a look-see.*"

Rush's screen changed to bring up the ship's internal schematic, flickering through the deck plan to lock in on the area where Greer's team were. "It looks like there are two shuttles there, attached to individual docking sleeves. Airlocks at each access point."

Eli nodded, looking at the same display. Red warning glyphs were blinking steadily on the edges of the screen. "Well, if I'm reading this right, that whole section of the ship is leaking air like a screen door."

Greer led the way at a swift pace, with Franklin following and Lieutenant James bringing up the rear. The civilian's dour manner was starting to grate on the Marine some. "We're all gonna die," he said.

"Shut up, Franklin," Greer retorted. He had no time for whiners.

"I'm just saying what everyone's got to be thinking," came the reply.

He gave the man a fierce glare. "I said, *shut up*, or you're gonna be the first." That seemed to do the trick, and Franklin's face colored.

Up ahead, Wallace's floating camera thing was bobbing gently by an opening in the wall. Greer's first impression was of an airlock setup; the SGC gave all off-world servicemen training in basic airlock operation for shipboard emergencies or situations on worlds with hazardous atmospheres.

James was by the far wall. "There's what looks like a video screen set into a panel here."

Greer looked into the drone's lens. "This is the door?" he asked. It was partially open, and on closer inspection the frame around it seemed to be slightly distorted, as if it had suffered an impact. The air near the hatch was much colder than the rest of the corridor.

"*That's it,*" said Eli, over the open channel. "*Can you close it?*"

Greer moved to the panel and tapped the same controls he'd seen Franklin use on the other bulkhead doors. The hatch grumbled and rattled in place, but it did not cycle shut. He shook his head. "It won't close."

Franklin took a step into the shuttle itself, shining his flashlight into the gloom. "It looks like the whole front of this thing is compromised," he began. "Could have been an asteroid strike from outside, possibly…"

Greer followed him and Franklin stopped, looking over the spiderwebbed glass of the canopy. Both men saw great petals of torn metal where something of great force had ripped into the shuttle's nose and opened it to space. Beyond, a flickering bubble of energy was all that was keeping them from being blown out into the void. Greer resisted the immediate urge to back out.

"*I can't close it from here, either,*" reported Eli. "*There's something wrong with the mechanism.*"

The Marine cast around and found he'd stepped through a second hatchway inside the cabin of the smaller craft and not noticed it. "There's another door on the back of the shuttle, but no control pad," he noted.

"*Maybe we can close it off locally.*" Greer heard Rush's voice in the background. "*Don't touch anything. I'm coming down.*"

"He's coming down," James said dryly. "I feel better already."

Rush insisted that Eli remain in the control room, but as he wasn't — as Eli oh-so-eloquently put it — *the boss of him*, he went along anyway, eager to take a look at what he'd discovered via the kino. Anything to keep his focus off imminent death was a good thing, he reflected.

The shuttle had the same technological hallmarks as the rest of the ship, the same boiler-plate and drop-forged look to everything, which made it doubly disturbing to consider what amount of force would have been needed to smash through something so sturdy. The pattern of the wreckage seemed to chime with Franklin's idea of an asteroid hit. Even a tiny, dime-sized micrometeor could have done massive damage if it had collided with the shuttle's prow at a high enough velocity. The shock from the hit was clearly what had warped the outer door, and without some heavy duty metalworking gear, there was no way they could fix it.

The chair Eli had seen through the kino was in the middle of the shuttle's cockpit, likely set up for a pilot-commander. Rush settled himself into it without hesitation and began to work a set of keypads in the arms of the seat, while Franklin probed at the edges of the impact strike.

"The shield keeping the air inside is obviously not a hundred percent effective," said the scientist.

Rush's head bobbed in agreement. "No, it probably wasn't designed to compensate for the amount of damage the ship has sustained."

"Gotta wonder where that damage came from," said Greer. "Might not all be from space rocks."

Franklin clearly didn't want to consider that option at the moment. "Is there a way of boosting the shield? At least in the areas where we need it the most?"

Panels of data were appearing now, and Eli watched as Rush paged quickly through them. "We haven't found a way yet. It seems to be operating at maximum capability as it is."

Eli saw him touch a glowing glyph; then from behind them the open inner hatch of the shuttle let out a creak of metal and slammed shut. Immediately vents in the walls hissed and Eli's ears popped as the air inside the small craft was drawn out. "Open the door!" he shouted, his voice almost a squeal.

Rush tapped the glyph again and the process reversed itself, the hatch sliding back open again.

"Well," Eli managed, panting. "That's not good."

"What just happened?" said James.

"It looks like we have a way to seal off the leak," Rush replied.

"But only from *in here*," added Greer.

Rush nodded. "I didn't say it was the best way."

Young looked up as the hatch opened and Tamara stepped in. He shifted slightly and did his best to ignore the shooting pains in his back, but he was pretty sure that Johansen saw the tightening of his jaw. "Lieutenant," he said, with a nod.

"How are you doing?" she asked.

He pointed downward. "I can do this now." His feet moved a little, twitching in his boots. "Couldn't do that an hour ago."

She gave him a weary smile of encouragement. "That's great. That's a very good sign, sir."

"I'm still waiting on Doctor Rush."

Tamara nodded. "I told him you wanted to see him. He said he'd get to you just as soon as he could."

Young grimaced. "Yeah, I just bet he did." He took a breath and looked Johansen in the eye, measuring the woman's expression, gauging her stress level. "I don't have time for this, do I?"

Tamara leaned against a table and her shoulders sagged.

"Two problems," she began. "We're venting atmosphere from a damaged shuttle. But even if we can seal that off, the life support system is past its expiration date. We'll build up our carbon dioxide to lethal levels in a day, just by breathing in and out."

"That explains my headache," noted the colonel.

"You already had one," she replied.

Young thought for a moment. "Soda lime. Maybe one of the cases—"

She shook her head. "Left behind at Icarus."

He let that sink in. It was worse than he had expected, but they couldn't afford to lose focus now. "We'll find a way. That's what we do."

Tamara looked away. "Most of us aren't even supposed to be here."

Young pressed on. "How did the ship get damaged?"

"We don't know," she told him. "It certainly looks like it's been through a battle, at least in the sections we can access. We're still cut off from most of the vessel. It's huge."

"This shuttle," said Young. "We can't just close the hatch?"

The medic shook her head. "Eli says the outer door is stuck fast. There's an inner hatch, but that can only be shut from the inside. They tried jamming something into the shuttle doorway to keep it open long enough to let the person inside get out, but it just opens again. Some sort of safety mechanism, like in an elevator. Rush says he can't override it."

The colonel considered her report. "And the air... How much longer do we have?"

Tamara's aspect turned grim. "Every other leak we can find has been shut off. As it stands, Rush says if we don't get the shuttle hatch closed, we've got just over an hour."

Rush craned over Franklin's shoulder, watching the man as he removed the panels around the hatch control mechanism out in the corridor. The other scientist continued to work inside, despite all the compelling evidence to the contrary, convinced that he could find another way to access the shuttle hatch controls from out here.

He's wasting time. All our time, Rush thought to himself. From what he could determine, the shuttle was a completely separate vehicle from the main body of the starship, with its own operating systems, controls and apparatus. There appeared to be no cross-connections with the panels in the corridor, doubtless as some kind of safety measure to prevent accidental opening of the airlock and the resultant explosive decompression.

Perhaps, given enough time, Franklin's dogged refusal to see sense might be proven right — Rush imagined it was probably possible for someone who knew what they were doing to dig down into the shuttle's hardware and jury-rig a method for remote access. But the escapees had only just scratched the surface of the Ancient systems underpinning this vessel, and with the limited amount of equipment they had with them, it could take weeks, even months before they knew enough to run that kind of bypass. There was only one way to solve this problem, and it was the simplest and most expedient method; it was also the most ruthless.

Lieutenant Scott had arrived, and Greer gave him the basics of the situation in his usual terse, aggressive manner. Scott's expression never changed, but his eyes betrayed him to Rush; the young officer was thinking exactly the same thing that the scientist was.

"Bad air is better than no air," said Eli, studying the video screen on the wall. The monitor was showing an interior view of the shuttle's cockpit.

"A day is better than an hour," Scott added, reluctance heavy in his voice.

Rush folded his arms. They all knew what needed to be done. There was no sense denying it. "Someone has to go in there and close this door."

"And die," said Franklin pointedly. "Just so we're all clear about what you're saying here."

"That part, we all understand," said Scott, staring at the doorway.

He gathered them in the control room to go over the situation one more time. Scott could have made a decision then and there, down at the shuttle, but the truth was he wanted to put it off, to have a moment to try and assimilate what he was being asked to do. With Colonel Young still off his feet and command still technically resting on the shoulders of one Matthew Scott, where they went from here was up to him.

And ordering someone to kill themselves was not something that the lieutenant had any kind of handle on. Oh, back in training they had talked about how an officer would eventually find himself in a situation like this, where he might be forced to order men on missions that would more than likely result in their deaths. They talked about the greater good and duty and all that stuff. But that applied to combat, to battle with the enemy, to soldiers who had taken an oath to put their life on the line for their country. What was before him here and now was nothing less than an order to commit suicide. A cold equation, one life in exchange for fifty or so others.

And even then, it wasn't really a trade of life for lives — it was literally a trade for *breathing room*. Locking off the shuttle would net the rest of them no more than a day more at most, and that still might not be enough time to solve the bigger problem of the busted air scrubbers. Whomever stepped up to this might give their life for nothing, just so the rest of them could see the end coming and die a little slower.

And how could he ever order someone to do it? To look a subordinate in the eye — Riley or Greer, Spencer or even

Vanessa — and tell them to go in there? What was he supposed to do, throw it open to volunteers? Draw straws, run a lottery? Or was it that the responsibility fell to him, and him alone? As defacto commander, perhaps the only choice he had was actually no choice at all.

Tamara and Rush stood there, along with Eli and the senator's daughter, all of them waiting for his decision.

Eli was speaking into the glassy eye of a kino, reporting to it like he was the presenter on some documentary show. "My head is pounding," he told the machine. "Heart rate is accelerated. It's getting hard to breathe, as our very lives are vented out into space."

Rush rolled his eyes at Wallace's dramatic delivery and Scott took a step toward him. "That is going to get old very fast," he warned.

Eli pointed at the drone. "This needs to be documented."

"No one is going to see that," said Scott.

"How do you know?" Eli insisted. "We made it here. Someone else could too. If we die, maybe it will help them to know what happened to us."

"We're not dead yet," said Rush firmly.

Eli turned back to the kino to continue his narrative. "I'm starting to have slightly blurred vision," he noted.

Scott snapped Eli's name angrily and he stopped voicing his train of thought for the camera. "So," the lieutenant continued, "how are we going to decide *who*?"

Rush smiled without humor. "I assume we're not going to get any volunteers." He glanced at Chloe. "Do the rest of the civilians know the situation?"

She gave a shaky nod. "Some of them. I told my father about the shuttle, Miss Wray too...." She paused, working to draw herself together. "What's another day going to buy us?"

"Time," insisted Rush. "To find a way to survive." He

looked over to Tamara. "Do we have our list yet?"

Scott saw a hollowness in T.J.'s face as she handed Rush a sheet of paper with a hasty roll-call scribbled across it. "I marked the names of anyone injured," she said softly.

Rush scanned the paper. "We need to know their background, experience, skills—"

Scott broke in before he could go on. "It doesn't take any special skills to die from asphyxiation, Doctor."

Rush eyed him. "I'm saying it shouldn't be someone who has potentially valuable knowledge, or abilities we might need to survive beyond this."

Eli's reaction to the man's statement was everything that Scott was keeping inside; incredulous, aghast and disgusted all at once. Rush's callous criteria meant that, of course, he would automatically be exempt from being a candidate. Scott wondered how he would have felt about things if he was just one of the line grunts and not a goddamn genius; but part of him could also see he had a valid point.

Chloe didn't hide her revulsion either. "Are you really suggesting what I think you are?"

Scott glanced at the scientist. "Half the people on this ship already want to kill you. This won't win you any friends."

Rush dismissed his comments. "I don't care what people think of me."

"So that means you get to decide the value of one person's life over another?" said Scott. The question was as much for him as it was for Rush, however.

"You can't ask someone to sacrifice themselves," Chloe broke in. "*Period.*"

Rush gave the girl a cold, level stare. "Politicians ask military personnel to sacrifice themselves for the good of others all the time." He didn't look away, pressing his point home. "If someone doesn't close the door to that shuttle, we are all going to die...*period.*"

And then all eyes were on Scott again.

"Lieutenant?" said Tamara. "How do you want to proceed?"

He opened his mouth to speak, but he couldn't find the words. Finally, he looked away. "I need to talk to the colonel."

Young listened and said nothing as Scott and Johansen brought him up to speed. As he let them talk, he saw the burdens of the last few hectic hours showing heavily on both of his junior officers, and felt a pang of sympathy. T.J. wasn't even supposed to be here, and Matt Scott was still green in a lot of ways; but today they'd both been forced to dig deep and face challenges neither of them had been trained for. They were dealing with it all as best they could, and that would have to be enough.

"Franklin is still working at the airlock controls locally," said Scott, "but it doesn't look good, sir."

"Camile's explaining the situation to everyone else on board," added Tamara. "Someone may come forward to—"

"I'll do it." Young said the words automatically, without questioning himself.

Scott shook his head. "Sir..."

"This isn't the kind of thing I can ask somebody else to volunteer for," he continued.

"If we're going to make it past this, we're going to need you," Scott insisted.

"I don't know about that." He looked to Tamara and then back to Scott. "I just don't know."

"Sir," repeated the young man, and there was a plea hidden deep in the word.

"I'm not sure anyone should do it," Tamara broke in before either man could say more. "I don't want someone sacrificing their life for me. I say we either figure this out together while we still have time, or we all die trying."

Young shook his head. "It needs to be done, and I'm doing

it." He put his weight forward on his legs and tried to stand, but his muscles wouldn't respond.

"You can barely stand up," said Tamara, "let alone—"

"Help me," he grated.

She went on, ignoring him. "Sir, the paralysis is not permanent, you know that now. You are going to recover…"

He tried again to stand and fell forward, stumbling to his knees. Young shot a look at Scott. "Help me, Lieutenant."

Scott stood, impassive. "No, sir, I will not." In that moment, something changed behind the young man's eyes.

"I gave you an order," said the colonel.

Scott nodded once. "I know. You can have me court martialed when we get home, sir, but I will not help you kill yourself."

Young heard the steel behind the words, and he knew that not even the commander-in-chief would shift Scott once he'd dug in his heels. The lieutenant could be stubborn that way; in fact, it was one of the reasons Young had selected him for Icarus Base. "Then at least help me get on my feet."

Scott threw Tamara a nod, and she reached down to give Young a hand.

Without warning, there was a pounding on the hatch and Scott opened it to find Chloe Armstrong standing in the corridor outside. She was distraught, her hands fluttering in front of her face like panicked birds. "What's wrong?" asked the lieutenant.

"My father's not in his room!"

Tamara shared a loaded look with Scott. "In his condition, he shouldn't be up and around."

Scott placed a hand on Chloe's arm. "Don't worry, we'll find him." He turned to Tamara, nodding toward the colonel. "In the meantime, you make sure he doesn't go anywhere."

"I don't understand…" said Chloe. "He wouldn't just leave me…"

"He's injured. He can't have gotten far." Scott reached for his radio.

Young saw a sudden realization dawn on the girl, and she went pale. "I... I told him what was going on..."

"Greer, this is Scott," said the lieutenant. "Come in. Greer, do you read, over?"

"You'd better get down there," Young told him.

Scott nodded and broke into a run, with Chloe racing a few steps behind him.

Greer had his radio set to hands-free, and Scott's voice issued out from the walkie's speaker grille. *"Senator Armstrong is missing. He may be headed your way."* The lieutenant's words were coming in hard chugs of breath; he was running. *"Greer, do you read me, over?"*

At the Marine's side, bent low near the open panel beneath the video screen, Franklin had his hands raised, still grasping the tools he'd been using to delve into the guts of the door control mechanism. Greer moved slowly and carefully, taking great pains not to move his hands anywhere near the butt of the G36 rifle slung over his shoulder.

His fingers reached the push-to-talk button on the radio and he keyed it. "He's here," he reported.

A few feet away down the corridor, Armstrong stood, his face pale, patches of sweat blooming through the material of his five thousand dollar suit. He had one hand clamped to his side, in obvious agony. The other was held out before him, and in its shaky grip was a Beretta automatic.

"He's got a gun," Greer continued, his eyes never leaving those of the other man. Scott didn't respond; if the lieutenant wasn't already double-timing it down to the shuttles, then he surely was now. The Marine released the radio and moved his hand slowly away. "Where'd you get that, sir?" he asked. "You know how to use it?"

"I know," Armstrong said, through gritted teeth.

Greer kept his voice neutral and calm, but he made it clear he was reaching slowly for his weapon. "Look, I don't want to shoot you. I don't think you want to shoot me." His fingers reached the grip of the G36 and he took hold of it.

"Get out of the way." Armstrong ground out each word like it was broken glass. The man had to be hurting, putting all he'd got into standing up.

"Just give me a little more time," said Franklin. "Let me try and fix this."

"I don't have much," Armstrong gasped, forcing a brittle smile.

The senator's gun hand was twitching, and Greer was afraid the man might let off a shot without intending to. The problem was, if he shot Armstrong, even giving him a glancing round in the leg or the arm, the shock might be enough to kill the senator then and there.

Over Franklin's radio, Eli Wallace called out, clearly oblivious to the unfolding drama in the corridor. "*Guys? Did you stop what you're doing? I'm not seeing any change. Whatever you just tried, it's not working.*"

Then Greer heard Rush say something in the background. "*The problem is obviously mechanical.*"

Armstrong walked slowly, painfully toward them. "That's it?" he said, gesturing with the gun toward the open panel where Franklin had been working.

The scientist nodded, shooting Greer a questioning look. "Uh, yes. It looks like some kind of hydraulic system. I'm still trying to backtrack all the conduits…" He trailed off, eyes flicking to the pistol aimed toward him.

The Marine watched Armstrong as he swayed on his feet. The senator was getting worse by the moment. Greer had seen death coming up on people before, and he saw it again now, in the gray pallor across Armstrong's face, the distant glitter in his eyes. He had no doubts he was looking at a dead man walking. Greer released his grip on the G36; no threat he could make with the gun was going to have any impact on Armstrong. The senator briefly met his gaze and an unspoken communication passed between them. He could see the need in the man's eyes, the need for his end to *mean* something.

Greer looked toward Franklin. "You can't fix it." It was a statement of fact, and with that the scientist slowly shook his head.

Armstrong looked at Greer and he understood. He released his grip on the pistol and handed it over. Taking a shuddering breath, he nodded toward the shuttle. "Tell me what to do."

Scott rounded the corner into the corridor at full tilt, his boots pounding down the metal decking toward the bulkhead hatch and the shuttle beyond. Chloe was with him every single step of the way, her hair flying back from her head, her body propelled forward by the sheer hysterical energy of her panic.

He saw Greer and Franklin at the hatchway, both men sullen and silent. And as he came close, there on the video screen the live feed from the interior of the damaged shuttlecraft. A figure was settling into the command chair, a pale face ghost-like on the digital screen.

Chloe screamed. "Dad! No!" She was reaching out to him as she ran. "*Wait!*"

Armstrong moved, and from inside the shuttle, Scott heard the groan and crunch of the inner hatch as it closed.

His daughter threw herself against the iron door, banging her fists on the metal. She pressed her face to the tiny window in the hatch and screamed louder. "Dad! *No!*"

Panting hard, Scott rounded on Greer. Breathless, he couldn't find the words to demand an answer. *Why did you let him do this?*

Greer met his gaze. "He was dead on his feet." The simple truth of the sergeant's words shut down all of Scott's momentum, his every question.

The lieutenant's gaze slipped to the video screen, and on it he saw the man settle back in the seat as the air faded all around him. There was no sound, but Scott saw Armstrong's lips move, and knew the shape of the words. *I love you.*

Chloe's face was streaked with tears. "Open it!" she cried. "Please, open it!"

Franklin shook his head. "I can't."

Before Scott could stop her, she was on him, tearing his radio from his gear vest. "Eli, help him!" She yelled into the pickup. "Not him, please, not him! Open the door, please!"

Eli sounded stricken as he told her the hard, unforgiving truth. "*I'm sorry, I can't! There's no way to do it from here.*"

"Chloe…"

Her pretty face, marred by fear and dread, seemed to crumble as at last she understood that nothing would stop this from happening. The radio fell from her nerveless fingers and the girl burst into wracking sobs. She staggered forward, desperate for support, and Scott took her and held her as Chloe Armstrong's world came crashing down around her.

Alone in the dark, silent shuttle, her father surrendered his life for his daughter's.

CHAPTER NINE

Rush watched the display on the deck plan change. The schematic showing the area around the shuttles was alight with warning symbols, and the zone that indicated the damaged shuttle itself flashed red, showing the incidence of air loss. As he studied it, the glyphs blinked out one by one, and the red zone changed color to a solid blue, matching that of the airtight corridors all around it.

He felt the ball of tension in his chest relax — but only a little. This was just the solution to the most immediate problem; the question of how to repair the air scrubbers was still hanging over them.

"Well… He bought us a day." Rush looked up and saw Eli's stunned expression. The young man was having trouble dealing with what had just happened, but Rush didn't have the luxury of that. He needed to remain pragmatic and concentrate on making sure that no one else died. He had to—

There was a flash of movement at the corner of his eye and Rush turned. Armstrong's daughter thundered into the control room and flew at him, her expression twisted in furious anger, her hands coming up to grab at him.

He barely had time to defend himself before Chloe was raining down blows on him, kicking and scratching and punching, fuelled by distress, turning it all on him. Rush hesitated, seeing Scott coming in a few steps after the girl; if he defended himself, there was no telling how the situation would escalate.

"You did this!" she screamed, throwing vicious, heedless punches at his face. "You killed him! *You've killed all of us!*"

He tasted blood on his tongue, but then Chloe was reeling away, dragged backward by Scott. She relaxed in his arms, and he loosened his grip; then a heartbeat later she tried to lunge back at Rush, swiping at air.

"Chloe, stop!" said the lieutenant, but his words fell on deaf ears. Johansen entered the control room and Scott called to her. "Little help here?"

The medic reached out to the girl. "Chloe…"

The anger still hard in her eyes, the violence in Chloe's manner finally ebbed and she shrugged herself free of Scott's grip. Breathless and crack-throated, she glared at the two officers. "Get away from me." She turned back toward Rush and Eli. "All of you."

He'd expected a reaction to Armstrong's death, of course, but not something so extreme. The girl's bright, politic manner clearly concealed a fierce spirit. Rush filed that thought away for later consideration. For now, he had to stamp down on any suggestion that the senator's choice could be laid at his feet. "Miss Armstrong…" he began, attempting a soothing tone. "You're in shock. I understand. Everyone deals with tragedy in different ways. You're looking for someone to blame."

Chloe's glare was icy. "I'm not looking," she told him.

"I am sorry about your father," he continued. "He certainly would not have been my choice, he was a good man…" Rush paused, feeling for the right words. "But this is not my fault. I didn't create the situation that forced us here. There was no other way."

His statement had the opposite effect he wanted it to, and for a moment it seemed as if the girl was going to take another run at him. Johansen saw the flash of anger in her expression and moved to where she could intercept Chloe if the need arose.

Rush pressed on, trying to make her understand. "It may not matter to you right now, but this ship may be the most important discovery mankind has made since the Stargate itself. You know that the Icarus Project was something your father believed in, enough to risk his career to support it."

Chloe was silent for a long moment; her father's advocacy for the project had not been without its problems, and it was an open secret in the upper echelons of the SGC that Alan Armstrong had used up a lot of his political capital getting Icarus the funding it needed. "What difference does it make if we all die?" she said, at length.

He tried a different tack. "A number of people died in the attack on the base." Faces drifted through his thoughts; good thinkers, highly competent scientists, colleagues whose insights Rush had respected; many were not among the escapees and he assumed the worse. "People I worked with closely for the last few years, people I knew well."

"I'm sure some had more value than others," Chloe shot back.

That gave him pause, but he kept talking. "As human beings, all of them were invaluable. I promise you, I am going to do everything I can to make sure no one gave their life in vain." He took a step toward her. "Please, just give me a chance."

She didn't say another word. Instead, Chloe turned, swallowing her anger and pain, and left the room. Rush reached up to wipe a comma of blood from his lip, and watched her go.

Camile Wray looked down at her hands and stared at them as if they belonged to someone else. It was a small thing, a silly thing really, but she'd always worked hard to keep her hands looking good. Manicures and skin creams. A careful daily regimen. It was true what they said, that a woman's hands were the first to betray her age, faster then her eyes, her face. She managed a wistful smile; Sharon always made fun of her for thinking that way, gently mocking her vanity, always reminding her that it was quite acceptable for women like them to grow old, as long as they did it *dis*gracefully…

The smile became brittle, broke apart. Camile's hands were dirty, the nails cracked, the skin torn in places; and with a deep sigh, she wondered when she would ever feel Sharon's touch on them again. She looked up at the metal walls around her, at the small knot of people taking refuge in the storage space. *We are so far from home,* she thought. *We're all lost together.*

Camile thought on that for a moment. What would her part in all this be? Back on Icarus, she was a functionary at best, and if she was honest, a paper-pusher with ideas above her station. Right from the start, she'd felt as if her posting to the isolated research base was a make-weight assignment, far from the center of things, away from the corridors of power where the policy of the International Oversight Advisory was shaped. But if a man such as Richard Woolsey could be promoted to command of a facility like the city of Atlantis, then Camile Wray believed she could do the same, if not better.

But now they were here, and that goal was beyond her. *Or was it?* She looked at her fellow escapees. Scientists, mostly, and soldiers. Both persona types locked in their ways, at opposite ends of the spectrum. In the days ahead, someone like her, someone with her skills at handling people, could prove invaluable. She could have purpose.

Behind her, the hatch opened and Young hobbled into the compartment, walking with difficulty. Wray kept her expression neutral as she noticed the Marine, Greer, at his side. "Colonel…"

Young took them all in with a look. "Senator Armstrong is dead."

Camile's eyes widened. "My God. What happened? I'd heard he was injured…"

"He's bought us some time," said the colonel, and abruptly Camile understood what Armstrong had done.

"To do what?" she said.

Young answered without answering; he seemed to make a habit of that when he dealt with Wray. "We're working on it. First up is trying to dial the gate back home." He winced as he spoke, clearly in pain.

Some of the others were talking eagerly, clinging to the faint hope the word 'home' engendered. Camile moved closer, studying Young. "Should you even be on your feet?" she asked.

"No," said Greer, with an edge of annoyance.

Young threw the sergeant a look. "Well, I *am* on my feet, and right now we're going to try to get home." His gaze met hers. "I need your help, Camile. You know these people. Spread the word. Try and keep things as positive as you can."

A dozen questions popped into her head. Was he serious about the Stargate? How much air did they have left? Was he just lying to keep people calm? *Do we really have a chance at survival out here?* But she asked none of them, because Wray knew as well as Young did that right now, the Icarus refugees needed hope almost as much as they did air. "I can do that," she said.

He gave her a nod. "Good. Thank you."

He found her on the observation deck.

Scott peered into the starlit room to see Chloe sitting on the floor, staring out into space. Out beyond the window, the sweep of the Ancient ship framed the strange shimmering colors of the Doppler-shifted stars. For a moment, he considered leaving her where she was, letting her have her quiet, her moment of reflection; but he couldn't walk away.

He thought of the intensity of emotion that had washed out from Chloe when he held her as her father perished. The poised and perfect young senator's aide he had met less than a day ago was breaking apart, and she had no one to help her shoulder the pain. Scott walked in and took a seat on the floor next to her, offering what he could just by being there. He said nothing and let Chloe find her way.

After while, she spoke, quiet and heavy with emotion. "I've never done anything like that before." She showed him the bruises on the knuckles of her hands from the wild punches she had thrown.

"He'll be fine," Scott assured her. "Rush isn't quite as noble as he says he is, but I don't think he really intended for us to get stuck this way."

"You think he had no choice?"

Scott considered that. "If he's lying, then he's a lot crazier than I want to believe." That thought made him uncomfortable, and he pushed it away.

Chloe fell silent for a long moment, before taking a low breath. "I just… I can't believe my dad is gone. I watched him die and I still just can't accept it."

He could hear the emotions in her voice, the disbelief and the pain. Scott glanced at her. "Tell me about him."

Chloe looked back, her brow creasing in confusion, as if she thought that was a odd thing to ask of her. "Why?"

He looked back toward the stars. "The man died so I could live. I'd like to know more about him. I owe him that much, at least."

"Like what?"

"Anything."

Chloe thought on that for a little while, and he saw the faint ghost of a smile on her face. "No matter how tired he was, how long he had worked or what was going on in his life, he always had time to listen to me," she said. "I'd go on and on."

"About what?"

She looked away. "Everything. The world, school, friends, guys…" The smile grew a little more as she remembered her father, reconnected with him. "He never preached, never told me what to do even though sometimes I wished he would. He just listened." Chloe took a breath and there was a faint catch in it. "Then he'd tell me he loved me. When that didn't help, he'd break out chocolate ice cream."

In spite of himself, Scott smiled. "I'd kill for some right now."

Chloe went on, the words she needed to hear coming from her own lips, not his. "The worst was if I had a fight with my mom. He never took sides." She shook her head. "God, my mom... He was her whole life. She probably thinks we're both dead."

Scott watched the play of emotions on her face. "I didn't know him, and now I wish I'd had the chance. All I do know is that he wanted you to go on. He loved you."

"I know." Her voice seemed to come from very far away.

He wanted to say more, but he had nothing else to give her. Anything else would have just been empty platitudes, and Chloe deserved more than that. Scott slowly got back to his feet. "I gotta get back to the search. Are you going to be okay?"

She gave him a look. "I don't know."

He felt the same way. "Fair enough."

Eli felt numb.

He'd experienced death in the same way that most people his age had; through the funeral of an elderly relative or the distant, removed passing of someone they knew at second hand. But Eli had never been so close to something like this, to a man making the choice to end himself by his own hand. People had died back there on Icarus, and Eli knew that on a disconnected, intellectual level; but he hadn't known them, hadn't seen their last moments as he had with Armstrong, watching him seal himself into the shuttle via the unblinking eye of the kino, watching Chloe's sorrow and fury at her father's sacrifice.

He stared at the console before him without really seeing it, dimly aware of Rush, Brody and Park busying themselves at the control room's other panels. Senator Armstrong's death made the threat facing all of them shift from an abstract to terrible reality. Maybe on some level, Eli had believed that they would never have to really face up to their own mortality; but now that was all torn away, and the truth of it was bearing down on him.

"Eli…"

He looked up and found Rush staring at him. "What?"

"What are you doing?" The scientist looked irritated. "We need to keep working, searching the ship's systems."

He shook his head. "I just watched a man die. Give me a break, okay? Don't you care?"

Brody and Park paused, watching the conversation. Rush shot them a look that said *Back to Work!* and then turned to Eli again. "Of course I do. But I'm concentrating on what needs to be done. I'm also learning as much as I can, as quickly as I can." He tapped the console in front of him. "That is, in addition to running nine separate searches in the database in the hope of solving our life support issues."

"Right," said Eli, frowning. "Have you found anything?"

Rush paused, and when he spoke again Eli detected a note of melancholy in his voice. "*Destiny.*"

He blinked. "As in ours?" Eli hadn't figured Rush as the kind to make portentous statements.

The scientist shook his head slightly. "It's the name of the ship, translated from Ancient. Fitting, don't you think?"

Park spoke up. "I never much liked the whole idea of destinies and fates and predetermined events, myself."

"Destiny and fate are two different things," said Brody. "Fate implies a path with no choice to it. Destiny is something else… Something you have to be a part of. Something with a choice to it."

Rush nodded. "I have also learned that the Ancients were never here."

That brought Eli up short. "Wait, I thought this was an Ancient ship. You said they built it, just like they built the Stargates."

"They did," said Rush. "They sent it out unmanned, planning to use the gate on board to get here when it was far enough out into the universe…but they must have learned to ascend before it was time."

Ascend? Eli wasn't sure what the word meant in that context, but he saw Brody and Park both nodding at Rush's theory. "They learned to *what*?"

"It's, uh, a bit complicated," noted Brody.

Rush took on a lecturing tone once more. "*Ascension* is a process in which consciousness converts to energy and no longer requires physical form."

He made it sound like he was talking about someone changing their shirt, not shifting from one state of being to another. Eli had read enough science fiction to grasp the concept of a corporeal entity transforming into pure energy, but the idea of a whole civilization doing it *for real* was a little harder to comprehend. But it did explain a lot; he'd wondered for a while why it was these so-called Ancients were willing to let Earthmen screw around with their funky technology and not kick up a stink about it. They were all gone, vanished off to Dimension X or some other higher plane of being. "That wasn't in the video," he said. Eli had been constructing his own theory about the builders of the Stargates ever since he'd first heard them mentioned, factoring in what he knew of conspiracy theories about Roswell, alien abductions and that kind of thing. Now it all seemed trivial and commonplace. *All that stuff with little gray men must have been some big disinformation thing,* he decided.

Rush gave him an arch look. "There's more than one video, Eli. Now, if you don't mind, we all need to get to work."

"Sorry…"

Young entered the gate room, and resisted the urge to glance over his shoulder at Master Sergeant Greer. The Marine was only doing his job, making sure that Young stayed standing, but the colonel was already starting to quietly resent having to lean on the young man for support. His legs felt like they were wrapped in needles, and every step he took, a little shock of agony went up his spine and rattled around his skull.

T.J. had offered him something for the pain, but he had told her to keep it. Medical supplies were too important to dole out without good reason; and Everett Young's reason wasn't anywhere close to good. But he couldn't stay in that cabin any more. People needed to see he was still alive, see that a senior officer was there to lead them. The alternative was to load even more pressure on to Scott, and he had enough; that or let Rush continue to pretend he was running this ship.

Sergeant Riley had contacted him over the radio, and the technician's excited tone was the first positive thing Young had heard since they'd fled here from Icarus. The colonel found him at one of the copper-sheathed consoles at the back of the chamber.

"I think I got it," he told him, as Young and Greer approached. "It wasn't even that hard to find. It's right here in the dialing program." Riley tapped the screen, and on it Young saw something that looked a lot like the activation subroutines in use at Stargate Command, only here the familiar strings of angular constellation symbols were replaced with combinations of dots, circles and wavy lines.

He gave the non-com a level look. "You're sure?"

Riley nodded. "Yes sir. It's an eight symbol gate address input."

"You can dial this thing to Earth?" said Greer.

The other man nodded. "There's no point of origin indicated, though, but that might vary based on the location of the ship. And unlike the Giza-type Stargates, there's only thirty-six symbols, not thirty-nine."

"Thirty-six," echoed Young, "Same as the Pegasus Stargates."

"That's right." Riley nodded again. "I'm assuming that the ninth symbol represents some x-factor distance equation."

Young suspected that the sergeant would start giving him chapter and verse on the whole structure of the new kind of gate they'd discovered on the ship, but he didn't have time to listen to it. "I don't care about the details," he said. "Start dialing."

Riley reached for the control pad, and then paused. "Don't we want to bring Dr. Rush in on this?"

Young gave him a look. "You said this wasn't that hard to find?"

"No sir."

The colonel nodded. "Then he probably already knows and didn't tell us." He pointed at the console. "Get to it, Sergeant."

Eli worked through a dozen more levels of the ship's — no, scratch that, the *Destiny*'s — subsystems, and it seemed like the deeper he went, the more he found. The size of the database on board the vessel defied measurement, so it seemed; and the problem was, with a library that big, locating a single book, such as the one labeled *How Not To Suffocate And Die*, was like finding your actual needle in a haystack. As much as he searched, however, he couldn't stop his thoughts from wandering back to the events that had brought them all here.

And Rush's comment continued to nag at him. *There's more than one video*. The question was, *How many more?*

"Who is this Lucian Alliance, anyway?" The question slipped out before he was aware of thinking it.

Rush looked up. "Where did that come from?"

"I want to know who to blame for this," Eli told him.

"If it *was* them..." muttered Brody.

"All right," said Rush. "I suppose your security clearance is a moot point now we're all out here. They're a largely-human coalition from various Milky Way planets, that formed in the power vacuum left when the Goa'uld were defeated."

"The Goa'uld..." Eli repeated. The name felt odd as he said it.

"An intelligent parasitic ophidian life form," offered Brody. "They used human hosts, and ran slave empires under the guises of mythological deities."

"Right. Of course." Eli decided to accept that at face value and move on.

"The Lucian Alliance are criminals, mostly," continued Rush. "A street gang with starships."

Eli considered that. "How did they find out about Icarus? Wasn't it like, double secret?"

"Yes." Rush frowned. "I suspect there was a leak somewhere. Someone working on the inside, feeding them information."

"On the base?" Eli felt a chill at that; the idea of someone willingly opening the door to the death and destruction he'd seen made him feel sick.

"Or Earth," said Rush, looking away. "The legend surrounding the ninth chevron has been floating around our galaxy for a very long time, in different forms."

Eli's hand closed around the remote control pad for the kino he'd left bobbing in the air nearby, and he activated it, careful not to let Rush see him do it. He had a sudden feeling that what the man said next would be worth recording.

Rush pointed at the star map screen. "We found it means a variety of things to different cultures. Historical remnants appear on worlds in our home galaxy and out in Pegasus. Some believed that the Ancients received a subspace signal so old that it must have originated from the first intelligence to arise after the Big Bang, and that the ninth chevron was the only way to reach them. Some said it was a key to the universe itself, and once unlocked, you would gain untold power." He paused, musing on his own words, apparently unaware of the kino drifting nearby. "If the Lucian Alliance learned we had discovered the address and a means to dial it, they would want that information."

"Enough to kill for it," Park said, grim-faced.

Eli couldn't help but glance around at the dull iron walls, the dim lighting and the bleak, metallic décor. "This ship is a source of untold power?"

A smile flickered over Rush's face. "No, not literally. It has more to do with what this ship is doing, it's mission of exploration and the information that the *Destiny* is capable of gathering."

He was starting to get the measure of it now. "If you know how to use it."

Rush nodded. "Yes. Perhaps the grand sum of that knowledge could lead to a powerful understanding of the universe."

Eli saw that look in the man's eye again, that glint of deep *need*. "That's what you're after, isn't it? That's why you risked everything to get here." His lips thinned. "You think this ship is going to make you all-powerful or something crazy like that." He had a sudden mental image of Rush plugging himself into some vast Ancient machine and transforming himself with a blast of cosmic energy, like something out of an old Jack Kirby comic.

Rush gave him a patronizing look. "Eli, if there was a way to safely send all these people home and return with a properly skilled team to pursue this mission as intended, why wouldn't I want to do that?"

Admittedly, he didn't have an answer for that. "I don't know."

"Now," he said turning to shoot a glare at the kino. "Shut that thing off."

Eli gave a sheepish grin. "You saw that, huh?"

Rush was going to say more, but a tinny chime from his console drew the scientist's attention. A new star map appeared on the display, and he quickly brought it up on the large holographic pane. Eli crowded in to get a better look, and Brody and Park followed.

"Planets," said Park. The imager projected a series of worlds on the monitor, one after another, lines of data scrolling quickly past each one before the display shifted.

"What is it doing?" said Brody.

Rush tapped his chin. "I attacked the life support problem every way I can think of. I asked the computer to look for any possible resources on board that might help us. But now it seems to be looking *outside* the ship."

Suddenly, the search program froze and an indicator panel appeared over the display. Rush's manner immediately became one of alarm. "No…" he muttered.

Eli looked back at the hologram; he was reminded of the kind of pop-ups he saw on his PC whenever the machine suffered a blue-screen-of-death crash error. Rush was already on his way out of the room, and Eli called after him. "What's wrong?"

"Someone's dialing the gate," he replied.

Young used the gate room console to support his weight, watching Riley as the sergeant's hands danced over the touch screen and interface wheel. He looked up to see Lieutenant Scott enter the chamber as the Stargate began to spin. Unlike other gates he'd seen, the chevrons on this one all lit up immediately, and instead of rotating an inner ring of symbols, the entire structure of the device spun, passing through a slot in the deck and a glowing orb at the twelve o'clock position. Each time a dot-dash symbol passed under the orb, the glyph would illuminate, sending the gate spinning back the opposite way until another fragment of the address locked in.

"Sir?" said Scott, coming closer. "Are we—?"

"Going home?" finished the colonel. "Let's hope so."

Some of the other evacuees had been drawn by the noise of the rumbling Stargate, and among them Young saw Rush arrive with Eli, Brody and Park in tow.

Rush looked surprised to see him "Colonel Young? You're up."

He returned a neutral nod. "Nice to see you too, Rush. I did order you to report to me."

The scientist ignored the comment, nodding toward the

gate. "What are you doing?"

"Trying to dial Earth."

Rush shook his head, his jaw stiffening. "This is a mistake—" he began.

Young spoke over him. He wasn't in the mood to be second-guessed by the man. "Riley thinks he found the address for home."

Rush's dismissive look at the sergeant made it clear what the scientist thought of that. "His understanding of Ancient is marginal at best, Colonel."

Riley shot him a look. "I know enough to recognize a reference to Earth."

"He said it wasn't that hard to find." Young said it without weight, but the unspoken half of the sentence hung in the air. *So why didn't you mention it, Rush?*

"No, no…" He was saying, shaking his head. "This is a complete waste of power we may need. You need to stop doing this, right now."

"We have the address back, all we need is the right point of origin," said Scott, weighing in.

Young nodded "And we've got thirty-six tries to find it."

Rush's voice turned icy. "We have barely enough power to operate the main systems! This ship simply doesn't have the capability to dial Earth!"

"Really?" The colonel eyed the scientist. "See, that's news to me."

"He didn't tell me that either," offered Eli. Brody and Park exchanged nervous glances but said nothing.

Rush shot Eli an irritated glance. "That's because I've only just learned so myself." He turned to Wallace, looking for support. "Eli, you know what I've been doing—"

"Even if it doesn't work," Young went on, "the people aboard this ship need to see us try."

The scientist was incredulous. "So you're going to drain what little power we have left for the sake of a morale boost?

That is absurd!"

He was going to say more, but the deck beneath their feet lurched and Young felt a brief sense of arrested motion wash over him. He heard a surge in rhythm of the ever-present engine noise, and suddenly the Stargate halted its spin and went dark. Riley muttered a curse and tapped fruitlessly on his console.

"What was that?" said Scott. "Felt like before, like something shifted…"

Young spoke into his radio. "Anybody got a visual outside?"

After a moment, Tamara Johansen's voice answered him. "*Colonel, I'm here with Chloe on the observation deck. It looks like we've dropped out of faster-than-light travel.*"

"Copy that," he said with a nod. "Stand by. Report if anything changes."

"It won't," said Rush, as he hurried to the console where Riley stood. "At least, not for the moment."

"Because we were draining power?" said the sergeant.

Rush pressed the other man out of the way with a brusque wave of his hand. "No. If I'm right, the gate should begin to dial any moment."

As if it had been waiting to hear those words, the white chevrons flashed on once again, and the Stargate started to spin.

"How did you know that would happen?" said Scott.

"In the control room, we saw a scan report," Rush told him. "The ship detected a planet with a Stargate on it within range, one that may have what need."

"What?" Young's brow furrowed. One second Rush was telling them they were deep in unknown territory, the next he was talking about the gate network. "How the hell are there even Stargates out here? Aren't we light-years from anywhere?"

"The Ancients launched a number of unmanned ships in

advance of this one," said the scientist, working the console. "They were programmed to gather data and resources to manufacture Stargates and then deposit them on habitable worlds. Any relevant information is relayed back here and helps plot the course of the *Destiny*."

"That's the name of this vessel," Eli offered. "*Destiny*. Little showy, if you ask me."

Now the man was talking about *other* Ancient ships apart from this one? Young felt like he was running to keep up. "So you're telling me this ship knows that we're in trouble?" On the console, a seven-symbol address had locked in.

Rush nodded. "Yes, exactly, because I *told* it we were. We're essentially flying on autopilot. The ship may have stopped when it was within range of a Stargate regardless of our need, but I have good reason to believe it is actively helping us to survive—"

The rest of his words were lost in the churning roar of the Stargate as it opened a wormhole through space-time, the strange shimmering energy wave swelling out before collapsing back into a rippling vertical pool of silver light.

Young stared into the event horizon, musing. "So what we need is on the other side of that wormhole?"

"At an educated guess, yes," raid Rush.

The glow was enticing, and Young walked stiffly across the deck toward it, turning Rush's words over in his thoughts. "Only one way to find out," he said, after a moment.

Riley shook his head. "Sir, you can't do that, you don't know what's on the other side. It could have locked on to a world with a toxic atmosphere, or a Spacegate…"

Eli drew a slim metallic device from his pocket. "We could use the kino to find out. Send it through ahead as a scout."

"I imagine that's the actual purpose of that device," said Rush, with a sniff.

"The what?" said Riley.

"This," Eli explained, manipulating a few controls on the

keypad-remote device. After a moment, the spherical drone arrived in the gate room, and drifted down toward the wormhole. "Okay, I got this." Aiming the remote toward the device, Eli steered it through the event horizon and off the ship.

Another screen near the main console immediately lit up. "I'm getting readings over here," said Riley.

The group crowded in to watch, and Young saw a panel of live video there, and another showing what had to be a direct stream of data telemetry. The video feed revealed a pale blue sky and shallow, rolling ridges of white extending was as far as the camera eye could see.

"Is that snow?" asked Park.

Rush was studying the sensor data. "We're getting temperature readings, gravity, atmosphere composition, barometric pressure…"

"It's a desert," said Brody. "Those are sand dunes."

Scott nodded. "So the ball is like a probe."

"Like a MALP drone," said Riley. "A 'hover-malp'."

Eli shook his head,. "*Kino* is way better."

From a hidden speaker grille, the sound of low winds issued out, and on the screen Young saw wisps of blown mineral sand flutter off the tops of the banks. "What have we got? Can we go there?"

Riley ran a finger down his screen. "Atmosphere looks like oxygen, nitrogen… Very little carbon dioxide. Extremely low humidity… Habitable, but just barely, sir."

"Excellent," said Rush.

Brody was leaning forward, pointing at another part of the display. Young saw more strings of dot-dash glyphs. "It looks like four other addresses came up here too. They could be other planets in range." He looked at Rush. "Maybe we should think about—"

"No." The scientist shut him down immediately. "They're locked out. The ship chose this one and the Stargate is open. All we need to do is step through."

Rush seemed to have an awful lot of faith in an millennia-old computer system that he'd only just discovered, but Young wasn't ready to go after the kino just like that. "We need to put a team together before anyone goes anywhere."

"Doctor Rush," said Brody. "There's something else." He pointed at another display. On it there was a string of Ancient letters flickering and changing in sequence.

"Looks like our time might be limited," said Rush.

"What is it?" The alien digits were unfamiliar to the colonel.

"It's a countdown," explained the scientist, translating it on the go. "We have approximately twelve hours."

"And what happens then?"

Rush looked around. "I suspect we jump back into FTL, and go on our way."

"The ship's giving us a deadline?" said Eli. "What happens if somebody is on the other side of the gate when it the clock hits zero?"

"They get left behind," said Park.

The colonel reassembled them in the control interface room. Scott, Greer, Johansen, Spencer and Curtis represented the military contingent, while Rush and Eli stood with Brody, Volker, Park, Franklin and Palmer.

Rush was nodding toward Palmer. "She's a geologist, so obviously she should go. This mineral may not be so easy to identify. Franklin and Brody are the best of the rest of what we have."

Franklin made a face. "Thanks for the ringing endorsement."

Volker's lip curled. "He didn't even *mention* me."

Young considered Rush's words. "Palmer and Franklin will go with Scott and his team. The others stay. We're still going to need good people here working on the problem from this end."

Eli gingerly raised a hand. "I'd like to go."

"Really?" The colonel couldn't help but be a little surprised. Wallace didn't seem the type to take risks if he didn't have to.

"If I can help..." he said.

Rush cut him off. "I don't think so."

Eli shot the other man a narrow-eyed look. "Why, you don't think I can handle it?" He pointed at Franklin. "*He's* going."

"I've been off-world before," said the other scientist. "How many planets have you been to?"

"Three," Eli said defiantly. "Counting Earth. And this one. If I go."

Young considered Wallace for a moment. For someone who had been torn away from his cozy, normal world and thrown in at the deep end among all this madness, Eli was actually handling it pretty well. He'd shown ingenuity and quick thinking, and the colonel decided there and then to give him the benefit of the doubt. "You *have* made a habit of pulling our asses out of the fire," he admitted. "You want to go, you're going." Lieutenant Scott seemed surprised, but Young didn't acknowledge him, and went on. "The only one I'm questioning right now is you, Doctor Rush."

Rush snorted. "Besides Palmer, I'm the only other person who knows what we're looking for." He pointed toward the countdown timer, visible on a repeater screen. "We have less than half a day to find what we need and get back to the ship. You need me out there."

Young studied the consoles laid out around the room. "You sure you can't stop this ship? Disable the countdown, anything?"

The scientist shook his head. "No. We're just along for the ride, for now."

"Then we may all be better off on the planet," said Young. "Maybe we need to come up with an exodus plan."

Rush nodded in agreement. "Yes, that's another reason I

should go. Someone needs to assess whether long term survival there is even an option."

The man had a point, it had to be said. "Okay," said Young, "but I want everyone to be clear that Lieutenant Scott is in charge of this mission." He got a round of nods from the assembled group. "Good. Sergeant Greer has pooled kit from all the men. Take what you need, gear up and move out."

The team dispersed; all except Scott, who hung back to have a moment alone with his commander. "What is it, Lieutenant?"

"Sir, about Eli…" he began.

Young held up a hand. "He volunteered."

Scott frowned. "He's not trained for this."

"No, he isn't," admitted the colonel, "just like a lot of the people we've got on this ship. I'm going need to know what they're made of, if we expect to survive out here."

"He's going to slow us down," insisted the junior officer.

"If he does, send him back to the gate." He gave Scott a measuring look. "If we're going to make it through this, and I don't just mean the next few hours, we're going to need everyone on board to step up."

"I understand, sir." Scott gave a reluctant nod and turned to go.

"One more thing," said Young, halting the lieutenant on the threshold. "Keep an eye on Rush."

Scott gave a nod. "Way ahead of you, sir."

Eli felt kinda weird in the mishmash of United State Marine Corps-issue digital desert camouflage and normal Eli-wear he'd been asked to don. The clothes were ill-fitting on him and scratchy, and the boots — donated by one of the other Air Force non-coms — were tight on his feet. But still, he'd have been lying if he didn't admit that despite the life-or-death nature of the sortie they were about to embark on, despite everything that had happened, he was *thrilled*.

It was a strange mix of fear and anticipation, not the kind of tingle you got from a really good slasher flick or that moment before the big drop on a rollercoaster. Eli felt it deep in the pit of his stomach, in the nerves of his arms and the tightening of his fingers. A crazy grin was threatening to erupt on his lips and he had to pull it back, pack it away. This was serious. It wasn't a day trip. They were on a *mission*.

He looked up at the shimmering puddle of light and that understanding hit him hard; and suddenly the fear got the upper hand, just for a moment. *What the hell am I doing?* screamed a voice in his head. *Am I insane? What was I thinking, volunteering for this? That's an alien planet on the other side of that thing! Someplace no human being has ever been to!*

And then the moment ebbed away, and Eli was back in control. Yeah, he was going in harm's way, he knew that. But what other choice was there? Stay on *Destiny* and watch that clock tick off the time until the gate snapped shut and sent them off to die? He thought about what would happen if they failed, imagining the *Destiny* a hundred years hence, the skeletons of the evacuees lying in its rooms and corridors, the ship like an intergalactic *Flying Dutchman*. He had do all he could to stop that from happening.

Scott walked up alongside him, carrying a heavy pack and a weapon, giving his team a final once-over. "Ready for this?" he asked.

Eli gave a crooked grin. "You think there could be dinosaurs?"

He got a wan smile in return. "Anything's possible." Scott turned to where Colonel Young was standing and threw him a salute. "We'll be back, sir," he promised.

Young returned the gesture. "Good luck."

Scott walked up to the gate, and Eli followed a step behind.

He took a deep breath of *Destiny*'s stale air, and crossed into the gateway.

CHAPTER TEN

The dry heat slammed into him like the blast from an open furnace, and Scott blinked at the glare coming off the stark white dunescape. His boots crunched on dust-covered stone and he pulled his sunglasses from his vest, stepping away from the Stargate and casting a wary look around.

He spotted the kino nearby, bobbing on the light breeze, humming to itself. Other than the machine, there was no other sign of life around the gate and the gray stone podium it stood upon. No welcoming party, no evidence of civilization, alive or dead. He took a deep breath. The air had a peculiar metallic taste to it.

Scott heard the murmur of the rippling event horizon, and turned to see Eli step out behind him and gasp. Following Wallace, the rest of the team emerged one by one, Greer and Palmer, then Rush and Franklin, with Marine Sergeant Curtis bringing up the rear. A moment after Curtis stepped out, the wormhole effect shimmered and vanished into a flash of quantum foam.

No one spoke, and Scott glanced around. He'd half-hoped that there would be something to aim for, maybe a landmark, but all he could see were the rise of the nearby dunes. The Stargate lay in a shallow basin, the yellow sun overhead beating down hard.

"Hot," he said aloud.

Eli came up alongside him, and he saw the ghost of a grin on the other man's face, his excitement at visiting a new world there for all to see. "Cool," he countered.

Scott glanced back at the group. "Franklin. Make sure we can dial back to the ship."

"Already on it," said the scientist. Franklin had the remote unit Eli had found for the kino, and he was paging through its display. According to Rush, as well as working the floating drone device, the remote would function like a hand-held dialing podium.

Palmer bent down and gathered up a handful of the white sand, letting the fine granules run away between her fingers. "This looks like gypsum. It's rare to find it in this form on Earth."

Rush nodded and unlimbered the pack on his back. "That would be good." He unzipped the bag and drew out components for their testing kit.

"Why is that good?" said Scott.

"We're looking for calcium carbonate," Palmer replied.

"Calcite," added Rush, producing a beaker and a chemical bottle.

"Gypsum is calcium sulphate, which is thirty-six percent calcium carbonate," continued the geologist. At her side, Scott saw Greer give a shrug; the Marine didn't seem that interested in turning this into a class field trip. Palmer took a measure of the sand and added it to some water from her canteen. "It dissolves," she said. Rush lit a small butane pocket torch and she took it from him, running it under the mixture she'd made.

Scott scuffed a rime of the white dust off his boot. "You saying we can use this sand to fix the scrubbers?"

"That *would* be convenient," noted Eli.

Palmer shook her head. "No."

"So, how is it good?" Scott frowned. What was it with science types? Why couldn't they just give a straight, to-the-point answer?

"It's a clear indication that the components we need may exist nearby," Rush explained.

Palmer nodded, her eyes fixed on the beaker. "For the sake of portability and efficiency, I'm hoping to find high concentration granular limestone. Hopefully, the closer we get to the source, the greater the concentration of calcium oxide in the sand will be."

Scott drew his binoculars, wondering if he would know 'high concentration granular limestone' if he actually saw it.

"We are looking for the dried lake bed or salt water body all this sand came from," Palmer continued.

Eli gave an *isn't-it-obvious?* shrug. "It's a desert,"

"Lime is formed mostly from the remains of marine organisms," said Palmer.

That caught Scott's attention. "You're saying there was life here?"

"Possibly," said Rush. "At some point in the distant past. Not likely anything we've seen before."

Nearby, Franklin had found what he needed and the gate was starting to spin, the chevrons glowing as the glyphs flashed on.

Palmer was still talking, warming to her subject matter. "The water may be gone now, but this desert was formed by water evaporating slowly on a playa floor, causing gypsum to be deposited in a fine crystalline form called selenite."

"Every day's a school day," muttered Scott and he started forward, walking up the incline of a tall dune.

"Where are you going?" called Eli.

He didn't look back. "Higher ground." He heard the heavy trudge of combat boots behind him and knew that Greer was following on.

The gate continued to dial, spinning clockwise and then anticlockwise, as the return address back to the *Destiny* locked in one symbol at a time. Eli looked away and back to Palmer, who took the reagent bottle offered by Rush and poured a few drops of a red liquid into the beaker containing her cooked solution of muddy white sand. She swirled it gently, like a wine expert prior to taking a sip. "What's supposed to happen?" he asked.

"If this sand is high enough in calcite concentration, the solution would absorb the acid I just added," said Palmer.

"Right." Eli had flunked chemistry; largely because of an incident involving a volatile formula he had pulled off the internet.

"The liquid would turn clear," added Rush.

The mixture remained a grimy crimson. "It's not," Eli said, attempting to be helpful.

With a sudden peal of sound the Stargate opened and all of them glanced up to see the event horizon solidify. Franklin waved the remote. "We're good," he said.

Eli heard Scott's voice over the radio channel and looked up to find the lieutenant and Sergeant Greer standing atop the crest of a tall dune; Scott's dark uniform stood out like a blot of ink against the ivory-colored sands. "*This is Scott,*" he was saying. "*Unfortunately, there's nothing useful in the immediate vicinity of the gate.*"

Colonel Young answered him. "*You have just under twelve hours, Lieutenant.*

Make them count."

"*We're moving out.*" Eli saw Scott give a nod, and then cast a long look around. Eli stood up and followed Scott's gaze. In every direction, off toward the distant horizon as far as the eye could see, the endless desert ranged away from them. "*Too bad we can't just use this sand,*" said the lieutenant. "*There certainly is enough of it.*"

The colonel moved through the corridors with difficulty, his legs still refusing to work the way they should, slowing him down, making every step a painful one. Much to his chagrin, he had accepted T.J.'s suggestion that he use a support, and she'd had Airman Becker cobble together a makeshift crutch for his use. He hated using it — of all the times, now was not a moment to be seen to be weak, not when strong leadership was needed — but it was either that or risk falling on his backside.

He turned the corner of a junction and hesitated, looking this way and that. The interiors of the *Destiny* had the same modular characteristics of a lot of Ancient technological design, but the downside was that if everything looked the same, it would be easy to get turned around. Looking right, he spotted a figure sitting on the floor, leaning up against one of the walls. "James?"

The lieutenant looked up at him, as if she was just noticing him for the first time. "Yes sir," she replied in a sullen, distant voice. Young was never a hard-ass about saluting, protocol and all that stuff, not when it wasn't important, but he sensed the faint, morose insolence lurking under her words.

"I'm looking for Chloe Armstrong," he told her. "You know where she is?"

James gestured to a closed hatch a short distance down the corridor. "She's still in there. Hasn't come out."

He took a step toward Chloe's quarters and paused, wondering what he was about to walk in on. He had no idea how the girl was dealing with her father's death. "How is she?"

The response he got from James wasn't the one he expected. "How is *she*?" echoed the woman, with building anger. "How about you ask *me* how *I* am?"

Young gave her a level look. They were all under a lot of stress right now and he was willing to give Vanessa a little latitude, but there were limits. "She's a civilian. You're trained for this, Lieutenant." James grimaced, and he kept on before she could speak again. "She just watched her father die."

James glared at him. "My father may as well be dead to me too, 'cause I'm stuck in some galaxy only God knows about…"

He frowned. "Yeah, okay, look—"

She kept talking. "I was supposed to go back to Iraq again, but they said Icarus was a better opportunity." Her surly manner evaporated, turning to despair. "We're all gonna die out here…"

"Hey," he said firmly. "I don't want to hear any more of that talk. We're going to work this out."

James gave him a weak, fake smile. "I'm just telling you how I am, Colonel." She stood up. "Since you asked." Before he could say any more, the lieutenant walked off down the corridor.

Young let her go; he'd have to deal with Vanessa James later, and anyone else whose manner was slipping down the road to despondency, before low morale became a problem for all of them. He hobbled to Chloe's hatch and knocked on it.

She didn't respond, and after a count of two, he entered.

The colonel found her perched on the edge of one of the beds in the sleeping alcove. She spoke without looking at him, and her voice was flat, cried out and exhausted. "I'm fine," she lied.

"No, you're not," he replied. "And neither am I. But we're all still alive because of what he did for us."

"For what it's worth—" Chloe began.

"It's worth a lot." Young insisted. "And as long as we're still here I promise you that—"

She turned to him. "Colonel, I've edited enough of my father's speeches to know what you're going to say."

He shook his head. "You don't have a clue what I was going to say, because I don't." He sighed. "I'm figuring this out as I go." After a moment, he went on. "I brought along an Ancient device from Icarus when we escaped. Communications stones. They'll allow us to talk to people back home."

Chloe gave a nod. "I know what they are."

"Good." He wondered how much of the Stargate program the senator had allowed his daughter to become privy to; but then she had been his executive assistant. *Probably has a higher security clearance than me.* "Well, I'm about to use one of them to report to my superiors on Earth and tell them our situation." He paused, framing his words. "I thought you might want to—"

She nodded again. "I want to tell her myself,"

"All right," he said. "Come with me. We've set up a chamber as a communications room."

On the U.S.S. *Hammond*'s return to Earth, everyone who had been involved in the defense of and then retreat from Icarus Base had been subjected to a thorough and exacting debrief, designed to garner as much information as possible from the officers and men for the intelligence analysts to work with. For most people, that left them feeling wrung out and ready to stand down, but David Telford had never really been the kind to let that sort of thing bother him. From his earliest days in flight school, through his service in the regular Air Force and then on to the SGC, Telford had always placed the mission ahead of everything.

Some people thought he was a hard-charger, that he was cocky. He didn't give a damn what 'some people' thought. He did his job, and did it well. If there were those who didn't like his manner, his directness, his tenacity, that was fine; because the mission was more important than them, as well.

He sat at rest in the chair before a bench of monitoring equipment, one hand resting on a whorled black stone. He had his eyes shut, but he could hear the soft click and whirr of the scanning devices, and the breathing of the two Marines standing guard across the room from him, by the door.

Telford heard the door open, and careful footsteps as someone entered. *A woman*, he guessed by the lightness of the tread and the sound of the shoes, *a civilian*.

"Is he asleep?" said a quiet voice.

He smiled slightly. "I'm meditating." Telford opened his eyes and found Doctor Mehta studying him. He'd met the attractive young Indian woman before in passing; she was a sociologist with the SGC's cultural analysis department, and

now she'd been hastily brought in on short notice to provide
a psychological viewpoint on the situation with the Icarus
survivors. It was a unique circumstance the escapees found
themselves in; if what Telford had been told was right, they
were so far from Earth that it could take centuries for them to
return home, even at hyperspatial velocities, but at the same
time they were able to communicate instantaneously.

"You've been sitting here since Rush made contact," said
Mehta. "Let somebody else take a shift."

He shook his head. While he didn't much like the idea of
his body becoming the temporary puppet of one Nicholas
Rush, should the scientist initiate communication again,
Telford wanted to be the first person to go back the other way,
to see where the survivors were and what had happened to
them. More than that, even if it had to be through the flesh
of someone else, he wanted to see what lay beyond the ninth
chevron — and what it was he'd lost the chance to explore.
"I'm not leaving this chair," he told her. "I spent the last six
months on this project, and I'll be damned if I will—"

He felt a sudden shudder run through his body.

Telford's eyes closed as though he was about to faint, but
then he opened them again widely, looking around with an
expression of surprise. Mehta had the impression of a man
who looked as if he had just woken up from a deep sleep.
"Colonel?"

"Doctor Mehta?"

"Yes sir. What's wrong?"

Telford looked down at his hands, trying them out, moving his fingers. "This is strange…" He stared at the monitor
showing the live feed from the room's camera.

There was something in the tonality of his voice and the
shift in his body language that made it immediately clear
something had changed; the closest thing she had seen to it
was in footage of sufferers of dissociative identity disorder.

"Dr. Rush, is that you?"

That question seemed to galvanize Telford's new 'passenger' and he shot her a look, "No. It's Colonel Young. And I need you to put me in a room with General O'Neill."

"All right," she began, nodding to one of the guards.

"Doctor," said Young/Telford. "I'm going to need you too."

"Sir!" Tamara rushed forward to gather up Young from where he had fallen on the deck. "Sir, I told you not to try to get up!" One second the man had been fingering one of those weird alien stones, the next he was trying to walk as if he had no wounds at all.

The colonel was lying on the floor, hissing in pain. "I'm not Colonel Young!" he snapped angrily. "The link worked. I'm Telford!"

"Right…" Tamara thought about that for a second, and then dismissed the questions churning in her mind. *Telford, not Young. Got it.* If this sort of thing was going to be happening a lot, she mused, it would take some getting used to.

"What did he do to himself?" Telford hissed, through clenched teeth.

"You… I mean *he's* got cracked ribs, more bruises than I can count and a concussion that resulted in neurapraxia…"

"That's just great…" he hissed, biting out the words. With effort, the man turned himself over and sat heavily on the floor, sweating and pale with pain and effort. "I need to get up. Can't waste time, I have to use every second I'm here, you understand, Lieutenant?"

Tamara nodded. Although she was still looking at Everett Young, Telford's manner and persona came through strongly. She turned. Chloe Armstrong had come in with the colonel, just before the 'link' had occurred. "Chloe, can you help me?" Then T.J. realized that she too was holding one of the smooth black stones. "Is that still you in there?" she added.

"I'm Doctor Mehta," came the reply. Chloe's face wore a different expression; gone was all her fear and sadness; now she seemed amazed by her surroundings.

A real doctor? Tamara wondered, hoping this person's qualifications included medicine. "Okay," she said, "Help me get him on his feet."

"General," said Young, extending his hand as his commander entered the room. "It's good to see you, sir."

O'Neill gave him an odd look, then took the hand and shook it. "Yeah, you too, Colonel. Well, not exactly *see* you…" He trailed off. "You know what I mean."

He nodded to the woman standing beside him. "Doctor Mehta kindly offered to allow Miss Armstrong the use of her…self."

The general immediately picked up on the inference in Young's words. "The senator?"

"I'm afraid he didn't make it, sir," said Young. "The fact is, I wouldn't be here talking to you if not for him. He gave his life to give the rest of us a fighting chance to survive."

"I'm sorry to hear that." O'Neill nodded gravely, and glanced at Chloe. "I had some of my favorite arguments with your father."

Chloe's slight smile appeared on Mehta's face. "Are you saying you won some?"

The general cocked his head. "That all depends on who you ask." He turned and spoke to a junior officer standing out in the corridor. "Major Green? Arrange a car for Miss Armstrong."

"Yes sir," said the major, reaching for an intercom phone.

"He'll escort you to see your mother, bring you back here when you're ready." O'Neill paused. "Please give her my condolences."

"Thank you, General," said Chloe. Young threw her a nod, and she left.

When the two of them were alone, O'Neill asked the question that Young knew was coming. "So… How bad is it?"

"It's bad," he replied.

"You should know we've already had an emergency briefing about all this," said the general. "Strom and the rest of the IOA are afraid that the attack on Icarus was just the opening shot in something bigger. They think those Lucian Alliance creeps might be making a move on us."

"Is that likely?"

O'Neill shrugged. "A day ago I would have said no way, but right now…" He paused. "The *Daedalus*, the *Odyssey*, *Sun Tzu* and *Apollo* are all on high alert. I've got people in the field trying to figure out if there's more coming, or if this was just an attack of opportunity."

"Anyone I know?"

"Jackson's out with Vala chasing up her former contacts in the Alliance. Mitchell and Teal'c are sharing what intel we have with the Free Jaffa Nation. In the meantime, Carter's on station at the moon base with the *Hammond* while we patch it up. I know she's already talked to McKay and his people about ideas for getting you all back, but don't get your hopes up."

Young's heart sank. "Sir, I don't know what Rush told you, but we may not have much time left."

Disappointment flashed on the other man's face. "Find a way."

"The ship is very old," Young insisted, "It's falling apart."

"Then repair it."

"We're trying," he said. "But even if we can get life support working, there's not much food and water—"

"Then go get some," the general retorted.

"We're not supposed to be there!" Young snapped, his irritation flaring. He paused before he spoke again. "Sir, these are the wrong people in the wrong place, and as a group they are just not qualified."

O'Neill made a face. "Please, I wasn't qualified to lead the first team through the Stargate…"

"Yes sir," Young began, trying to reinforce his point. "But I—"

The general kept talking. "I'm not really qualified for this job, either," he admitted. O'Neill gave him a hard look. "In the past dozen years or so, we've sent hundreds of teams through that thing, and let me tell you, in the grand scheme of things, *none* of us are qualified." He seemed weary for a moment. "You don't give up. That's the one rule that works out there."

Young nodded. "I never have. We're doing everything we can." He looked away, the grim truth settling in on him. "I'm just saying what it is. It may come to a point very soon where everyone on board should be given a chance to say goodbye… before it's too late."

The general was silent for a moment. "After we're done here… I can arrange a car for you, too, if you like."

Young managed a brittle smile. "I'll take you up on that, sir. Thank you."

They trudged through the lines of the sand, and Eli glanced down at his booted feet, watching a fat droplet of sweat fall from the tip of his nose and away. He blinked owlishly and tried to remember if there had been another time in his life where had felt this hot.

No. Nope. Nada. Even that time when he was eleven, when he went on vacation to Florida in the middle of summer, it had been cooler than this. The heat was like a palpable thing, radiating off the sand around him, coming up in waves. *Is it really possible for a person to melt?* he wondered. Eli didn't want to find out.

As they climbed slowly toward the top of a dune ridge, he saw Franklin blow out a labored breath and take a long swig from his canteen.

"Save it," Greer told him.

Franklin shook his head, "That's not very smart. At temperatures like these the human body needs at least—"

"Walk, don't talk." Greer shot Franklin a look that silenced him in mid-speech.

Eli licked his dry lips. "Just FYI, he's right about the whole human body and water connection...."

Scott glanced back at him from the front of the group. "Eli," he said firmly.

"I know, I know," he replied. "Walk, don't..." He gave up on finishing the sentence, breathing hard from the effort of climbing the incline. Finally, as they crested the ridge, he managed a sniff. "Oh look," he said, staring out at miles and miles of trackless white dunes. "More sand."

"This is pointless," huffed Franklin. "We should go back."

"To what?" said Palmer. "We just got here."

He looked toward Rush. "I still think we should be checking out the other planets in range of the ship."

"I still think you're *wrong*," said Rush. "The solution is here." He took a sip from his canteen. "We are going to find it."

They moved on, extending out into a single file line, crossing a wide swath of sand between the ridges. Up ahead, Greer walked the point, his rifle at his side. His pace was steady and constant, and Eli watched the Marine go, sure-footed and alert, while he slogged on, feet aching and brow filmed with sweat. Without really knowing why, Eli began to talk, half-aloud. "I know it was a mirage... But when we were walking over that last dune... I thought I saw the Statue of Liberty sticking half out of the sand." If anyone was listening to him, they didn't show it. He went on. "Just for a second there, I was all ready to yell; *damn you, damn you all to hell.*"

Rush turned and gave him an odd look.

Eli returned a weary grin. "Come on, that was funny."

"Was it?" Rush's words were the coldest thing for hundreds of miles around.

He paid no attention to the scientist's withering tone. "Because it would mean we were really on Earth... But in the future... And that apes had taken over... and buried the Statue of Liberty for some reason." It all seemed perfectly reasonable to him, but by Rush's expression, the other man clearly thought he was delirious.

"Have a drink, Eli," he told him. "You'll feel better."

That seemed like good advice, so he took it. After all, there was no telling what other things could be out here. *Tusken Raiders, giant sandworms, a double-decker bus...*

Up ahead, Scott called out. "Greer, hold up. Hold up!" Their slow train came to a stop, and as Eli drank, Scott looked out over the desert. "This isn't gonna work," he said.

"Not if we keep stopping," agreed the Marine.

Scott looked at his watch, mindful of the ever-encroaching deadline. "I'm saying we need to split up."

Greer nodded. "Fine with me."

"I agree," said Rush. "I'll take Franklin and—"

The lieutenant shook his head. "No, no, you're with me and Greer." Eli watched him range around, getting his bearings. He pointed. "The sun's been moving that way so we'll call it west... Eli, Franklin, Palmer, and Curtis, you head that way.

Palmer adjusted the straps on her pack. "We'll test every twenty minutes or so, and contact you if we find anything."

Scott gave her a nod. "After two hours, head southeast. That should take you back in the direction of the Stargate."

Eli held up a hand. "Wait a second, do we really think that splitting up is the best idea?"

"I say we head straight back," said Franklin.

Rush's lip curled at that suggestion. "There's no point in going over the same territory we just crossed."

"Or we could just stick together," Eli pressed. Splitting up was never a good idea. Anyone who had ever seen a horror movie understood *that* simple fact. Scott stepped to him and he lowered his voice. "Look, Matt," he said, using Scott's first name for the first time since they had met. "I'm sorry... I just have this really, really sick feeling that you're gonna go that way and we're gonna go this way and—"

Scott quieted him with a look. "Eli, listen to me. I need someone I can trust to lead the second team, okay? That's you. Curtis is a good soldier. A tough guy. He won't let anything happen to you."

The last thing Eli expected was to be promoted to team leader. "You're just saying that, right? The truth is, I'm slowing you down and you want to get rid of me."

He knew he was right when Scott didn't answer straight away. "I'm doing what I think will best accomplish this mission," said the lieutenant. "You asked to come. I'm telling you how you can help. Now suck it up." He patted him on the shoulder.

Fine. Responsibility. I can handle that. Eli took a deep breath and headed toward where Franklin and Palmer were standing. "Okay guys, we're going this way.

Let's move out." He gave Curtis what he thought was a serious, *we're-all-in-this-together* kind of look, but the sergeant said nothing.

"Radio if you find the lake bed," said Scott. "We'll double back, come find you."

Eli nodded, and forced a cavalier smirk. "If you see the Statue of Liberty you know what to say, right?"

Scott nodded. "Right."

Franklin and Palmer shook their heads, and as Curtis took the lead, Eli gave a last look at Greer and Rush as they stepped up to follow the officer. Scott said something, and Eli frowned as he caught it on the wind.

"Now we can make some time," said the lieutenant.

Chloe sat in the staff car's back seat and looked out of the window at the poplar trees, and the curve of the drive leading up to the house. Off to the right, just through the bushes, she could see the fence surrounding the tennis courts; no one ever really used them but her, despite all the times she'd talked to mom and dad about getting more fresh air and exercise. The Armstrong household rose up, all white walls and big windows, behind the courts. It wasn't as sprawling as their other home back in California, but Chloe had always liked the Washington place; she enjoyed the sense of age that the building had. In a peculiar way, the house had an air of permanence around it that no other place she had lived in had. Chloe always felt at rest there.

She tried to grasp a piece of that same emotion now, but it eluded her. There was a distance between what she saw around her that she couldn't fathom, an odd sense of disconnect that lay in the back her thoughts like the echo of a headache.

Major Green had gone inside ahead of her, asked her to remain in the car while he spoke with her mother. She had no doubts that her mom had already been informed about the attack on Icarus; her father kept nothing from his wife, and Patricia Armstrong knew as much about the Stargate program as Chloe did. That had been the source of the last argument they had, with her mother angrily demanding that she stay behind during her father's fact-finding mission. Mom gave her enough static about following Dad from state to state on his normal business, so a voyage to outer space was, naturally, a geometrically larger issue.

Chloe took a shuddering breath, wishing that she could be in that moment again, wishing that she could will her past self to convince her father not to go. Then none of this would have happened; but then everyone on *Destiny* would be dead.

She sighed and pressed her hand to the window. She felt the strange detachment once again; there against the glass were delicate, long fingers, the skin a rich tawny brown. Her eyes flicked up to the rear-view mirror and Doctor Mehta looked back at her from there.

I am here, she told herself. *I am not here.*

Faintly, Chloe heard someone call her name from inside the house, and she knew it was her mother. The front door suddenly burst open and Patricia Armstrong stepped out, her face marred by anxiety and dread. Major Green was behind her, reaching out but hesitant to lay a hand on the woman.

She approached the car with a look of confusion, and for a moment Chloe thought about staying inside the vehicle, afraid to face her mother, hiding behind the polarized windows. But then she reached for the handle and stepped out on to the gravel drive.

Her mother halted, her confusion deepening. She glanced at Green. "Who is this?"

"It's me," said Chloe. "I know I look different, and I sound different... But it's me."

She shook her head. "I don't know you." She looked at the major again. "I'm not interested in your wild stories, just tell me where my daughter is!"

"Mrs. Armstrong..." began Green.

"*Mom,*" said Chloe, tears prickling her eyes. "It's me." Her mother started shaking her head and Chloe pressed on. "Manny Krist," she said, pulling up a random name from her memory. "Remember him? You told me not to go out with him because he had no respect for women. I ended up throwing a glass of wine over his suit, and you clapped. We never told Dad what happened."

Her mother's face went from a moment of brittle understanding to a sudden flash of deep, deep terror. "Chloe?"

Major Green cleared his throat. "Perhaps we should go inside?"

They went to the living room, where the big bay windows had a view of the trees and the lawns, and Chloe listened to Green as he gave a terse explanation of why Patricia

Armstrong's teenage daughter now looked like a twenty-something woman from Delhi. Her mother said nothing, instead pouring herself a healthy measure of the good Scotch from a decanter. In the same motion, she drew a prescription bottle from the pocket of the elegant waistcoat she wore and shook a couple of pills into her hand.

Chloe frowned. "Mom, please," she began. "I have something to tell you." Her mother didn't respond; instead she knocked back the tablets with a long drink from the glass of whiskey. Chloe knew this behavior of old, and it made her feel sad to see it again. "Mom... *Stop.*"

Her mother seemed to become aware of what she was doing, looking down at the glass, and her cheeks colored. Neither woman noticed as Green quietly excused himself and went to stand out in the hallway.

"I'm sorry..." said Chloe's mother. "It's just ..." She halted, and it was almost as if she had to force herself to look in Chloe's direction. "The thought that you're actually on some spaceship so far away, I can't even imagine it."

"It's all true," Chloe told her.

"I remember when your father first told me about the Stargate," she continued. "He never kept secrets from me. Not in twenty-six years. He knew better."

"Mom..."

She gave her a pleading look. "Just tell me you're coming home."

Chloe's gaze dropped to the floor. "I... I don't know."

Her mother gave a shaky sigh and downed the rest of the contents of the glass in a single pull. Chloe had the terrible sense that she already knew where this was all heading.

"Mom, please," she went on. "The ship is old and damaged... We were losing air and somebody had to—"

She cut her off. "He's dead." Her mother put down the glass. "Your father is dead, isn't he?"

Chloe tried to find the words, but there was nothing

there. She couldn't even bring herself to nod; instead, the tears came.

Chloe's mother took a few steps toward her, and seemed to stumble. The emotion of the moment cut her down, and she collapsed to the floor, overcome by the pain of the terrible truth. She was silent too, the anguish so powerful it robbed her of her voice. Her daughter got down on her knees and held her tightly.

Long minutes passed in the hush of the open, airy room. There were no words strong enough to carry the depth of feeling that moved through mother and daughter.

At last, after what could have been hours, Chloe's mother whispered to her." I can't lose you too. *I can't.*"

Chloe shook her head. "You won't. I'm going to be okay." With care, she helped her mother back up, to a seat on the ornate couch, clasping her hands over hers.

Her mother dabbed her eyes and composed herself as one of the maids discreetly delivered a tray of refreshments. "Thank you, Martha," said Chloe. The maid, a woman who had known Chloe Armstrong since she was a little girl, gave her a quizzical look and walked away.

Of course, Chloe thought, *she looks at me and sees a stranger.* The moment brought the reality of her situation back into hard focus; as much as Chloe was with her mother at this moment, she was also very, very far away.

"Have some tea, Mom." She poured a cup of Chamomile and pressed it into her mother's trembling hands.

Chloe heard a tap on the doorframe and turned to see Major Green standing on the threshold. "I'm sorry. Excuse me, ma'am, but Miss Armstrong, we're going to have to leave soon."

"I have to…go back." Chloe said, with a nod.

Her mother got to her feet and gave the major a hard stare. "You get my daughter home," she demanded.

"Everyone is doing their best, I assure you," said Green.

"We're all very sorry for your loss—"

She cut him off. "Sorry... That's not good enough."

"Mom, it's not his fault."

Her mother kept her attention on the Air Force officer. "I am a personal friend of the President and of the First Lady."

"Yes, ma'am," Green nodded.

She pointed at Chloe. "You tell your superiors that if anything happens to her, I will go public with what I know about your Stargate. I don't care what happens to me. I only care about her."

"Mom," warned Chloe, worried at her parent's outburst. "I'm sorry, major, she's just upset."

But her mother was using the tone of voice she only called upon at times of utmost annoyance. "Trust me, Chloe, threats are all these people understand." She advanced on the officer. "My husband gave his life for my daughter. You get her back to me or the whole world will know what has really been going on these past years."

"Everyone is doing their best," Green repeated.

Chloe paused as she stepped back into the car, looking up to see her mother framed in the window, watching them. She glanced at Major Green. "She didn't mean what she said," Chloe told him. "My mother wouldn't do anything foolish."

Green nodded, but his expression was unreadable. "I'm sure she'll be okay, Miss Armstrong."

He closed the door after her, but instead of walking around to the driver's side, the major took out a cell phone and dialed it. He turned to face the house, his back to Chloe so she couldn't see what he was saying.

CHAPTER ELEVEN

Telford was laboring as he made his way down the corridor, grimly soldiering on after Lieutenant Johansen and the Armstrong girl — *correction, Doctor Mehta*, he reminded himself — as the medic led them deeper into the alien ship.

The colonel wasn't sure what he had expected to see aboard the vessel, this *Destiny*, according to Rush's translations. Maybe something that resembled the crystalline Ancient technology of the city-ship Atlantis, or the metallic structure of Asgard design. *Destiny* was nothing like that; it had an old, engineered feel to it. When he tried to put a shape on his first impression of the craft, he found himself imagining a ship built not with an eye towards esthetics and artistry for its own sake, but instead one made by craftsmen and engineers to do a difficult job of work. The interiors reminded him of submarines, of steelworks and garages, of aged machines powered by steam and coal and fire.

Telford tried to take it all in, but the lances of pain that shot through him with each footfall made it hard to concentrate. Even though he was feeling Young's injuries at second hand, the body he had temporarily usurped wasn't about to let him use it without making him pay for it. He gritted his teeth, dealing with the hurt.

Mehta was looking around. "Where is everyone?"

Johansen pointed ahead, down the corridor. "We've got all able-bodies searching the ship for anything that might have carbon dioxide sequestration properties to fix the scrubbers. The rest of the evacuees are in the crew quarters we found."

The corridor widened into a larger space, and Telford saw the distinctive shape of a Stargate at the far end of the chamber. The gate was active and the colonel noted straight away that the design of the vast metal ring was slightly different from others he'd seen. He recognized two familiar faces from Icarus Base — Adam Brody and Lisa Park — standing in front of a curved console. As they approached, the Stargate shut down with a shriek of noise, and a pair of vents in the floor either side of it discharged a blast of steam into the air.

Brody threw him a look. "Ah, Colonel. We were able to dial out to the planet again."

Johansen stepped in before Telford could answer. "Colonel Young and Chloe are using the communication stones. This is Colonel Telford and Doctor Mehta from Homeworld Command."

Brody blinked. "Uh… right, okay." He gave the colonel a measuring glance. "This might get confusing."

"Next time I'll wear a sign around my neck telling you who I am," Telford retorted. "Did you make radio contact with the off-world team?"

"Yes, nothing to report yet," said the scientist. "They've split up to cover more ground."

"How much time before the ship jumps back to faster-than-light?" said Mehta.

Park pointed at a screen where a series of Ancient digits flickered past. "Roughly nine hours."

Telford considered this. "Dial out every twenty minutes. Maintain regular contact with them."

The woman made a negative noise. "We do have power issues to be aware of, sir. Dialing the gate is a significant drain on what seem to be limited resources at this point."

He ignored another jolt of searing pain from Young's injury and braced himself. "Right now, the away mission is priority one."

Johansen heard the tightness in his voice. "Sir…"

He waved her away. "I'm fine," he insisted.

Mehta moved to look over the console. "I understand there are other Stargates in range, is that right?"

Brody nodded. "Four other addresses came up in the system, but we seem to be locked out from here."

"Have you tried working around it?"

Park folded her arms. "Doctor Rush didn't think that was a good idea." From her expression, it was clear the woman didn't fully agree.

"I think it makes sense to know what the options are," said Telford. "Do what you can to learn more about those alternates."

Brody spoke up again. "There has to be a good reason why these addresses are being disqualified."

Telford eyed him. Perhaps Colonel Young was willing to let the civilians call the shots, but he wasn't about to do the same. "In case I wasn't being clear, I was giving you an order. If there are good reasons, find out exactly what they are." He turned to Johansen. "Okay, let's keep moving, I want to see more."

The medic frowned. "You really should rest."

"Lieutenant…" he began, a warning in his voice.

"Sir, Colonel Young's body needs time to recover," she insisted.

"Just give me something for the pain."

Johansen shook her head. "The body feels pain for a reason, sir, I'd rather not mask it—"

"Just do it, Lieutenant," he snapped. Insubordination seemed to be spreading like a rash around here. "From the sounds of things, you need my help."

She relented. "Yes sir. My med-pack is back in the colonel's quarters. If you'll come with me?"

Telford gave a tight nod and walked stiffly after her. *Young better damn well take more care of my skin than he has of his own,* thought the colonel.

It wasn't one of the best residential districts outside of D.C., but it was better than most, maybe good enough for a generous critic to call it 'low-rent' — even if the rent actually wasn't that low. After the argument over his acceptance of the Icarus Base posting, Emily had finally made good on an old threat and moved out. Young didn't like this place; she deserved better. But as he was coming to realize, she had deserved better from him for a long time.

The staff car pulled to a halt and Young got out. His chaperone was one of O'Neill's men, a serious-looking major named Peterson, and the officer intercepted him before he could walk away.

"I'll go up." Peterson jerked his thumb at the apartment block. "I'll shout down when she's ready to see you."

If she'll see me, you mean. Young nodded and stood against the car, waiting. He glanced down, and it was Telford's face that looked back up at him from the reflection in the window. He wondered how the hell he was going to explain this to his wife. Would it be better for him to pretend to *be* Telford? Tell Emily he was 'passing on a message from Everett'? Or would that just be a kind of cowardice?

He blew out a breath. He could never lie to her. Emily was his wife, and she knew him better than anyone else, better than he knew himself. *She would know.* She would know it was him, no matter what face he was wearing.

He closed his eyes and tried to picture her. Tried to picture her smiling at him. It was hard to frame the moment in his mind, and after a while he sighed and gave up.

"Colonel," said Peterson, walking back down the steps toward him. He said nothing else, just gave Young a nod and a look that seemed to say *good luck, you'll need it.*

He took the stairs carefully, resisting the urge to break into a jog, grateful for the moment to be free of the pains of the injuries he'd sustained on the *Destiny*. His wife was at the door, and she seemed unsure of what to make of the man coming toward her.

He couldn't help but smile when he saw her. "Emily…"

Without thinking, he reached out to embrace her, but she backed off.

"Don't," she said, eying him warily.

For a moment he couldn't be sure of the reason why; *is she suspicious because she's seeing Telford, or because she knows it's me?*

"All I said was that you can come in," she continued, and stepped aside.

He gave a nod, the smile fading, and walked in. Inside, the apartment was compact but warm, and everything in it was Emily. He sat opposite her across a low table and felt a pang of guilt, of loss.

"Are you going to explain all this to me?" she said.

"I will," he said, and he did. Over the next twenty minutes he told her what his job with the Air Force actually entailed, where Icarus Base really was, what had happened there, all of it. Every piece of fantastic truth and grim reality. He told her things that nobody else could possibly know about them both, intimacies shared that only Everett Young could speak of.

When he was done, Emily's silence stretched away from him. He could see her struggling to process it all, daring herself to believe it.

She shook her head. "It's just... It's ridiculous. You're supposed to be my husband? You come here and tell me this...fantasy story?"

"It's true," he said simply, "All of it. Every word. I would never lie to you, Emily."

His wife heard the honesty in his voice and clasped her hands together. "Okay. Let's say it is true. Why are you here now? Why are you putting me through this?"

The question struck the breath from him. He had thought the reason was obvious. "I'm here because I wanted to..." He tried to form the words *say goodbye*, but he couldn't do it.

After a moment, Young shook his head and stood up.

This is never going to work. He'd made a grave error coming here, reopening this wound again. "I'm sorry. I…" He walked toward the door, then halted. "I want you to know that I didn't chose the job over you. Not when I left, and not now. I love you, Emily."

Young walked down the stairs in a daze, feeling hollow inside. *This was a mistake,* he told himself, *all you've done is create more pain for both of you. It would have been better for her to get a visit from an Air Force pastor and a couple of men with a folded flag.*

He crossed toward the car, where Peterson was waiting. The major looked at him as he approached. "I'm guessing it didn't go well."

Young's stony look was all the answer he gave; but then he noticed Peterson looking past him. He turned to find his wife had followed him down. The major got into the car to give them a moment of privacy.

He opened his mouth to speak, but Emily spoke first. "How does this change anything?"

Another unexpected question. "What do you mean?"

"Let's say I believe all this," she went on. "I don't really, but even if I did…

You *did* choose. You chose to go."

He shook his head. "I didn't choose *this.*"

Accusation was sharp in her tone. "You knew there was a chance you wouldn't be coming back."

"I am coming back, Em," he insisted. The words sounded weak in his ears.

"No, don't give me the party line," she retorted. "I'm not your troops. You wouldn't have come here like this to say goodbye if you really thought there was a chance."

He wanted her to believe him. "I'm doing everything I can. I'm going to do everything I can. I want nothing more than to get back here to be with you." He took a breath. "I want nothing more than for you to be here for me when I do come home. I'm just saying… I don't know when that will be."

Emily folded her arms and shook her head "You made your choice, Everett. I made mine. Nothing has changed. I really do hope you're going to be okay."

"Em…" He reached out a hand to touch her arm.

She stepped back, out of his reach. "Please. Let me go."

He stood and said nothing as she turned and walked back into the apartment.

Scott rested his hands on the assault rifle slung across his chest as Rush bent down in the sand before him. Working in the shadows cast by Greer and the lieutenant, the scientist was running the sample test again, swirling the blood-colored mixture of heated sand and acid reagent.

Rush held up the glass flask and sighted through it. The liquid within remained resolutely red.

"Struck out again," muttered Greer. "How many is that now?"

Scott ignored the comment. "All right, come on. We keep going."

The scientist paused for a drink, tipping back his canteen to take a long draught.

"You better save some of that," Scott warned him. "We got a way to go yet."

Rush screwed the cap back on to the bottle and clipped it to his belt. "We need to slow down."

Scott shook his head, walking up to the top of the closest dune. "What we need is to cover more ground."

The other man sighed. "It's going to be impossible to maintain this pace on the way back."

"Maybe for you," said Greer, with a sniff.

Rush shot a narrow-eyed glare at the Marine. "Both the lieutenant and yourself are boys playing soldier. But I've got no interest in that game."

Scott saw Greer stiffen at the insult. "I'm not playing anything," he said firmly. "I'm trying to save the lives of everyone aboard that ship."

Rush cast around. "If you continue at this pace, we're going to die out here." He upturned the beaker in his hand and angrily shook out the solution inside, spilling it across the sand in a ruddy patch.

Scott looked away. "Maybe we will—" He began; he suddenly trailed off as he caught sight of a strange swirl of sand blowing toward them. It looked like a tiny dust devil, and for a second Scott was certain that it was moving *against* the direction of the breeze over the tops of the dunes.

Rush was still talking, his irritation rising. "Look around, man. You're light-years from the admiring eyes of your father, or your drill sergeant or whoever's approval it is you're trying to get with all this macho posturing—"

Greer rocked forward and grabbed the scientist by the shoulders, dragging him to his feet. "That's enough outta you. Get up and move, *now*."

"Get your hands off me," snapped Rush, pushing Greer away. His temper flaring, the Marine immediately leveled his weapon at the other man.

Scott turned back from the sight of the swirl. "Hey, did you see that?"

"What?" Greer snarled.

The lieutenant's eyes widened as he saw how the situation was turning. "Sergeant, lower your weapon," he ordered, and Greer reluctantly obeyed.

"Did you see something out there?" asked the Marine, still glaring at Rush.

Scott looked back in the direction of the blowing sand, but the eddy of white dust was gone. It had to have been a mirage. "I don't know... nothing." Scott shook his head, dismissing the thought. "Let's move on," he ordered.

"One hour," insisted Rush, determined to have the last

word. "Then we start circling back."

Scott shrugged. "Fine. One hour."

The three men continued their course to the northwest, leaving behind the depression in the dune where Rush had scooped out his sample, and the streak of red fluid across the white sand.

Unseen by any of them, a complex, ever-turning matrix of spinning mineral particles rode up the curve of the dune, following the path they had taken. The swirl of sand moved over the patch of liquid, back and forth, dithering by it.

Then swiftly, far faster than the sunlight would have dried it out, the moisture was drawn off beneath the passage of the tiny funnel of dust.

With the fluids absorbed, the swirling sands drifted away, shadowing the footprints of Scott and the others.

Tamara opened the door to the sleeping chamber being used by Colonel Young, and Telford hobbled past her. His irritation was increasing by the moment, and his pain was doing the same, even if he refused to admit it to her.

The man's behavior was reckless; Young's body had suffered severe injuries and it needed time to heal. Telford was treating it like a rental car, pushing it too hard with no regard to the consequences. And when the communication was cut, it would be Young who would have to deal with those consequences, not Telford. She frowned. Tamara Johansen wasn't the type to buck the chain of command if she could help it, but right here and right now, she was the chief medical officer aboard the *Destiny*, and that gave her the right to protect her patients. No, scratch that, she was the *one and only* medical officer aboard the *Destiny*.

Telford rolled up his sleeve and offered her a bicep. Tamara rooted around in her pack, quickly loading an injector pen.

Doctor Mehta, who had followed them back, shot a look at the drug ampoule she was using and frowned. Before Mehta had a chance to comment, Tamara stabbed the injector into the arm and discharged it.

Telford blinked, suddenly looking confused and faint. "What have you...?" he managed; then the life went out of him and he slumped. Tamara caught the body — *Young's body* — and lowered it carefully to the bed.

Mehta gave her an accusing look "That was supposed to be for the pain. What did you give him?"

"A strong sedative, which we are desperately short on and I should not have had to use in this case, just so that Colonel Young can return to a body in working condition," she snapped back.

"You're out of line, Lieutenant," Mehta began.

Tamara shook her head. "Disregarding the health of another human being is out of line. I'm well within my rights as ranking medical officer. He'll be out for an hour or two."

As she made to leave, Mehta's expression became animated. "Wait! What am I supposed to do in the meantime?"

Tamara shrugged. "Honestly, I don't care. I have other patients to attend to. Unless you can help, just try not to get in anyone's way." She stepped out and let the hatch close behind her.

They could try to court-martial her if they wanted, she reflected, but considering she was already technically supposed to be out of the Air Force by now, and the fact she was a hell of a long way from any board of inquiry, Tamara wasn't going to let it bother her.

Eli reflected that his new role as 'squad leader' wasn't really being taken that seriously by Palmer and Franklin, and Sergeant Curtis seemed only capable of responding to him with a nod or a grunt. He started wondering if having a name for their group might have helped strengthen the bonds of shared duty. Maybe 'Bravo Team', or 'Unit Delta', that kind of thing.

"Stop here," said Palmer, and the group halted.

"Yeah," Eli added quickly. "Here. That's, uh, right."

The geologist ran the test for the umpteenth time; water, sand and heat, red acid stuff into the mix. Swoosh around the beaker and wait. And wait. *And wait…*

Palmer shook her head and sighed. "I take it that's not good?" said Eli.

"No," she retorted irritably. "Red means bad."

He turned and looked over at Franklin and Curtis, who were perched on the lip of a dune, conferring over the kino remote. The drone itself was sitting in his backpack, inactive and inert for the moment. Eli wondered how powerful the suite of sensors inside the device were; if only they had a manual, he was willing to bet it could find the limestone they needed on its own. Of course, right now the thing was little better than an RC toy. "Hey guys, another negative over here," he told them, walking over. "I'll radio Scott and tell him we're moving on."

Franklin didn't look up from the remote's screen. "Yeah, that's not what's going down."

That stopped him dead. "It's not?"

The two men stood up, and suddenly Eli felt an old and hatefully familiar sense of intimidation. "No," said Curtis.

"There are four other viable addresses in this thing." Franklin waggled the remote in his hand. "I think I found an override that will allow us to dial them from here."

"Yeah, but—"

Curtis cut off Eli's reply. "Look around. This planet is a dead zone."

He tried again. "But—"

"We should've been trying to dial these other planets from

the start," said Franklin.

Eli held up a hand. "Doctor Rush said that—"

Clearly, neither of them wanted him to finish a sentence. "We don't care what Rush said," Curtis replied.

Franklin nodded. "We don't trust him."

Eli looked to Palmer, wondering if that *we* included her as well. "He doesn't want us to all die."

It clearly *did*. "That doesn't mean we trust him to make the right decisions," she said.

"You too?" He frowned. "But what about the lake bed?"

She threw up her hands. "It could be hundreds of miles from here. We could be blowing our only chance of finding a decent place to evacuate to."

Franklin took a step forward. "Maybe the ship did bring us here because there's lime on this planet. For all we know, the Ancients had a way of locating it that we don't. But right now, that's not helping us."

Curtis was nodding. "For that matter, I'm sure they could have stopped the ship for more than twelve hours to find it, and recover it with the proper tools."

The other scientist was nodding too. "The fact is, the Ancients wouldn't have let the life-support system get that screwed up in the first place. Rush is set on fixing the ship. He's deaf to any other logic. We need to find a planet that we can survive on." He gave Eli a hard look. "This might be our last chance."

"That ship jumps to FTL, we could be dead before it drops out again," Curtis added.

Franklin pocketed the control pad. "We're going to the gate. I'm going to dial out and see what's there."

Eli shook his head. In a day that had more than its fair share of bad ideas, this was one to put right at the top of the list. He moved toward Franklin, drawing up as much of an assertive tone as he could muster. "Give me the remote," he demanded. Curtis had his gun raised in an instant, drawing a bead on Eli's chest. "Or not," he amended hastily. "That was optional."

"You give me the kino," said the sergeant.

"I'm supposed to be in charge," Eli piped. "Isn't this mutiny?"

Curtis's lip curled. "Not sure that applies on the other side of the universe. Now give it up."

It was like Eighth Grade lunch hour all over again. Eli glumly reached into his pack and removed the kino. Franklin snatched it from him and turned it over in his hands, studying it.

"Besides," Curtis continued, "my orders were to keep searching and then head to the gate." He looked at Palmer. "Are we done?"

She nodded. "We're done."

The sergeant lowered his weapon. "Go ahead and tell Scott we're headed for the gate, if you want." He gave a sneer. "My radio doesn't seem to be working." He set off, and Palmer fell in behind him.

Franklin glanced over his shoulder as he followed along. "We'll let you know if we find a planet everyone can survive on."

"That remote is our only way back to the ship!" Eli fumed.

Curtis kept walking. "Guess you'll have to get another one."

Scott took the tail-end charlie position, trailing Rush while Greer, as ever, took point. Rush was laboring now, panting and trying hard not to keep diving for his canteen every few minutes. The lieutenant kept one eye on him, but for the most part his attention was being pulled back the way they had come. There was a nagging feeling in the back of his head, the same sort of weird animal sense that warned you someone was watching you, following you.

Despite the oppressive heat, Scott shivered and he turned to look behind him. There was nothing out there, no one. Only the dunes and a swirl of sand twisting along the ridge-line, blown by the wind.

"Something wrong?" The scientist had halted and was staring at him.

Scott looked away. "No. It's fine."

Rush shrugged and bent down, unlimbering his sampling kit. "Well, then. This is as good a place as any to stop and test."

They stood in silence as Rush performed the analysis once more; and once more the red fluid did not turn clear. Rush shook his head in disappointment.

Scott adjusted his pack. "Okay. We've got to keep going."

Rush made no attempt to get up. Instead, he sat back on the sand, exhaustion heavy on his sunburned face, and took a drink before offering it to Scott. "Here. Take it. You look like you need it."

"I have my own," replied the lieutenant. "Come on. We're burning daylight."

"The daylight's burning us," replied Rush, shaking his head. "I can't go on. I know it's here. You have to find it." With effort, he got to his feet and put his canteen in Scott's hand. "Go on, take it."

Scott hesitated, on the verge of giving the man a rebuke; but then he checked himself. Rush was right, he *couldn't* go on. One look at him made that clear. The lieutenant accepted the water bottle, and started packing up the testing gear.

"We're just going to leave him here?" said Greer.

"I'll head back to the gate," Rush told him.

Scott gave a shake of his head. "Greer, go with him."

The Marine shot him a look. "What? I'm not leaving you alone."

"Make sure he gets back alive," Scott went on.

Greer snorted. "What difference does it make?"

The lieutenant picked up the pack and shouldered it. "Because if I don't find what we need, he's the one who's going to work out some other way to save his own ass...and yours along with it."

Greer shook his head. "You're losing it."

"I'll be okay," he replied. "You have your orders, Master Sergeant."

The radio crackled at that moment, and Eli Wallace's voice issued out from the speaker. "*Scott, this is Eli. Come in. If you can hear me, please respond.*"

Eli sounded scared. *Not good*, Scott thought. "This is Scott, what's up?"

The reply was breathy, as if Eli was walking and talking at the same time. "*We have a problem here. Franklin, Curtis and Palmer have given up and are headed back to the gate to try dialing the other addresses in the remote.*"

Rush stood up in alarm. "They have no idea what they could be walking into."

"*They have the kino,*" added Eli, hearing him over the open channel.

"There are a myriad of dangers the kino data cannot foresee," snapped Rush.

"*They don't think we're going to find the lime here. They want to look for another planet that will support life.*"

Scott listened, thinking. *An exodus site?* The idea had merit, but not if they went about it in some half-assed, screw-the-orders way.

"They're going to get themselves killed," Rush was saying.

Greer leaned in. "Don't we need that remote to get back to the ship?"

"Well... When we're past due, they'll dial in to check on us," Scott told him "We can radio for another one."

"That's not the point," maintained Rush. "The fact is, a few hours is nowhere near enough time to determine if a planet is safe, let alone viable for sustaining life. I promise you, the ship is our only real hope of ever getting home."

Scott nodded. "Greer, you stop them if you can. I'll go on, turn back when I have to. *Go.*"

Greer gave a sullen nod, then scowled at Rush and pointed in the direction of the Stargate "You lead."

Rush gave a hollow sigh and started walking, and Scott turned away, heading out into the endless dunes.

He walked on and on, across the shimmering fields of burning white.

The heat was almost unbearable, and it seemed like a cowl of heavy wool around him, stifling him, strangling his every footstep. It was hard to breathe, and each lungful of the strange, dry air felt like it burned him inside, sucking the moisture from his tissues.

Scott stopped for a small drink from his precious reserves of water, swilling the tepid, blood-warm fluid around his mouth. The urge to tip back the whole canteen and drain it dry was strong, but he resisted it. Instead, he paused to rest, turning in place to survey his surroundings.

A slight gust of wind pulled at the flaps of his duty jacket, stirring up scatterings of sand around his boots. Scott looked in the direction it had come from and saw the same swirl of dust he'd seen before. It came closer, dancing over the curvature of the dune, no taller than the height of a small child. He froze, unsure of what he was seeing. Was it some kind of atmospheric phenomena, some quirk of this alien world's environment? *Was it…alive?*

The swirl—he didn't know how else to think of it—whipped around his ankles and he felt the faint prickle of static electricity. Then it was moving, back and forth, drifting to a halt in front of him.

Something seemed to be attracting it to him. Scott glanced at the canteen in his hand and held it out at arm's length.

Carefully, he let a few drops of water spill out onto the dune, and took a step back.

The swirl of sparkling sand moved again, spinning toward the patch of water, dancing around it. As Scott watched, the liquid vanished, drawn into the vortex of the tiny dust-devil. *Thirsty little guy,* he thought. *Just like me.*

The lieutenant carefully moved into a crouch, bending closer to get a better look. When he was a hand's length from it, the swirl suddenly spun away, drawing more sand up with it as it went. Scott frowned as the thing retreated and his gaze dropped.

The sand had blown away, forming a shallow depression in the lee of the dune, and there beneath the white dust was the pale, ashen face of a dead man, a priest's collar visible at his neck.

Scott's shock was a physical jolt, and he threw himself back from the sight, gasping out a dry, crack-throated wheeze. He blinked and forced himself to look again; there was nothing there but a drift of bone-white granules. Scott shuddered and gathered his wits, taking a long breath before getting back to his feet. He was more tired than he realized; the fatigue was starting to play tricks on him.

Off toward the horizon he found the swirling dust-devil vortex once more, this time dancing to and fro along the top of a sandy ridge. As he watched, it dissipated and vanished.

After a long moment, he hefted the pack and began to walk in that direction.

Rush took a step and staggered on a loose drift of sand, wavering on the edge of losing his balance. He grimaced and lurched forward, regaining his stability in an inelegant fashion.

Behind him, Greer trudged on, sure-footed and steady. Rush wondered if the Marine felt the heat as much as he did; *probably,* he reasoned, *but he's just too obtuse to show it.*

"I need water," Rush told him.

Greer made no move to answer his request. "We're almost there. Keep walking."

"I guess I assumed since I gave Scott my canteen, that we'd share."

Greer snorted. "You were wrong about that."

What made you think you'd get any succor from this man, Nicholas? He heard his wife asking the question as they walked on in silence. "I should have known…" muttered Rush.

Greer eyed him. "Yeah, you think you know me pretty well, don't you?"

Rush gave a humorless chuckle. "Remember, Sergeant, I helped choose the personnel for Icarus Base. I read your file. You were not on my list, by the way."

"You think I care?" came the reply.

Rush looked back at him. "You seem to think that because you were born into impoverished circumstances, it gives you the right to be angry at the world."

"You think that's why I'm angry?" Greer's voice took on a dangerous edge.

He gave a noncommittal shrug. "Without the military, you'd probably be in jail, or worse."

Greer made a spitting sound. "That's what all you rich people think."

"Rich?" Rush turned and laughed at him. "My father worked in a shipyard, Sergeant." His temper was rising. "I earned a scholarship to Oxford while I was working two jobs. I earned the right to make decisions without having to explain myself to you or anyone else."

It was Greer's turn to shrug. "Doesn't look like it to me."

The man's tone made his annoyance flare and he halted in front of him "I need water," he demanded.

"Keep walking." Greer came face to face with him, daring Rush to argue.

Enough was enough; if this thug wasn't going to let him

drink, then he would have to take what he needed. Rush pushed forward and grabbed at the canteen.

Greer blocked him. "Don't ever touch me!" he snarled, and shoved back.

Rush's response was immediate, and — judging by the millisecond of shock on the Marine's face — a lot more aggressive than Greer had expected.

The two of them tangled in a push-and-shove match, each pressing against the other; but Greer's training gave him the edge, and the sergeant knocked Rush's leg out from under him, sending the scientist over and sliding down the side of the dune. Furious, Rush scrambled back, trying to get to his feet. He looked up and found the muzzle of Greer's rifle an inch from his forehead.

"Do that again," growled the Marine, "and I will put a bullet in your face and forget about you."

Rush rose slowly. "You need me. Otherwise, I suspect you would have done that by now."

Greer seemed to be considering it; then in the next moment his let the rifle drop on its strap and started walking again.

"Give me some water," Rush grated.

The Marine did not. "Right now, I'm praying to God above that dehydration will shut you the hell up. Walk, or die here. Take your pick, Mister Decision-Maker."

Rush's eyes narrowed, and after a moment, he began to walk.

Eli came to the top of the dune just as the Stargate flashed open, and with care he picked his way back down the slope of shifting sands. He saw Curtis and Palmer looking over Franklin's shoulder as he worked the remote. The kino zipped through the open wormhole and vanished.

"Looks like it's worth a shot to me," said Franklin.

Curtis nodded and hefted his rifle. "Let's do it."

Eli tried to call out, and the first time all his parched throat let out was a squeak of dry air. He was on the verge of stumbling over, his stamina all but spent, his body pushed way beyond its physical limits. He tried again. "Wait! Stop!"

They ignored him. "It's not perfect but it's better than here." Franklin was reading planetary data off the remote. "Vegetation, water, air…" He looked up at Eli as he came panting toward them. "It's not too late to come with us."

He shook his head, breathing hard. "Don't… Don't do it…"

But they were already walking away. "We'll dial back as soon as we know it's safe to evacuate everyone."

"You'll never get home…" Eli called after them.

Curtis was taking the lead, and Palmer was a step behind as they walked up the stone ramp leading to the gate. "You don't know that," Franklin retorted. "Maybe there's a way to use the gate system to connect the dots."

Dots? What dots? Eli blinked. Right now, the only dots he could see were those in front of his eyes. He gave a shaky gasp. "There has to be a reason the ship locked out those addresses!"

Curtis and Palmer disappeared through the puddle, and Franklin gave a dismissive wave of the hand, stepping up after them.

The sharp crack of a gunshot sang through the air and splinters of stone exploded in front of Franklin's feet. Eli spun about to see a figure atop one of the nearby dunes; Sergeant Greer, his rifle raised to his shoulder, his aim steady.

Eli turned back to Franklin and saw the train of thought on his face. The man looked at Greer, at the Stargate, back to Greer again. "Don't do it!" Eli warned.

Behind them, Rush came scrambling up the sandbank just as Franklin bolted for the open wormhole. "Shoot him!" shouted the scientist.

The gun barked a second time and Eli saw a sudden flower of red blossom on Franklin's shoulder. The man gave a thin, reedy scream, twisted and fell in a heap on the ramp. The shiny metal remote pad fell from his fingers with a clatter.

Eli ran as quickly as he could toward the gate. Franklin was pale and semi-conscious, bleeding heavily from the glancing bullet hit, but still alive. He hesitated, unsure of what to do, while ahead of him the gate gave a shriek of air and deactivated.

A shadow fell across him and Eli looked up to see Greer and Rush. "Why'd you do that?" he demanded.

"He told me to," said Greer, nodding noncommittally toward Rush.

"We just saved his life," insisted the scientist.

Eli found that a little hard to take. "By shooting him?"

"He'll live," said Greer, dismissive.

"You just stranded Curtis and Palmer." Eli pointed at the gate.

"We can send them another remote," Greer bent to recover the device Franklin had been using. "I wasn't taking any chances."

Abruptly, Eli realized they were a person short. "Where's Scott?"

"Still looking for limestone," said Rush.

Eli felt his gut tighten and he checked his wristwatch; he'd set a timer before they'd left the *Destiny*. "It's almost half-time," he said. "We have less than six hours left before the ship leaves."

Greer grabbed his radio. "Lieutenant Scott, this is Sergeant Greer, come in."

Eli frowned. "I hope he's turned back by now."

"Lieutenant, come in," Greer repeated. The only reply was static.

Rush bent down and began to work on Franklin's wound. "He's either out of radio range or is lying face down in the sand. Dead, or soon to be."

Eli made a choking noise. "Yeah, that's the spirit. Think positive."

Greer checked his rifle and slung it over his shoulder, dropping the rest of his pack on the stone ramp. "I'm going back for him."

Rush didn't look up. "That's suicide."

"I'm not leaving him out there."

Eli nodded. "I'll go with you."

Greer shook his head. "You're just going to slow me down. *Again*."

Eli's shoulders sagged. "Right…"

"Someone needs to get this man back to the ship," Rush broke in. "He needs proper medical attention."

The Marine gave Eli an appraising look, then handed him the remote. "Dial," he said simply, then indicated Rush with a jut of the chin. "He can take Franklin back. You wait here for me."

"I can do that." Eli studied the remote, remembering the activation sequence. "You have five hours and change to find him and get back here."

"It has not been a pleasure knowing you," muttered Rush.

Greer's lips thinned and he reached for the holster at his belt. He pulled out his pistol and offered the weapon to Eli.

He took it gingerly. Eli had played enough *Call of Duty* games to know a Beretta handgun when he saw it; it was heavier than he expected. "What do I need this for?"

"Just in case," said the Marine evenly.

"In case of what?" Greer began to walk away, and he called after him. "I don't even know how to fire this thing!"

The other man stopped, took the gun and worked the slide to put a bullet in the chamber. Then he flipped off the safety catch and cocked the hammer before slapping it back into Eli's palm. Now all he needed to do was pull the trigger.

"You better be here," said Greer.

Eli gave a nod. "I will," he promised.

The Marine broke into a loping run and swiftly climbed the dune slope before disappearing from sight.

Eli held the pistol, the metal warm in his hands. He could smell the lubricant oil on it. He slowly turned to Rush. "I have a gun," he said firmly.

The scientist rolled his eyes and went back to bandaging Franklin's wound.

CHAPTER TWELVE

Matthew Scott walked on.

It had become a mechanical, mindless process, one foot in front of the other, over and over, trudging across the ivory sandscape. As he struggled to sustain his consciousness, it became a contest of sheer applied will. His training, his stamina, his spirit, any combination of all these things, they were the force keeping his feet moving, long past the point where his body should have failed.

And the heat; the punishing, endless heat tore into Scott through his sweat-soaked uniform. Dimly, he could feel it killing him by inches.

At the edges of his vision there were blurs, ghostly shapes that could have been heat-haze mirages or specks of dirt caught in his eyes. He sensed a strange pressure in the back of his skull and something pulled him, compelled him to turn around. He did so, stumbling and righting himself before he could fall.

There was no shock this time. It didn't seem to register with Scott that what he was seeing was wrong, that it was utterly impossible. The distances of time and space made it so. He was *here*; he could not be *there*, where ever *there* was.

Father George was pacing him, step for step. He saw how the priest's careful tread was placing him in the boot prints Scott was leaving behind, the winding snake of his route crossing over the ridges of the white dunes.

He blinked, looked away. *No.* He wasn't there. It was an illusion, just like seeing the old man's face beneath the sand. It was his mind, starved of water, the dehydration attacking his reason.

Scott's gaze rose from the sands around his feet to see ahead of him. On the next rise over, the swirling vortex of dust glittered as it caught the hard sunlight; then it was gone again and Scott could not be certain that it was ever actually there. He shook his head hard, sweat flicking away from his brow, and blinked.

He felt the presence again, heard the crunch of the mineral sand beneath the soles of sensible black church shoes. Father George was at his side now, still matching him step for step, walking in parallel. He looked calm and collected, as if he were out for a walk on some cool summer evening, utterly out of place in this searing furnace of a landscape.

Scott halted and looked at the man. He seemed solid, tangible. The priest walked on a few steps, then seemed to notice he was going on alone. He stopped and gave Scott a paternal smile.

Then he spoke. "You must keep going, my boy." His voice was rich and resonant. "Don't give up."

The emotion that came to him first was an ugly one, a rise of sullen frustration. "I don't need you to tell me that," he croaked. Scott fumbled for his canteen and found it, working off the sand-caked cap and raising it to his lips. He found only a little water in there, and savored a mouthful of it. The priest's smile remained, and he mirrored Scott's actions, reaching into the pocket of his jacket to produce a silver hip flask. He raised it in a wry gesture, like a toast, and took a long pull. Scott thought he could detect the ghost of a scent on the wind; the peaty odor of strong whiskey.

"I'm not going to let anyone else down the way I let you down," he husked, looking away from the figure. "You really don't have to follow me around to remind me."

With a sigh of effort, Scott began walking again, and moved on toward the distant ridgeline, past the priest, who favored him with a sad smile.

He spoke again as Scott left him behind. "He has his plan for all of us."

The transition ended, Young's sight of the inside of the comms lab in the Homeworld Command facility blinking away, and darkness sweeping in. He remembered the last thing he had felt; Jack O'Neill shaking his hand, the concerned look in the general's eyes; then the pain came back, washing slowly over him like a tide of needles, and he hissed, opening his eyes.

"Colonel Telford?" Tamara Johansen was by his side, worry clear on her face.

"Young," he corrected. "It's me, T.J." He blinked. *Back again*, he thought. He took a breath of air and tasted the stale, coppery flavor of it; the CO_2 problem hadn't been solved while he was gone, then. Young looked around, seeing the now-familiar steely walls of a *Destiny* crew cabin.

"Glad to have you back, sir," said Tamara. She sounded like she meant it.

He stretched and felt an odd lethargy in his limbs, a tiredness that dragged on him like a heavy weight. "Why do feel like I've been drugged?"

"It was for your own good, sir," said the medic.

A walkie on a low table near the bed gave a crackle. "*We have an incoming wormhole.*" He recognized Brody's voice.

"Something's up," he began, trying to lift himself. A sudden spasm of pain shot through him and he winced. "Son of a … What the hell was Telford doing?"

Tamara frowned. "He didn't exactly drive easy, sir."

"Right…" Young let the lieutenant help him to his feet. "Next time I'll return the favor… Smoke a box of cigars. Get him a tattoo, maybe…" He looked around. "Where's Chloe?"

"She, uh, came back some time before you did, sir. She looked…scared."

"Yeah," said Young quietly. "There's a lot of that going around." He grabbed the radio and started walking.

Camile had walked as far as she dared to go through the corridors of the *Destiny*, and now she was coming back full circle, mentally plotting out the map of the 'local' area around the gate room. Most people had retreated to the crew quarters, shut themselves in and tried to find ways to make the passing of the time seem painless. Doctor Boone had apparently come across a deck of cards and a muted game was under way in one of the storage rooms; other people were sleeping to conserve what little air remained, some writing notes to their loved ones even though it was unlikely they would ever be read.

Wray wondered if she should be doing the same; but she had never been one to wait for things to happen. Something in her knew that she would face her end the same way she faced her life; on her feet, without apology.

She heard noises coming from the gate room, the low rumbling of the Stargate as it turned about itself. Her pace quickened; it could only mean the party sent down to the planet were coming back, and hopefully, they had their salvation with them. Turning the corner she came across Vanessa James, who stood at indolent rest outside the chamber.

"Lieutenant," she said, by way of greeting.

"Camile," came the reply.

She paused on the threshold. The woman was clearly there to stand guard, but Wray couldn't be certain if that meant the chamber was now off-limits. "Is there any word yet?"

James shook her head. "No."

"People want to know what's going on," she continued.

The woman looked away. "I don't know." She gestured at the gate room. "Go see for yourself."

Wray took a step, then halted. James's brooding manner was not characteristic of the young woman, not by a long shot; but then a crisis such as the one they were going through affected different people in different ways. "How are you holding up?" she asked. "You okay?"

The response was flat. "I'm fine."

"You know you can talk to me, right?"

That got her a nod, and Wray understood that was all James would offer for the moment. "Thanks," said the lieutenant, her gaze drifting away.

She went on into the gate room, just in time to see the wormhole form with a grumbling thunder of noise. Wray stood back from where Adam Brody and Sergeant Riley stood working the control console.

With a shudder of silver light, two figures stumbled through the Stargate and dropped to the deck a few steps in. It was Doctor Rush, and propped on his shoulder Wray saw Jeremy Franklin, groggy and marked with blood. She gasped; had they encountered something hostile on the desert world? "Is he all right?"

"What happened?" said Brody.

Rush lowered Franklin to the floor. "Greer shot him," explained the scientist. "I need water," he went on.

.Riley handed him his canteen, clearly expecting him to give it to the injured man, but instead Rush tore open the cap and drank it all in a single go.

"That was my ration for the day...." said the sergeant, clearly aggrieved. Rush waved him away with a noncommittal nod, which seemed to be his equivalent of a thank you.

Wray stepped aside as Colonel Young arrived with Lieutenant Johansen. "What's going on?" said the colonel, raising his voice to be heard over the screech of the dissipating wormhole.

Rush gave a dry chuckle. Wray could see his face was flushed with sunburn and the effects of dehydration. "We've all had a lovely day at the beach. How about you?"

Young shot him an acid glare and beckoned Wray forward. "Camile. Help us."

"We need to move him," said Tamara, indicating Franklin. "He's losing a lot of blood."

Wray swallowed hard and nodded, taking the unconscious man's shoulders, while Brody and Tamara lifted from his legs.

The coppery tang of blood reached her nostrils, and she did her best to ignore it.

Matthew Scott walked on.

Slower now. Each step a leaden effort. Each footfall a mountain climbed. He was fading, becoming a faint copy of himself, losing breath and energy and life. The white sands and the blazing sun were burning him, bleaching all color from him.

His boot went down awkwardly against a drift of sand and he stumbled. Gravity pulled him to his knees and he swayed, part of him unaware of the fall, the automatic part of his brain still trying to walk on and on, running him like a robot made of meat and bone.

Then he fell, all the way, into the sand. It came up to meet him, threatened to smother him. Scott took a shuddering breath and looked up. There was something out there, a shape he knew, a symbol, a man. Both and neither. He blinked away the blurs and saw the shadow of a figure hanging from a wooden cross.

He looked away and suddenly a rise of old memory came to him, strong and fluid. Desperate for even a moment's respite from the heat, he let himself sink into it.

The church.

It was always the church. Everything that went wrong in his life inevitably ended up back there. He was only a youth.

Sixteen. By the span of years, maybe not so long ago, but in terms of experience, in terms of maturity...it seemed like a lifetime.

The empty pews all around him, the cool, open space of the nave, the arched roof over his head. Light, colored by stained glass, drifting in over him. At his back, a man's breath. A hand reaching for his shoulder, offering him support. His throat thick with emotion, his fingers trembling. A face still wet with tears.

Then the admission. The damning truth from his own lips.

"I failed," he says. His voice is small and faint, but it carries across the silent reaches of the chapel. He looks up and sees Father George. The priest's face shows nothing but compassion.

"He has his plan for all of us."

But that's wasn't answer enough. Not enough for him. He felt like his young life was ending, breaking apart piece by piece. And in a way, it did end.

"I have sinned, Father. I failed you. I failed myself." He nods towards the altar, and beyond, the figure up upon the cross. "I failed him."

Then the words. "We have Redemption through his blood, even the forgiveness of sins."

Redemption. The word means many things. Deliverance. Salvation.

Rescue.

Only three remained here now; an entire world, and on it only three lives as human beings might reckon them. Each of them waiting for an ending, each moving toward it on their own way.

Scott's head lolled forward and consciousness left him, his body dropping into the grip of it, lost. He lay there in the ashen sands, fallen, clinging to the edge of his life, each breath laboring from his lungs, each a tick of the clock one moment nearer death, for his life and the lives of everyone aboard the *Destiny*.

Out beyond him, unseen, past the drift where he had collapsed, the sand dunes fell away. The landscape there became flat and featureless, and glittering in the sunlight, the vast plain of a bone-dry lake bed that had not known the touch of water upon it for thousands and thousands of years.

Only three remained here.

Greer marched, ignoring the cries of his body, the aches and the pain and the ever-present drag from his limbs, the need to stop, stop and fall. He denied them all, kept on, kept on marching. Like a soldier. Like a machine. Standing tall. A man on fire.

That was who he was, this was what he did. Ronald Greer was a Marine, and he was of the few, the proud, the always faithful. He would not allow himself to falter. This was not an option. The life he had left, and the new life the Corps had given him, all these things had forged a will in Greer like tempered steel. Even now, out here in a wilderness so far from home his mind got lost trying to grasp it, he was still that man. And he would leave no one behind.

As he marched, he carried a voice with him, crackling through the air. *"Curtis, Palmer, this is Eli, if you can hear me, come in, over."*

Only three.

Eli Wallace stood beneath the glare of the sun, looking into the ever-changing, shifting silver of the gateway. On the other side of that shimmering portal, another world like this one, alien to everything he had ever known. Somewhere, through that gateway, other lives had been cast like thrown stones.

"Curtis ... Palmer... please respond." He said their names into the radio, repeating them over and over; and with a slow chill that crept through his bones in defiance of the crippling heat, he wondered if his words were now just a eulogy. They had taken a risk against all odds and he had let them do it. If they were dead, did he share in that? Eli stared at the radio, willing it to respond to him, waiting for the sound of a voice.

Silence answered him, and he sighed, fighting down the fear that he would follow them, that all of them would follow, soon enough.

With howl of energy, the pool of silver evaporated, and the Stargate became a inert ring of gray metal once more.

Young stood back across the room and gave Tamara space to work. Franklin lay on one of the crew beds, his face sweaty and pale. The colonel could hear him moaning softly in the depths of a fever.

"Greer's shot is still in there," said the lieutenant. "I have to get that bullet out, and soon."

"Then do it," he ordered.

Tamara hesitated. "I'm going to use a lot of the morphine I have left."

"Whatever you have to do," said Young. "Get to work."

She gave him a tight nod and began sorting out equipment from her medical kit. Young studied Franklin for a moment. Part of him wondered if Tamara's effort would actually be worth anything; if Scott didn't get back with the minerals they needed, it wouldn't matter if Franklin came through or not. He'd die either way, along with the rest of them.

Young shook his head slightly, banishing the callous notion. He couldn't afford to let himself start thinking that way. He couldn't look at human beings and see only numbers, pluses and minuses on some great, abstract scale. The colonel turned away and found Rush and Wray standing by the door.

Wray was attempting to interrogate Rush, while the doctor probed gently at his sunburned skin, looking at his hands.

"Your man didn't have to shoot him," she said, turning a glare on Young. "He shouldn't be allowed to carry a weapon."

The colonel ignored the latter comment, looking at Rush. "Greer said Rush told him to do it."

"Franklin would be dead now if we hadn't stopped him," said the scientist.

"How do you know that?" demanded Wray.

"Eli redialed the address of the planet Curtis and Palmer went through to," Rush explained. "He was unable to raise them on the radio or get any response from the kino they sent in advance. I'm sure he's still trying even as we speak." He looked away. "But wherever they went, I don't think they're coming back. That's why those gate addresses were locked out. The *Destiny* knew they were dangerous."

Wray seemed unconvinced of the starship's good intentions, and Young couldn't disagree with that. "So, what's our next step?" she said. "If we wait for the ship to arrive at another destination, we could be out of breathable air."

"That's likely, yes," agreed Rush. "But I don't believe evacuating through the gate is an option. Not one that will end well. Realistically, we can't possibly know what a completely alien planet would have in store. Not without—"

Young's tolerance for Rush's manner was running thin. "You're the one who said you wanted to go assess the long term viability, Doctor."

"I wanted to go because I believed what we needed was there," Rush retorted. "And I still do!"

"Then maybe you should have stayed," Young shot back. "Kept looking."

The scientist shrugged. "There's still time. You could send others."

The colonel nodded. "I intend to. I'm sending another team out to look for Greer and Scott. And then—"

Rush didn't let him finish. "Colonel, we've only just begun to understand the potential of this ship." His attitude changed, becoming earnest, almost pleading. "We can't abandon it. If there is one, I promise you, this ship holds the key to our way back to Earth."

Young folded his arms. "Then prove it."

Cradled in the immense fields of white, Scott felt detached, adrift from the here and now. He tried to reach out and grasp the real, but it slipped through his fingers like the pallid sands. He couldn't hold on; and gradually he drifted back. Back to the moment.

Back to the church.

Father George sits side by side with him on the pews. He isn't looking straight at him. He's letting Scott breathe, letting him deal with it in his own time.

But the question came soon enough.

"Do you love her?"

"Do I...?" He is so brittle at that moment that he is afraid he will shatter if he answers. "I don't..." And when at last he does reply, it is to a different question. "She's not going to have it."

The old man felt that. Like a punch in the gut, it hit him hard.

"You're sure?"

"She's sixteen. We don't even really know each other."

The silence goes on, and it is like darkness. Filling the chapel, blotting out the light in the room.

"Is there any chance she will change her mind?" He asks this, but the old man knows the answer already from the cast of Scott's face.

"No."

And then the other question. The real one. The one the future turned on.

"What are you going to do, Matthew?"

"I don't know." The truth is so heavy upon him. "About anything."

"I see." But he doesn't, not really.

"I thought I did. I thought he was my calling. But now..."

He looked at me with such sadness then. Not disappointment, but something worse than that.

"I'm sorry," he says.

It's the last thing Scott expects to hear. "Why? I'm the one who is weak. It's my fault."

"No... it's not."

He looked away, like he was lost in thought, staring into a distance only he could see. And I was blinded by my tears.

"It's not yours." Scott reaches for him, searching for connection, for something solid.

But then he is sand, dissolving before my eyes, crumbling, dissipating, gone.

He is sand.

Sand—

It was part of the dream, the memory; or perhaps it wasn't. Later he would think on it and try to find the places where one ended and the other began, but it did not resolve itself. In Scott's mind it stayed murky and unclear.

The swirl of sand had returned once more, twisting around him. It spun up in front of him as he lay on the slope of the white dune. The vortex turned faster and faster, seeming to take on power and build energy before a sudden release of force. The swirling mass punched down into the sand, and from beneath a dark stain grew. Welling up from below the surface, liquid rose. Bubbling, flowing, a pool of ink-gray water emerged around Scott's face, soaking into his jacket, touching his arid, burned skin.

He roused. Blinked and coughed, swallowed by reflex and gasped. Scott lifted himself up on shaky arms, his eyes widening.

Water. There was *water* here, hiding beneath the sands. *And water meant—*

Fueled by a surge of adrenaline, Scott drew on his reserves of strength and plunged his hands into the damp sand. Using his fingers like blades of a spade, he tore out great clods of the wet powder, desperately digging in.

When he found it, he gave a wordless noise of elation. Under the sand, beneath the layer of the dry lake bed, a granular mass of crumbly sediment was visible, pale and powdery. It was soft, and it broke apart easily in his hands.

Scott dove for his pack and upended it, spilling out the testing kit on to the dune. He was aware that his hands were shaking, and concentrated on steadying himself. Carefully, he scooped a measure of the sediment into a flask, then gave up the last splash of water in his canteen to the mix. He swirled it, firing the pocket torch and placing the flame at the flask's underside.

He snatched at the bottle of reagent, dropping the colored acid into the solution. The fluid turned red and he worked it, swilling it around and around with the torch flame licking at the bottom of the flask. Scott held his breath, and like a magician's trick, the crimson thinned, became insubstantial…and then clear.

He wanted to yell out but he could barely speak. Getting to his feet, he saw the dull glitter of the lake bed beyond and gave a weary nod. Palmer had been right all along.

"This is Scott," he husked into his radio. "Anyone read? Come in." He released the push-to-talk button and static chattered back at him. He tried again. "I found it. I found the lake bed." He looked down. "I've got the lime."

Still no reply. Drawing back his cuff, Scott looked at the dusty face of his wristwatch and blinked, unsure if he was reading it right. He rubbed at his eyes, trying to focus.

The time. He felt sick inside as it dawned on him. "Oh God…." *I'm too late.*

No matter how fast he could go, he would never make it back to the Stargate before the time limit expired. He called into the radio again. "If you can hear me... *wait*. I'm coming. Just wait!"

With frantic speed, Scott tore the collapsible entrenching shovel from its pocket on his back pack and desperately began digging up great divots of the crumbly sediment, shoveling the powdery material into his bag as fast as he could.

The heat had pushed Eli into a dozy reverie, and he sat on the stone ramp, trying to shade himself with a sliver of shadow from the Stargate; but the gateway's sudden reactivation shocked him into motion and he broke into a scrambling run, out into the sand. Each time he'd seen the flash of energy when the gate opened it had made him jump, and he couldn't help but wonder what would happen to someone standing in front of it when it 'kawooshed' open. *Nothing good*, he imagined. Then another unpleasant thought struck him; *what if you were stepping through when it closed?* He made a sour face, thinking about *The Fly* again.

The gate spun, the chevrons glowing, and Eli took a tighter grip on Greer's pistol; at this point he was way beyond knowing what to expect. The wormhole opened and he raised the gun in a shaky, two-handed grip; then he almost dropped it in relief when he saw a familiar face come through. It was the woman Scott had shared a smile with in the corridor, back on Icarus. *Lieutenant James, yeah, that was her.* It seemed like a lifetime ago.

"Hi," he managed.

She nodded to him. "Why don't you let me have that?" James plucked the gun from his hands and made it safe.

Two more people followed her through, men in Marine gear with the names 'Spencer' and 'Gorman' on their jackets.

Eli felt a little giddy and gave a crooked smile. "Table for three?" he croaked. "I'm sorry, but we only have outdoor seating."

James handed him a water bottle. "Take this," she said.

"You sound like you need it."

Eli attacked the canteen greedily and gulped down mouth-fuls of water, nodding. It was the best drink he'd ever had. "Next planet we find," he managed, between swigs, "Nice and cold, please."

"We're going to make a sweep for Greer and the lieutenant," she told him. Spencer and Gorman were already heading out at a fast clip, and James jogged up to follow them. "Oh yeah, we brought you this, too." She dug in her pack and tossed something toward him.

Eli reached out to grab the object but it slowed to a halt and hovered in the middle of its arc; a replacement kino. "Thanks," he called, but they were already over the dune and gone.

He paused, staring at the Stargate, thinking of the shade and the cool of the *Destiny*. He could dial back, step through and get out of this murderous heat, just step-step-step and he'd be there. He drank the rest of the water slowly, then finally turned away.

Eli had promised Greer he would be here when he got back; somewhere out there the Marine was keeping a promise not to leave a comrade behind. Eli nodded to himself. He wasn't going to let some sunburn make a liar of him.

Through fire, Scott lumbered across the dunes, drag-ging the heavy pack behind him across the sand in jerks of motion. Every inch he advanced was pain, his joints tight with the effort. The pack felt like an impossible tonnage, and in his mind's eye he imagined it was loaded down with great ingots of heavy steel, the weight of them so great it threatened to sink through the mantle of the sand and drag him down with it into a bottomless abyss.

He shot an angry look into the sky, flinching away from the pale yellow sun riding high in the cloudless blue above. Scott wanted to shout at it, *Do your worst!* but he couldn't form the words. His mouth was as arid as the sands, and the brief surge of groundwater that had soaked his tunic had already evaporated away.

A sudden, panicked thought worked its way through his mind and Scott turned to look back at the pack; he had a horrible vision of it split open, the precious mineral sediment inside scattered out behind him like a contrail. But the pack had not broken and his load was still intact. If he could just get it back to the Stargate before it was too late. Before the time ran out. Before *he* ran out.

Scott planted his foot wrongly on his next step and fell hard, losing his grip on the pack's straps. The impact of the sand slammed into his body and his breath crashed from his lungs in an aching rattle. He tried to lift himself up, but his muscles twitched and spasmed. Scott sank back into the embrace of the desert.

Camile clasped her hands together to give them something to do, to stop her from wringing them over one another. Nervous energy was warring with her body's fatigue from the ever dwindling oxygen supply, and caught between the two, she roamed the decks of the *Destiny*, doing what she was best at — observing people, measuring them and following their thoughts.

She went from room to room. In the quarters, there was mostly silence from each open door, not even the murmur of quiet conversation now. From one room she heard the faint tremors of a man softly crying, and she walked on. Wray saw survivors lying on bunks, or huddling in hallways. As she passed them by they looked at her, the questions open on their faces. *What's going on? Is there any word?* But she had no answers to give them; Wray knew as much — or as little — about their fate as they did.

Unseen at the door of the room Colonel Young had taken, Wray watched Tamara Johansen work to mend Jeremy Franklin's bullet wound. The lieutenant had co-opted Chloe

Armstrong to assist her, and the young girl struggled on, her face tight and pale with aversion at the blood and torn flesh in front of her. Tamara dug into the meat of the man's shoulder and drew out the flattened head of the rifle bullet. Camile had to turn away at the sounds of her working on the ripped, injured flesh.

Wray went on to the gate room. She'd hoped that the wormhole they had opened earlier might stave off the pounding headache tightening around her head, as whatever air passed through the Stargate might bring some tiny measure of fresh oxygen through; but she had learned to her chagrin that the wormhole only worked one-way, so while *Destiny*'s bad air bled out, nothing had come through to replace it across the shimmering silver membrane of non-matter. For now, the gate remained closed.

Brody stood with Sergeant Riley and a few of the other civilian scientists, nursing the workings of the air purification unit that had been pulled from the ship's walls.

"We still have options," Brody was saying. "I mean, I think there must be replacement stores of this material on board the ship." He poked at the black slurry caking the scrubber unit. "It simply doesn't make sense that the Ancients would send this vessel into space without them."

"That's as maybe," said Volker. "But if we can't find this missing storehouse of magic chemicals, it may as well be on the other side of the universe."

"What if we can get into some of the other scrubber units?" said Riley. "They can't all be filled with this goop. If we can find some good ones, maybe swap out the units in here..."

"And then what?" said Brody. "We have fresh air in the gate room for a while, but nowhere else?"

"We move everyone back in here, seal it off," said Riley. "It's not an ideal solution, but—"

Volker shook his head. "We've looked already. There are no 'good' units left. All of them are stale."

The conversation went on, and Wray noticed Doctor Rush a few feet away from the group. He stood at the control console, a dour expression in his face, before shaking his head and looking away.

She walked to him. "Doctor."

"Miss Wray."

She nodded at Brody and the others. "I imagine they could use your help."

He didn't look up. "I'm not really one for hopeless causes."

"You think we don't have any hope?" Wray heard the tremor in her own voice.

Rush gave her a sideways look. "I think what they're talking about is a waste of breath." He looked away again, dismissing her.

She frowned and took a step toward the Stargate. The metallic ring arched high up over her and for a moment she lost herself in it.

It was something so incredible, so beautiful; and yet this device and all it represented would be responsible for taking their lives unless they could take control of their fate... Their destiny.

Wray glimpsed movement on the upper balcony; in the shadows she saw Colonel Young resting on the coppery rail, staring down at the Stargate. She had no doubt that at this moment, he shared the same fears and hopes that she did.

Greer felt himself waver slightly in the burning heat, for a split-second stepping off the line and almost losing the path of his straight-arrow march; but he caught himself in time and straightened out, his jaw stiffening.

The Marine hunched forward, pushing on towards the crest of the next dune. He would not allow himself to weaken; he had not earned that right. *In the Corps, you need permission to die,* his Gunny had once told him, *you don't got that, you keep your*

CHAPTER THIRTEEN

"Incoming," called Sergeant Riley, and Young looked up with a jolt. He'd been miles away for a moment, at first mulling their options, then slowly coming to the grave realization that they had none; then drifting, back to that moment with Emily. He had promised her he would be coming home, and now it seemed that he lied to her.

He pushed the dismal thoughts from his mind and made his way down the curved stairs from the gate room's upper balcony, his knee joints complaining with every step he took at speed. Ahead of him, the Stargate had started to spin once again, the white chevrons blazing like beacons in the dimness.

Rush was standing at the control console, watching the origin symbols lock in one by one. "It's Eli," he confirmed. He looked up and saw Young was watching him. "We have less than three minutes before the ship jumps again."

The colonel nodded. "If they don't come through with what we need…"

"I have some ideas," Rush replied. "You may not like them."

The gate locked in place and the wormhole flashed open. Young's lips thinned; "We wait until the last possible second, do I make myself clear?"

"Of course," said Rush, as if he were surprised that the colonel would suggest anything else.

Young walked up to the gate as Corporal Gorman stepped through, and then Sergeant Spencer a beat behind him. Both of the men gave him a weary nod; their expressions spoke volumes, and Young's heart sank.

James came through a moment later and halted, giving him a grim look. "I'm sorry, sir," she said simply.

He nodded. "You did your best, Lieutenant. Stand down."

"Sir," she replied and walked away, past Rush, Brody, Riley, Wray and the others who were gathering around the console, watching the ticking countdown clock on the auxiliary screen.

Ninety seconds now, by my estimate, thought Young. When time zero showed on the monitor, the *Destiny* would shut that gateway forever and blast away from this star system at superluminal speeds. Any chance the desert world might have had to save them would be lost.

He raised his radio to his lips. "Eli, do you read me?"

"*Right here*," came the weary reply.

"Don't wait," he said. "You make sure you get through with enough time to spare."

Eli's reply was lost in the sudden clatter of an alarm tone that began to sound through the gate room and the corridors. On the screen, the countdown timer was flashing red.

"Alert signal," called Riley. "The ship is preparing to jump to FTL."

"Less than one minute remaining," said Rush.

Young nodded. "Eli? It's time."

"Okay," said Eli, retreating up the stone ramp. "Just a second."

"*You don't have a second*," said Young's voice. "*Get back here, that's an order.*"

He was still working the kino, eyes glued to the remote, even as he took steps toward the wormhole. The field of vision from the drone device swept the landscape, looking for any sign of Scott and Greer.

The image panned over the tops of the dunes, and blurred past something. "Whoa!" said Eli, stabbing at the control and reversing the scan. The image bobbed back and found its target.

Two men, running as fast as they could, hobbling, headlong. Scott and Greer, a heavy pack being dragged between them.

"I see them!" he shouted, fumbling with his radio. "I see them. They're carrying something…"

Greer's voice broke in over the open channel. "*We've got it!*" he bellowed. "*Don't go! We've got it!*"

Eli gauged the distance between the men and the gate and his gut filled with ice. Only moments remained, but it wouldn't be enough. With damning certainty he knew there was no way Greer and Scott would reach the Stargate before the *Destiny* cut off the wormhole. "They've got the lime," he reported. "And they're not going to make it…"

The hooting alarm was becoming more and more strident as the time-to-disconnect shrank toward nothing. Rush looked up as Riley made the call. "Thirty seconds!"

If they left the others behind, it would be death sentence for all of them, not just the men the stranded on the planet, not just Curtis and Palmer, but every single person who had fled from the destruction of Icarus Base; and Nicholas Rush was not about to die, not after so much, not after finally finding his destiny. He refused to be denied it.

"Somebody give me a radio," he snapped. Their only hope now was to ask someone to risk their life for all of them. Lieutenant James handed him her walkie and he spoke into it. "Eli, it's me, Rush. I want you to stick your arm into the event horizon…the 'puddle'…"

Rush felt every eye on him. "*Seriously?*" came the young man's reply.

Young stepped closer, and he could see that the colonel understood what he was attempting. "Are you sure?" said the officer.

Rush released the talk button. "No," he said honestly.

"He'll be torn apart…" whispered Wray.

Rush disregarded her words, continuing. "But I would

bet there's a safety protocol that will prevent someone from being cut off from the ship while en route."

"Like elevator doors," muttered Brody. "Same thing."

"What if there isn't?" said Young.

Riley called out the count. "Twenty seconds."

He had no time to debate the merits of his theory, and spoke urgently into the radio once more.

"Eli, do it!"

He stood at the very surface of the fluid-like event horizon, seeing a weird, distorted reflection of himself in the matrix of the wormhole. Turning, Eli saw Scott and Greer, both of them dredging up whatever energy they still had left in them for one final, headlong sprint. But they were still some distance away. Still *too* far away.

Eli gave a deep sigh. *This is without a doubt the most insane thing I have ever done*, he told himself. With a wince, he extended his arm and pushed it through the surface of the rippling portal, all the way down past his elbow, then filled his lungs for a frantic shout. *"Come on!"*

A strange cold-hot prickling tingle enveloped his limb, and he could still feel it intact in there, wherever *there* was, maybe trapped in some weird state of pre-dematerialization, waiting for the rest of him to come through.

Over the radio, he heard Sergeant Riley begin a ten second countdown.

" Five. Four. Three." The sergeant read off the time as the Ancient digits dropped toward nothing. "Two. One. *Zero*."

Rush found that he was holding in his breath, and he released it slowly. A second elapsed, then two, then three, and still the alarms blared. He could feel a low rumble through the deck beneath his feet, but the Stargate remained active, the chevrons shining brightly. *I was right...*

"Got something here," said Riley. Rush saw on his console

that the countdown clock display had now been replaced by a panel of warning text flashing an angry crimson. Judging by the tremors from the distant engines, it didn't appear that the FTL jump had been aborted, only delayed — the question now was, *for how long?*

Young barked into his radio *"Eli!* Eli, are you still there?"

In the next moment, two dust-caked figures crashed through the open wormhole and collapsed to the floor in a crumpled heap. A heavy back pack came with them, landing with a dull thud on the deck plates. Rush was already moving forward as Eli came stumbling through a heartbeat later, staggering to his knees. He was barely through before the event horizon disintegrated behind him and the gate went dark.

Rush couldn't help but grin as the young man rolled over on to his back and clasped desperately at his arm, grabbing at it to be certain that the limb was still attached to him. "Well done, Eli," he said quietly.

Around them, the walls moaned as the ship shuddered, mustering itself for a discharge of power. The engine note built to a rattling whine that culminated in a sudden, giddy sense of motion-without-motion, and Rush swayed a step before steadying himself.

"Great," coughed Eli from his position on the floor. "Warp speed."

"Good work," said Young as he approached. "All of you."

"Hey, thanks," Eli replied. "Is it okay if I pass out here for a little while?"

He didn't feel like he needed the crutch that Becker had made him any more, so Colonel Young left it back with the supplies and took a slow and steady walking tour of the *Destiny.* Everybody on board had come to within a few breaths of dying and all of them had faced it with a strength he hadn't credited. Alan Armstrong had given his life to keep them alive. Scott and Greer had performed above and beyond the call of duty. T.J. had stepped up when she was needed the most. Eli Wallace had shown great bravery in a moment when a lesser man would have shirked the responsibility. Even Rush, after everything the man had done and despite whatever selfish agenda he was pushing, had come through in the end.

He stopped to watch Rush supervising Volker and Park as they assisted in the revitalization of the carbon dioxide scrubbers. Scott's find on the planet had provided them with more than enough of the limestone compound for their immediate needs, and with it they'd cooked up a batch of milky fluid that would do the job and keep everyone breathing for the foreseeable future. They filled the filter pods and slotted them back into the walls, one after another.

Young passed by the control room chamber, and found a tired but elated Eli working with Brody. On the main holographic display, the life support system indicators that had remained an ominous red began to switch over to a stable green as each one of the air scrubbers was replenished. He kept walking, on toward the crew quarters, and in the corridor he felt the faintest breath of a fresh breeze against his cheek.

Young stopped and looked up toward the atmosphere vents and took a deep breath, allowing himself to savor it. Moving on, past the storage compartment where Camile Wray had gathered a few of the civilians, he heard them laughing with relief as clean air started coming from the vents. She saw him pass by and they shared a nod. For all of them, Young included, it seemed like an age since they had been able to breathe deeply.

Across the corridor was the room he'd rested in earlier — not that there was a lack of places to sleep here. Young wondered if Rush had been right about the *Destiny* never actually having a crew in the first place. If that was so, then why have the rooms at all? It was one more question about this craft that needed to be answered. Perhaps, now they weren't struggling for their next breath, they could think about finding some answers.

He entered and Tamara looked up from where she sat next to Franklin. The scientist's shoulder was heavily bandaged and the detritus from her work on his injury lay in a blood-stained pile on the table. She gave Young a weary nod and he returned it.

"How is he doing?"

Tamara sighed. "He'll be okay once the sedatives wear off and he wakes up. It'll hurt him like hell for a while, though, and his arm probably won't work as well as it did. I'm just a meatball surgeon, but I did my best."

"I know you did," said Young.

She went on. "I took a look at Scott and the others. The lieutenant has some wicked sunburn. Can't help him with that, though. He'll have to tough it out. I sent Chloe to get him rehydrated."

"What about Greer and Eli?"

"You know Marines, sir. There's a reason they call them 'leathernecks.' As for Eli, he's holding up pretty well. Just glad to be alive, I guess." Tamara seemed to sense what Young's next question would be and she moved to deflect it. "I made sure they all got enough to drink, but we need to be firm on the rationing. There's no telling how long its going to be before we can get more food and water—"

"Don't worry about that for now," he said. "How about you, T.J.? How are you doing?"

She looked away and blew out a breath. "I… I don't know when I last slept. Broke my watch coming through the Stargate. I guess I'm just strung out…" Tamara managed a weak smile. "But I'm alive. Where there's life, there's hope, right?"

"So I've heard."

The smile faded. "But I can't help thinking about Andrea Palmer and Sergeant Curtis. And Chloe's dad. Sir, we've been out here no more than a day or so, and we've already lost three people."

Young gave a solemn nod. "I know how you feel. But there's nothing we could have done."

She looked away. "How are we going to survive? We've got air now, but we need food, water, we need to figure out how this ship operates…"

"One problem at a time," he told her. "One day at a time. That's what we have to do." He paused. "Palmer, Curtis, Senator Armstrong… They all made their choices. Now we have to make ours. Do we pull together and get through this, or do we fall apart?"

After a moment, Tamara nodded. "Not really a choice at all, is it?"

"No," he agreed.

Eli looked up as Rush entered the control room, passing Brody on his way out. "Hey, we're not dead. That means this was a good day, right?"

Rush gave a snort. "That all depends on how you define *good*, Eli."

He held up his hands. "I have both my arms; I am alive. Yeah, I'll go with *good* for that."

The other man fell silent and studied him. Then he spoke again. "Thank you for trusting me. I know there's not a lot of that going around at the moment."

"Hey, if anyone knows how Stargates work around here, it's you, right?"

"Yes," replied Rush, without weight.

"And it's not like I had a lot of options," admitted Eli. "Suffocate on the ship, die of thirst on the planet, lose an arm. None of those are exactly enticing." He paused, considering his motivations for a moment. "The truth is, I knew you weren't going to let us all die."

Rush raised an eyebrow. "Why? I doubt Sergeant Greer

would have agreed with that."

Eli gestured around. "Because of all this. The *Destiny*." He nodded to himself. "Without that mineral stuff, everyone would have died, you included, and you don't want to lose one second of being here, do you?"

"Of course not," Rush replied. "I'd be a fool not to. This ship, everything it represents…" His gaze turned inward. "We have to *know* it, Eli. We have an opportunity here greater than any other explorer in human history. We can't refuse it."

Eli saw that odd light in Rush's eyes again, and something occurred to him; a sudden, cold realization. *He doesn't want to go home.*

The man blinked and went back to working the console, the moment vanishing. "We should keep digging through the layers of the system," he said, all business again. "We've only just scratched the surface here."

"Yeah," said Eli, for the moment keeping his thoughts to himself. "You're right about that."

Scott lay on the bunk and watched the patterns of the stars flash past the window in the far wall. He lay in the cool darkness of the room and didn't move; parts of his skin felt raw and tight, and he had to be careful how he sat on the bed. Even the slightest touch of cloth on his sunburn felt like someone rubbing sandpaper over him. He couldn't remember ever being this exhausted, not even after the worst days of basic training. Scott felt like he had been crushed up, wrung out and thrown away; but he was still breathing, so that had to count for something.

The streaks of starlight flying by had a lulling, almost hypnotic effect on the lieutenant — or maybe that was just the fatigue. He felt his thoughts drifting, falling back to those moments on the desert world.

Scott had not dwelled on thoughts of Father George for a long time, and to relive those moments so vividly now, to sense the old man's presence close to him... He couldn't help but wonder what it could mean. Part of him wanted to rationalize it away; it was heat stroke, some kind of hallucination brought on by dehydration, maybe. Another part of him, something he'd buried deep, kept to himself, had other answers that he didn't want to think about.

And then there was the strange dust-vortex shape he had seen, the 'swirl'. He hadn't spoken to anyone about it yet, and he wondered what he could say if he did. Scott was convinced that the twisting spiral of sand had been real, even if everything else wasn't. He remembered the static charge he'd felt when it touched him, the way it consumed the water he dripped from his canteen. He had not imagined that; he had not hallucinated the way it had helped him, saved his life — *and everyone else's*, he thought.

Perhaps it had been some kind of alien life form, something native to the white deserts, possibly sentient, possibly not. Then again, Scott thought about the stories he'd heard, the barrack-room rumors about the aliens the SGC called the Ancients. Weren't they supposed to be made of pure energy? He wondered if that could be possible, that the people who had built this starship might still be out here somewhere, watching over the craft, taking an interest in the new arrivals huddling in its corridors. And then there was the other possibility. Scott had grown up listening to stories of angels, of ethereal beings that gave assistance in times of great need. Maybe there hadn't been any harps and haloes, but he couldn't deny that *something* had looked out for him.

There was a knock at the door and he looked up as Chloe entered, holding a full canteen. "Hey," she said softly. "I brought you some more water."

He nodded at the bottle by his pallet. "It's okay, I still have some."

She came in and stood by the end of the bed. "You really

need to drink it. Lieutenant Johansen…. I mean, Tamara, was pretty insistent about it."

Scott nodded wearily. "I'm fine." He suddenly felt awkward, unsure what to say to her. His mind flashed back to that moment in the corridor outside the shuttle bay, when Chloe had held on to him for dear life, as if he were the rock in a storm raging all around her. In that instant, a connection had been forged between them.

After a moment, she spoke again. "Everyone appreciates what you did."

He sat up. "Did Rush say how long it will last?"

"He's not sure."

Silence stretched out between them, and he couldn't let it go on. Scott's experience on the planet had left him feeling hollowed out, alone, and he saw the mirror of his own feelings in Chloe. "How are you?" he asked. She shook her head and gave a numb shrug. "My parents died in a car crash when I was four years old." He said it without thinking, uncertain of where the impulse came from.

Chloe looked up at him, with genuine regret. "I'm sorry."

Now he had started talking about it, he found he couldn't stop. "There was a priest who raised me… He pretty much drank himself to death when I was sixteen."

Her hand went to her mouth. "My God."

"I'm sorry," he told her. "I'm not trying to diminish what you're going through."

"I know," she gave a slow nod. "I understand."

Scott looked past her, to the window. "I think my point is, some things you never get over. That's just the way it is." She came closer and sat on the side of the bed, taking his hand. "You go on through," he continued. "As best you can."

Chloe nodded. She opened her mouth to speak, but said nothing.

He looked at her. "We're going to be okay. I believe that."

She forced a smile.

"I believe," he repeated, looking back out at the darkness and the light.

Against the reach of the endless night and the ocean of stars, the ship thundered on, its voyage unending.

Collected in one small area of its hull, the humans gathered together, ranging themselves against the unknown, struggling to understand the fate that had brought them to this place, working to learn the secrets of their new home.

Beyond them, the iron flanks of the vast vessel, this *Destiny*, ranged away in curves and constructs, devices and systems yet to be discovered, yet to be deciphered. But in among the sculptured lines of the Ancient ship, there lay something that did not belong.

Small, so much so that a casual glance might have missed the sight, but distinct enough that a second look would have revealed it. Something deceptive in its design, something alien and foreign, latched to the hull of the *Destiny* as a pilot fish might cruise on the skin of a cetacean. With a blink of fire, a ring of thrusters on the aft of the craft suddenly ignited and it detached, falling free, dropping into the faster-than-light slipstream of the larger vessel.

For a moment it kept pace with the *Destiny*, matching its incredible velocities point for point, riding alongside it; then the craft veered away at a sharp angle, vanishing into the red-shifted light of the passing stars.

The *Destiny* and the lives aboard her traveled on, the vista of the universe opening before them.

ABOUT THE AUTHOR

James Swallow is the author of several books and scripts, and his fiction from the worlds of *Stargate* includes the novels *Halcyon*, *Relativity* and *Nightfall*, and the audio dramas *Shell Game*, *Zero Point* and *First Prime*, as well as short stories for the official *Stargate Magazine*.

As well as a non-fiction book (*Dark Eye: The Films of David Fincher*), James also wrote the *Sundowners* series of original steampunk westerns, *Jade Dragon*, *The Butterfly Effect* and fiction in the worlds of *Star Trek* (*Synthesis*, the award-winning *Day of the Vipers*, *Infinity's Prism*, *Distant Shores*, *The Sky's The Limit* and *Shards and Shadows*), *Doctor Who* (*Peacemaker*, *Dalek Empire*, *Destination Prague*, *Snapshots*, *The Quality of Leadership*), *Warhammer 40,000* (*Black Tide*, *Red Fury*, *The Flight of the Eisenstein*, *Faith & Fire*, *Deus Encarmine* and *Deus Sanguinius*) and *2000AD* (*Eclipse*, *Whiteout* and *Blood Relative*).

His other credits include writing for *Star Trek Voyager*, and scripts for videogames and audio dramas, such as *Battlestar Galactica*, *Blake's 7* and *Space 1889*.

James lives in London, and is currently at work on his next book.

SNEAK PREVIEW

STARGATE ATLANTIS: HUNT AND RUN

by Aaron Rosenberg

"Did you hear that?"

Rodney glanced up. "Did I hear what?"

"That." Ronon wasn't even looking at him—the big muscle-bound Satedan was staring off into the surrounding hills, his whole body tensed, head up, nostrils flared. He looked like a hunting dog and any second Rodney expected the big man to go bounding off and return with a duck hanging from his mouth.

"I didn't hear anything."

"There!" Now Ronon did glance at him, more of a glare really from beneath those heavy brows. "That. That was gunfire."

Rodney frowned. Had he heard something just then? It was hard to be sure. He thought he might have, but maybe it was just because Ronon had told him there was something to hear. Sounds—or the absence thereof—could work that way. You could hear things just because you were listening for them. Especially if they were already supposed to be faint.

"I don't know," he admitted finally, much as he hated that particular phrase. "Maybe." He glanced around. "You think Sheppard and Teyla are in trouble?" Ronon wasn't listening to him. He had gone back to gazing at the horizon. "Ronon?" Rodney didn't care for it when the big oaf stared at him, but he liked being ignored even less. "Are they in trouble?"

"Yes, they're in trouble," Ronon replied after a minute. He shook himself and turned his attention fully upon Rodney, making him squirm. "And so are we. We need to leave here. Now."

"I've only just started isolating the damaged areas," Rodney protested. "It'll take me another few hours to get the Jumper operational again—at the least!"

But Ronon wasn't listening. He simply grabbed Rodney's arm and began hauling him away from the ship. "We can't stay here," he explained softly as he moved toward the hills.

"What? Wait!" Rodney tried to free his arm, but it was like a fly struggling against a vise grip. "We can't just leave the ship here."

"That's exactly what we can do," Ronon retorted. "We're too vulnerable here."

"Then we should get it up and running as soon as possible," Rodney argued. "The sooner we're off this world the better."

Ronon was already shaking his head, and he hadn't stopped moving. "Too late for that," he said. "There's no time."

"Are we going after Sheppard and Teyla, then?" That did make some strategic sense, Rodney admitted to himself—three guards instead of one would afford him more protection while he worked. He could get the comm link up and running first, and let Sheppard or Teyla call in to Atlantis while he moved on to the navigation and propulsion systems. But his self-appointed shepherd was shaking his head again.

"We can't go after them."

"What? Why not?" Rodney struggled against the Satedan's grip again. "Come on, you said they were in trouble!"

"They are."

"So we need to help them!"

"It's too late for that," Ronon replied. He still hadn't slowed down. The Jumper was almost completely lost in the shadows behind them now, because this world's sun was already drifting down toward the horizon.

"Too late?" Rodney felt a chill wash over him. "You mean they're—?"

"I don't know," Ronon admitted. "Either they've won free, in which case they'll find us later, or they've been captured, in which case we will need to plan their rescue."

"You don't think they're dead?" That was a relief. Rodney might enjoy busting Sheppard's chops from time to time—okay, so most of the time—but he actually respected the commander. And Teyla was one of the few people in Atlantis he actually liked.

"Not dead, no. They're bait."

"Bait? For what?" The chill grew worse. "For us?" He yanked on his arm again. "I can walk on my own, you know—I'm not an infant."

Ronon released him suddenly, making him stumble and barely catch himself. "Then keep up." The Satedan drew his sword with his newly freed hand—the other already held his pistol—and lengthened his stride. Rodney had to jog to keep pace.

"So you think they've been captured?" Rodney asked again a few minutes later. They were in the hills proper now, and it was getting dark enough that he barely caught Ronon's answering nod. "And whoever did it is using them as bait to lure us in?" Another faint nod. "Why?"

"They know we're still out here," Ronon answered absently. "They need to take care of that. This is how they do it."

Rodney studied the bigger man's back. "You seem awfully sure of that," he noted. "What's going on here?"

"I'm trying to keep us alive," was the answering growl.

That kept Rodney quiet for a minute—but only a minute. "No, really," he started again as they clambered over some rocks and up a small cliff face. "You know something. Don't you?" He felt as much as saw Ronon tense. "I'm right, aren't I? Of course I am. You do know something. I thought so.

You've been acting strange ever since that ship." He grabbed Ronon by the shoulder, but quickly let go as the bigger man swung back to face him. "Tell me."

"I recognized the trap," Ronon admitted softly. "The 'ship in distress' gambit. I've seen it before." He shook his head, his long braids whipping about. "It took me too long, though. I should have noticed it at once."

"You saved our lives," Rodney pointed out.

"But not our ship," Ronon snapped. "And we're still stuck here. Still being hunted. I was sloppy."

"Okay, so you were sloppy. You still saved us. Again." Rodney glanced around, not sure what he expected to see— the sun had set completely now, and it was dark enough that he could barely make out his companion's glare in the deepening night. "But that's not all of it, is it?"

Even without being able to see it fully he knew Ronon was glaring at him—he'd come to recognize the feel of that particular response. "No," the Satedan ground out after a long pause. "I know who's after us."

"You do?" That didn't exactly make Rodney feel better. "By reputation, or personally?"

Again the hesitation before Ronon answered. "Personally. And we have to watch our every step from here on out."

"Who is it?" Rodney wanted to know. Well, no, deep down he didn't want to know at all. But he needed to know.

The answer was one he hadn't expected. "Runners."

"Other runners?" Rodney stared at him. "Like you?"

He felt the air move as Ronon shook his head. "No. Not like me. Not any more."

"Then like what? Who are they? How do you know them? What do they want?" Rodney was both horrified and fascinated. Before they'd met Ronon they'd never even heard of a Runner, but apparently the concept was legendary among all the worlds touched by the Wraith—a lone individual, caught by the Wraith but released and then hunted down.

For sport. Most Runners didn't last very long, a week or two at most—they were said to be chosen for their cunning and their skills but the Wraith had been hunting and killing for centuries.

Ronon had been a Runner for seven years.

If these others were even half as good at hunting and fighting as he was, they had a serious problem on their hands.

"Not now," Ronon answered shortly. "Not here. We're not safe."

Rodney took that in. "Okay, yes. Safe. Safe would be good." He was babbling, he realized, and forced himself not to say another word. Instead he followed as Ronon continued into the mountains, taking a winding path Rodney knew was meant to throw off anyone trying to track them. At last they paused, and Ronon knelt, brushing dirt and small rocks and dead brush back from the stone wall beside them. Behind the debris was a small dark opening.

"Get in," he told Rodney. His tone made it clear this wasn't a request.

Rodney's first impulse was to argue. He didn't like small dark spaces, and he didn't like being ordered around, and he didn't like not being told everything at once. But he also didn't like being shot at or taken captive, and he was fairly sure he would like being killed even less, so he held his tongue, dropped to his knees, and crawled through the opening.

It widened slightly about twenty paces in, and the ceiling rose enough that he could sit up without bashing his head on the rocks above. Beyond that it narrowed again. Far enough, Rodney decided, and leaned back against the cool stone. He heard rustling from the opening.

A moment later Ronon joined him. "I covered the opening again," he explained quietly, his voice little more than a gruff whisper. "They won't find us here."

"Good." Rodney closed his eyes and took a deep breath. Then he opened them again and fixed Ronon with the sternest glare he could muster, especially considering he could barely see the big lug. "Now talk. Who are these Runners, how do you know them, and why are they doing this to us?"

For a second he thought Ronon was going to refuse. But then the big Satedan seemed to reach a decision. He nodded slightly, and grimaced as if in pain. Then he began to speak.

"It was seven years ago," he started, his voice soft and his eyes somewhere far away. "I had just been captured by the Wraith..."

STARGATE ATLANTIS:
HUNT AND RUN

April 2010

For more info, visit www.stargatenovels.com

STARGATE
SG·1

STARGATE
ATLANTIS

STARGATE UNIVERSE

Original novels based on the hit TV shows STARGATE SG-1, STARGATE ATLANTIS and STARGATE UNIVERSE

AVAILABLE NOW

For more information, visit www.stargatenovels.com

STARGATE SG-1: FOUR DRAGONS

by Diana Botsford
Price: $7.95 US | £6.99 UK
ISBN-10: 1-905586-48-5
ISBN-13: 978-1-905586-48-6
Publication date: June 2010

Jack takes matters into his own hands to save Daniel

STARGATE SG·1

FOUR DRAGONS

Diana Botsford

Based on the hit television series developed by Brad Wright and Jonathan Glassner

Series number: SG1-16

Shortly after Daniel Jackson returns from his time among the ascended Ancients, he volunteers to join an archaeological survey of Chinese ruins on P3Y-702.

But after accidentally activating a Goa'uld transport ring, Daniel finds himself the prisoner of the Goa'uld Lord Yu.

Blaming himself for Daniel's capture, Jack O'Neill vows to go to any lengths to get him back — even if it means taking matters into his own hands.

Order your copy directly from the publisher today by going to **www.stargatenovels.com** or send a check or money order made payable to "Fandemonium" to:

USA orders: $10.82 ($7.95 + $2.87 P&P). Send payment to: **Fandemonium Books, PO Box 2178, Decatur, GA 30031-2178.**

UK orders: £8.30 (£6.99 + £1.31 P&P). **Rest of the World orders:** £9.70 (£6.99 + £2.71 P&P). Send payment to: **Fandemonium Books, PO Box 795A, Surbiton KT5 8YB, United Kingdom.**

Or check your local bookshop — available on special order if they are out of stock (quote the ISBN number listed above).

STARGATE SG-1: THE POWER BEHIND THE THRONE

One man's hero is another's villain

STARGATE SG·1

THE POWER BEHIND THE THRONE

Steven Savile

Based on the hit television series developed by Brad Wright and Jonathan Glassner

Series number: SG1-15

by Steven Savile
Price: $7.95 US | £6.99 UK
ISBN-10: 1-905586-45-0
ISBN-13: 978-1-905586-45-1
Publication date: May 2010

SG-1 are asked by the Tok'ra to rescue a creature known as Mujina.

The last of its species, Mujina is devoid of face or form and draws its substance from the needs of those around it.

The creature is an archetype — a hero for all, a villain for all, depending upon whose influence it falls under.

And the Goa'uld Apophis, understanding the potential for havoc Mujina offers, has set his heart on possessing the creature...

Order your copy directly from the publisher today by going to www.stargatenovels.com or send a check or money order made payable to "Fandemonium" to:

<u>USA orders:</u> $10.82 ($7.95 + $2.87 P&P). Send payment to: Fandemonium Books, PO Box 2178, Decatur, GA 30031-2178.

<u>UK orders:</u> £8.30 (£6.99 + £1.31 P&P). <u>Rest of the World orders:</u> £9.70 (£6.99 + £2.71 P&P). Send payment to: Fandemonium Books, PO Box 795A, Surbiton KT5 8YB, United Kingdom.

Or check your local bookshop — available on special order if they are out of stock (quote the ISBN number listed above).

STARGATE SG-1: VALHALLA

by Tim Waggoner
Price: $7.95 US | £6.99 UK
ISBN-10: 1-905586-19-1
ISBN-13: 978-1-905586-19-6

Upon the legendary fields of Valhalla, the spirits of Viking warriors do eternal battle in service to their god, Odin. By night they feast and toast the fallen, but at dawn the dead are restored to fight until the end of times.

Series number: SG1-14

When SG-1 find themselves trapped in this endless battle, prisoners of Odin, they must discover the strange truth about Valhalla before it is too late — and then confront the giant, Surtr, a terrible and immortal enemy bent on revenging himself against his god.

In order to defeat Surtr, Carter suggests using a naquadrium power cell Jonas Quinn has developed on his home world, but when she and Colonel O'Neill arrive on Langara they realize their problems have only just begun…

Order your copy directly from the publisher today by going to www.stargatenovels.com or send a check or money order made payable to "Fandemonium" to:

USA orders: $10.82 ($7.95 + $2.87 P&P). Send payment to: Fandemonium Books, PO Box 2178, Decatur, GA 30031-2178.

UK orders: £8.30 (£6.99 + £1.31 P&P). **Rest of the World orders:** £9.70 (£6.99 + £2.71 P&P). Send payment to: Fandemonium Books, PO Box 795A, Surbiton KT5 8YB, United Kingdom.

Or check your local bookshop — available on special order if they are out of stock (quote the ISBN number listed above).

STARGATE SG-1: HYDRA

by Holly Scott & Jaimie Duncan
Price: $7.95 US | $9.95 Canada |
£6.99 UK
ISBN-10: 1-905586-10-8
ISBN-13: 978-1-905586-10-3

Rumours and accusations are reaching Stargate Command, and nothing is making sense. When SG-1 is met with fear and loathing on a peaceful world, and Master Bra'tac lays allegations of war crimes at their feet, they know they must investigate.

But the investigation leads the team into a deadly assault and it's only when a second Daniel Jackson stumbles through the Stargate, begging for help, that the truth begins to emerge. Because this Daniel Jackson is the product of a rogue NID operation that spans the reaches of the galaxy, and the tale he has to tell is truly shocking.

Facing a cunning and ruthless enemy, SG-1 must confront and triumph over their own capacity for cruelty and violence in order to save the SGC – and themselves…

STARGATE SG-1: DO NO HARM

by Karen Miller
Price: $7.95 US | $9.95 Canada |
£6.99 UK
ISBN-10: 1-905586-09-4
ISBN-13: 978-1-905586-09-7

Stargate Command is in crisis—too
many teams wounded, too many
dead. Tensions are running high and,
with the pressure to deliver tangible
results never greater, General Hammond is forced to call in the Pentagon strike team to plug the holes.

But help has its price. When the team's leader, Colonel
Dave Dixon, arrives at Stargate Command he brings with him
loyalties that tangle dangerously with a past Colonel Jack
O'Neill would prefer to forget.

Assigned as an observer on SG-1, hostility between the
two men escalates as the team's vital mission to secure lucra-
tive mining rights descends into a nightmare.

Only Dr. Janet Fraiser can hope to save the lives of SG-1—that
is, if Dave Dixon and Jack O'Neill don't kill each other first…

STARGATE SG-1: THE BARQUE OF HEAVEN

SG-1 are trapped in a brutal Goa'uld trial

STARGATE SG·1

THE BARQUE OF HEAVEN

Suzanne Wood

Based on the hit television series developed by Brad Wright and Jonathan Glassner

Series number: SG1-11

by Suzanne Wood
Price: $7.95 US | $9.95 Canada | £6.99 UK
ISBN-10: 1-905586-05-1
ISBN-13: 978-1-905586-05-9

Millennia ago, at the height of his power, the System Lord Ra decreed that any Goa'uld wishing to serve him must endure a great trial. Victory meant power and prestige, defeat brought banishment and death.

On a routine expedition to an abandoned Goa'uld world, SG-1 inadvertently initiate Ra's ancient trial – and once begun, the trial cannot be halted. Relying on Dr. Daniel Jackson's vast wealth of knowledge, Colonel O'Neill must lead his team from planet to planet, completing each task in the allotted time. There is no rest, no respite. To stop means being trapped forever in the farthest reaches of the galaxy, and to fail means death.

Victory is their only option in this terrible test of endurance – an ordeal that will try their will, their ingenuity, and above all their bonds of friendship…

Order your copy directly from the publisher today by going to www.stargatenovels.com or send a check or money order made payable to "Fandemonium" to:

<u>USA orders</u>: **$10.82 ($7.95 + $2.87 P&P). Send payment to: Fandemonium Books, PO Box 2178, Decatur, GA 30031-2178.**

<u>UK orders</u>: **£8.30 (£6.99 + £1.31 P&P). <u>Rest of the World orders</u>: £9.70 (£6.99 + £2.71 P&P). Send payment to: Fandemonium Books, PO Box 795A, Surbiton KT5 8YB, United Kingdom.**

Or check your local bookshop – available on special order if they are out of stock (quote the ISBN number listed above).

STARGATE SG-1: RELATIVITY

by James Swallow
Price: $7.95 US | $9.95 Canada |
£6.99 UK
ISBN-10: 1-905586-07-8
ISBN-13: 978-1-905586-07-3

When SG-1 encounter the Pack—a
nomadic space-faring people who
have fled Goa'uld domination for
generations—it seems as though
a trade of technologies will benefit
both sides.

Series number: SG1-10

But someone is determined to
derail the deal. With the SGC under
attack, and Vice President Kinsey breathing down their necks, it's
up to Colonel Jack O'Neill and his team to uncover the saboteur and save the fledgling alliance. But unbeknownst to SG-1
there are far greater forces at work—a calculating revenge that
spans decades, and a desperate gambit to prevent a cataclysm of
epic proportions.

When the identity of the saboteur is revealed, O'Neill is faced
with a horrifying truth and is forced into an unlikely alliance in
order to fight for Earth's future.

**Order your copy directly from the publisher today by going
to <u>www.stargatenovels.com</u> or send a check or money order
made payable to "Fandemonium" to:**

<u>USA orders</u>**: $10.82 ($7.95 + $2.87 P&P). Send payment to:
Fandemonium Books, PO Box 2178, Decatur, GA 30031-2178.**

<u>UK orders</u>**: £8.30 (£6.99 + £1.31 P&P).** <u>Rest of the World
orders</u>**: £9.70 (£6.99 + £2.71 P&P). Send payment to:
Fandemonium Books, PO Box 795A, Surbiton KT5 8YB,
United Kingdom.**

Or check your local bookshop – available on special order if they are
out of stock (quote the ISBN number listed above).

STARGATE SG-1: ROSWELL

by Sonny Whitelaw & Jennifer Fallon
Price: $7.95 US | $9.95 Canada |
£6.99 UK
ISBN-10: 1-905586-04-3
ISBN-13: 978-1-905586-04-2

When a Stargate malfunction throws Colonel Cameron Mitchell, Dr. Daniel Jackson, and Colonel Sam Carter back in time, they only have minutes to live.

But their rescue, by an unlikely duo — General Jack O'Neill and Vala Mal Doran — is only the beginning of their problems. Ordered to rescue an Asgard also marooned in 1947, SG-1 find themselves at the mercy of history. While Jack, Daniel, Sam and Teal'c become embroiled in the Roswell aliens conspiracy, Cam and Vala are stranded in another timeline, desperately searching for a way home.

As the effects of their interference ripple through time, the consequences for the future are catastrophic. Trapped in the past, SG-1 can only watch as their world is overrun by a terrible invader...

STARGATE ATLANTIS: DEATH GAME

by Jo Graham
Price: £6.99 UK | $7.95 US
ISBN-10: 1-905586-47-7
ISBN-13: 978-1-905586-47-9
Publication date: July 2010

Colonel John Sheppard wakes up on an alien world, in the wreckage of a Puddle Jumper— and can't remember how he got there.

   As he puts the pieces together, he discovers that his team is scattered across a tropical archipelago, unable to communicate with each other or return to the Stargate.

   Prisoners of the local population, Sheppard and Teyla are taken as tribute to the planet's Wraith overlord, while McKay, Ronon, and Zelenka team up to mount a daring rescue...

STARGATE ATLANTIS: HUNT AND RUN

by Aaron Rosenberg
Price: £6.99 UK | $7.95 US
ISBN-10: 1-905586-44-2
ISBN-13: 978-1-905586-44-8
Publication date: April 2010

Ronon Dex is a mystery. His past is a closed book and he likes it that way. But when the Atlantis team trigger a trap that leaves them stranded on a hostile world, only Ronon's past can save them – if it doesn't kill them first.

As the gripping tale unfolds, we return to Ronon's earliest days as a Runner and meet the charismatic leader who transformed him into a hunter of Wraith. But grief and rage can change the best of men and it soon becomes clear that those Ronon once considered brothers-in-arms are now on the hunt – and that the Atlantis team are their prey.

Unless Ronon can out hunt the hunters, Colonel Sheppard's team will fall victim to the vengeance of the *V'rdai*.

STARGATE ATLANTIS: BRIMSTONE

A fiery fate awaits the Atlantis team

STARGATE
ATLANTIS

BRIMSTONE

David Niall Wilson &
Patricia Lee Macomber

Based on the hit television series created by
Brad Wright and Robert C. Cooper

Series number: SGA-13

**by David Niall Wilson &
Patricia Macomber**
Price: £6.99 UK | $7.95 US
ISBN-10: 1-905586-20-5
ISBN-13: 978-1-905586-20-2
Publication date: February 2010

The Stargate Atlantis team discover a city on a moon that's about to plunge into its own sun. But the city which looked as if it had been abandoned long ago turns out to be inhabited by descendants of the Ancients who have fallen into decadence and debauchery.

Faced with a dissolute society disinterested in their own fate and unable to escape, the team must fight their way free before being plunged into a fiery death.

Order your copy directly from the publisher today by going to www.stargatenovels.com or send a check or money order made payable to "Fandemonium" to:

<u>USA orders</u>: **$10.82 ($7.95 + $2.87 P&P). Send payment to: Fandemonium Books, PO Box 2178, Decatur, GA 30031-2178.**

<u>UK orders</u>: **£8.30 (£6.99 + £1.31 P&P). <u>Rest of the World orders</u>: £9.70 (£6.99 + £2.71 P&P). Send payment to: Fandemonium Books, PO Box 795A, Surbiton KT5 8YB, United Kingdom.**

Or check your local bookshop – available on special order if they are out of stock (quote the ISBN number listed above).

Stranded on an icy world

STARGATE
ATLANTIS

DEAD END
Chris Wraight
Based on the hit television series created by
Brad Wright and Robert C. Cooper

Series number: SGA-12

STARGATE ATLANTIS: DEAD END

by Chris Wraight
Price: £6.99 UK | $7.95 US
ISBN-10: 1-905586-22-1
ISBN-13: 978-1-905586-22-6
Publication date: November 2009

Trapped on a planet being swallowed by a killing ice age, Colonel Sheppard and his team are rescued by the Forgotten – a race abandoned by those who once protected them, and condemned to watch their world die.

But when Teyla is abducted by the mysterious 'Banshees', Sheppard and his team risk losing their only chance of getting home in a desperate bid to save Teyla and to lead the Forgotten to a land remembered only in legend.

STARGATE ATLANTIS: ANGELUS

by Peter Evans
Price: £6.99 UK | $7.95 US
ISBN-10: 1-905586-18-3
ISBN-13: 978-1-905586-18-9

Series number: SGA-11

With their core directive restored, the Asurans have begun to attack the Wraith on multiple fronts. Under the command of Colonel Ellis, the Apollo is dispatched to observe the battlefront, but Ellis's orders not to intervene are quickly breached when an Ancient ship drops out of hyperspace.

Inside is Angelus, fleeing the destruction of a world he has spent millennia protecting from the Wraith. Charming and likable, Angelus quickly connects with each member of the Atlantis team in a unique way and, more than that, offers them a weapon that could put an end to their war with both the Wraith and the Asurans.

But all is not what it seems, and even Angelus is unaware of his true nature – a nature that threatens the very survival of Atlantis itself...

Order your copy directly from the publisher today by going to www.stargatenovels.com or send a check or money order made payable to "Fandemonium" to:

<u>USA orders</u>: $10.82 ($7.95 + $2.87 P&P). Send payment to: **Fandemonium Books, PO Box 2178, Decatur, GA 30031-2178.**

<u>UK orders</u>: £8.30 (£6.99 + £1.31 P&P). <u>Rest of the World orders</u>: £9.70 (£6.99 + £2.71 P&P). Send payment to: **Fandemonium Books, PO Box 795A, Surbiton KT5 8YB, United Kingdom.**

Or check your local bookshop – available on special order if they are out of stock (quote the ISBN number listed above).

A terrifying weapon threatens the Pegasus galaxy

STARGATE ATLANTIS

NIGHTFALL

James Swallow

Based on the hit television series created by
Brad Wright and Robert C. Cooper

Series number: SGA-10

STARGATE ATLANTIS: NIGHTFALL

by James Swallow
Price: £6.99 UK | $7.95 US
ISBN-10: 1-905586-14-0
ISBN-13: 978-1-905586-14-1

Deception and lies abound on the peaceful planet of Heruun, protected from the Wraith for generations by their mysterious guardian — the Aegis.

But with the planet falling victim to an incurable wasting sickness, and two of Colonel Sheppard's team going missing, the secrets of the Aegis must be revealed. The shocking truth threatens to tear Herunn society apart, bringing down upon them the scourge of the Wraith. Yet even with a Hive ship poised to attack there is much more at stake than the fate of one small planet.

For the Aegis conceals a threat so catastrophic that Colonel Samantha Carter herself must join Sheppard and his team as they risk everything to eliminate it from the Pegasus galaxy...

STARGATE ATLANTIS: MIRROR MIRROR

by Sabine C. Bauer
Price: £6.99 UK | $7.95 US
ISBN-10: 1-905586-12-4
ISBN-13: 978-1-905586-12-7

When an Ancient prodigy gives the Atlantis expedition Charybdis — a device capable of eliminating the Wraith — it's an offer they can't refuse. But the experiment fails disastrously, threatening to unravel the fabric of the Pegasus Galaxy — and the entire universe beyond.

Doctor Weir's team find themselves trapped and alone in very different versions of Atlantis, each fighting for their lives and their sanity in a galaxy falling apart at the seams. And as the terrible truth begins to sink in, they realize that they must undo the damage Charybdis has wrought while they still can.

Embarking on a desperate attempt to escape the maddening tangle of realities, each tries to return to their own Atlantis before it's too late. But the one thing standing in their way is themselves...

Order your copy directly from the publisher today by going to www.stargatenovels.com or send a check or money order made payable to "Fandemonium" to:

USA orders: $10.82 ($7.95 + $2.87 P&P). Send payment to: Fandemonium Books, PO Box 2178, Decatur, GA 30031-2178.

UK orders: £8.30 (£6.99 + £1.31 P&P). **Rest of the World orders:** £9.70 (£6.99 + £2.71 P&P). Send payment to: Fandemonium Books, PO Box 795A, Surbiton KT5 8YB, United Kingdom.

Or check your local bookshop – available on special order if they are out of stock (quote the ISBN number listed above).